TRUST

LISA SELL

BLOODHOUND
— BOOKS —

First published in 2020 by Bloodhound Books

www.bloodhoundbooks.com

Print ISBN 978-1-913419-38-7

ALSO BY LISA SELL

Hidden

*For Dave, who gave me the courage to start writing,
and the support and love to keep doing it.*

1

Once upon a time there was a girl.

She wasn't beautiful or kind, and certainly not a storybook princess. If you met her, you never forgot her.

The girl was called…

It no longer matters. The old name died in the face of others' rejection. If they didn't want her, she would be someone else. She took another, more suitable, identity.

The girl became Red.

This isn't a fairy tale and the story hasn't ended. It's coming. Red is writing a tale of horror. People will suffer and die.

Once upon a time there was a girl who only wanted love.

They trampled over her affection and ground it into the dirt. Now she's grown up and ready to make them pay.

Revenge is Red.

2

SARAH

A trail of blood leads up the path to my front door. Carnage awaits us on the doorstep.

'That flaming cat's been bringing you presents again,' Hayden says, pushing the mutilated bird aside with his foot. 'I'll sort it out after we've put the shopping away.'

I let Hayden into my house while I linger outside. The bird's innards spill from its body. Three dead crows in one week. The other two I excused as my neighbour's cat, intimidating mine into being a better hunter. Now I'm not so sure. Aren't crows supposed to signify death?

Hayden was in such a rush to get inside he didn't see it. The trail along the path isn't linear. In the middle is a tiny smudged word, written in blood.

Red.

3

RED

R ed has made her mark.
It begins.

4

SARAH

I try to keep it light, after seeing the dismembered bird. 'Did I mention how much I hate food shopping?'

'Only about fifty times in the supermarket until we got back.' Hayden's reply is muffled by his head being inside a cupboard.

'Are all the tins' labels facing forward?'

Hayden's head pops around the cupboard door. His hair's ruffled after spending the day raking his hands through it, trying not to murder gobby pupils. 'Yes, the tins are in order. I annoy myself, let alone everyone else. To be fair, I had to rearrange the cupboard first. You're a messy cow.'

'True but you still love me. Do you line up your classes outside, facing the same way before a lesson too?'

Hayden blushes. I focus on inhaling a family-size bar of chocolate instead of continuing the teasing. I secretly admire how organised Hayden is. One of us has to be. I write in my phone calendar reminders to eat meals, which I then ignore. Sometimes, after the last appointment of the day, my mind is so full of other people's ailments and illnesses I don't have time to sort myself out. Being a GP is demanding.

I look around my kitchen and revel in the comfort of home.

There's warmth surpassing the boiler belting out heat. It's inside me and I will hold on to it. Maybe there wasn't a word written in the bird's blood. I'm tired and my eyes probably deceived me. The word *Red* coming from my overworked mind, making a link with the blood. It's safer to focus on home and the man I love.

As soon as I saw this place in Stadhampton, a pull of belonging hooked me in. I'd not felt it since I went to live with the Jessops, my adoptive parents. Oxfordshire is where I belong, despite living in various parts of the country before. As a trainee and newbie doctor, you go where the opportunities are.

Hayden whistles something resembling a cheesy pop song. He's in his element in my kitchen because he cooks in it the most. Once again I'm reminded why I love him, beyond doing the jobs I detest. Hayden is the most caring person I know. He's also the most stubborn and fiery.

'New and improved.' Hayden sneers at his favourite biscuits. 'Why can't they bloody well leave things alone? I expect these'll taste awful.'

'Try one. They might be nicer.'

'I bet they're not.'

I won't get involved any further with Hayden's biscuit crisis. When his parents fostered me, Hayden and I regularly fell out. Being young, the opposite sex, and me being a year older contributed. Since we got together, he's mellowed but it's still best to let him have a rant and get it all out. We try to avoid arguments by agreeing I'm always right and he's never wrong.

I'm not great at dealing with conflict. My birth parents often argued. They were young when they had me and were always moving from one place to another. It wore them down, along with the drugs that ravaged their brains and bodies.

I can't recall my father, James, ever saying a kind word to me. He was driven by selfish needs. Kayleigh tried to establish closeness between us but her love for heroin was stronger. It made the moments when she spent time with me something I'll always treasure.

Kayleigh occasionally pops into my mind. She gave me up so I could have a better life than one of moving from squat to squat. I hope her life improved too, although the odds were against her. James can rot in hell for all I care. He saddled me with his shame. I sometimes consider trying to find Kayleigh but the possibility of her still being with James deters me. Not all reunions are bad though.

'How did I get so lucky to find you again?' I ask Hayden, giving him a kiss on the cheek.

'Not so much luck as that twat, Richie, dropping the white-board holder on my head.' Hayden scowls at the memory of the errant pupil who rolled down the shonky equipment, almost knocking Hayden out. I'm quite partial to Richie. Richie's actions brought Hayden to my surgery to check if he had a concussion. We hadn't seen each other since I left Hayden's family home when I was thirteen.

'Thank the gods of teaching that the little git's not in my class this year. Although I guess he should be an honorary guest at the wedding, seeing as he got us together.' Hayden looks at me, waiting for a reaction.

We've been here often recently. Hayden should know by now I won't engage with commitment talk. Where there's serious-ness, the cat is a diversion. Weatherwax laps up the chin rubs. She's much cuddlier than her Pratchett namesake.

Chocolate flakes stick to my fingers as I dab at the table, trying to preserve the oak, already gouged from cat shenanigans. The kitchen is traditional and unpretentious, with the odd labour-saving machine. A technology king, Hayden's almost convinced me the modern can live in harmony alongside more old-fashioned ways. Hayden focuses on the future. He's a few steps ahead in everything. I tend to dwell on the past. There are memories so piercing they slice through me when they creep in. I try not to let them but they always find a way.

Hayden joins me at the table. 'Penny for them?'

'You know my bad memories aren't worth a penny.'

'Let's shake them loose then.' Hayden's spider fingers tickle my ribs until I have to retaliate.

'Ow!' Hayden rubs his tricep. 'Pinching isn't cool.'

'Sorry, I didn't mean it. I'd never intentionally hurt you.'

Hayden draws me close. 'You're nothing like your birth parents.'

In the past year I've enjoyed discovering how much Hayden learned about me from when I was living with his family. Hayden was the archetypal sullen and disengaged boy. When he shares anecdotes of the short period I lived with the Lawsons, I love hearing them. I wondered back then if Hayden registered I was alive.

Hayden understands I need to hear I'm not capable of hurting others. I have to accept tainted family blood doesn't run in my veins. Hayden thinks he knows the depths of how far James made me sink. If Hayden knew the truth about what I did, he'd want nothing to do with me.

5

RED

Playing voyeur ignites a familiar spark within Red. The shine of knowing something her targets don't will never fade.

Waiting can be boring but is always useful. The darker early evenings provided cover as Red waited for Sarah and Hayden to return from the supermarket. Getting caught by the neighbours with dead birds could be awkward.

Sarah kisses Hayden's cheek. Seeing them together always stirs Red's hatred. Affectionate touches and intimate gazes confirm the strength of their relationship.

Hayden should have been Red's, not Sarah's. Soon, Hayden won't belong to anyone. You can't claim ownership of the dead.

6

SARAH

Hayden forms his hands into a steeple, placing us in a more serious mode. I know what's coming.

'Food shopping would be much quicker if we did it for both of us,' Hayden begins.

'A bit awkward having to cart it to two places though.'

Hayden slaps the table. 'You always do this.'

'Do what?' I ask, knowing exactly what I'm doing; buying time.

'Living together, we could do most things in one, including the shopping. We're so busy at work. Check out that lot.' He points at the *Macbeth* essays that have been taunting him. They move from his home to mine on a daily basis.

In theory, I want nothing more than to live with Hayden. Waking up with him lying next to me is my favourite part of the day. I tell his sleeping face I love him and no one could ever match up. When I speak those words, I feel safe.

My dedication to Hayden isn't in question. I'm apprehensive of what might tear us apart. The closer I get, the harder not being together would be. Life isn't certain. I'm not sure if I can ever tell Hayden my secrets. I've been abandoned too often to place complete trust in anyone.

Hayden clutches my hand. 'Please give it some consideration. The only way to move on is to let go. Take a chance on me.'

I ignore his awful Abba rendition. The hand covering mine is a handcuff and a lifeline. I can choose which one it could be.

'Not yet. We're fine as we are,' I say, moving my hand away. 'It's only been a year. Let's enjoy what we have for now.'

'It's not like we were strangers when we met.'

'We've changed from the kids who met under crappy circumstances.' I'm not succeeding at keeping my annoyance at bay.

Hayden hooks a finger under his collar.

'If you're hot, adjust the thermostat,' I say.

'I'm fine. It's not that. Don't shoot me down but I think you need more counselling.'

I can't believe his suggestion. Hayden knows I pride myself on getting through counselling. When I became a partner at my practice, a fellow partner, Phoebe, suggested I have therapy. We studied at med school together and she's aware of some of my background. I wanted to be a partner so much I agreed. I can't spill out my emotions like that again. Every truth shared was a stab to my heart and a twist in my conscience. I ignore Hayden's suggestion. I'm in a stable place and can ask for help when I need it. Can't I?

'Please stop pushing me away.' Hayden's eyes, signifying belonging, reel me in. I'm almost set to give up the keys to my house and whole life when his phone rings.

Hayden answers his phone in the lounge. It must be his mum, Mags. Since my recent argument with my foster mother, Hayden decided it's best to separate the women in his life. He always takes calls with Mags away from me. Until now it's suited us. Hayden's tense responses, trailing through the open door, give me the courage to intervene.

I stomp into the room, ready to defend Hayden. 'What's Mags done?'

Hayden stares at his mobile as if it might explode. He doesn't move as I grab the phone, daring to speak to Mags. The silence of an ended call is a relief. We both said hurtful things the last time we spoke. I couldn't bear to hear it again.

I lift Hayden's face to look at me. 'What's happened?'

'They've found her. A body was discovered at the old allotments in Great Parston.'

'Is it...?' I don't finish my question. It can only be Tamsin.

Hayden's anguished expression confirms it. His sister who disappeared in 2002 is dead.

7

TAMSIN

28TH JUNE 2002

When I'm Doctor Who, I fight baddies. The Daleks and Cybermen can't hurt me if I'm wearing my stripy scarf. Tom Baker is my favourite because he's Hayden's too. I've got all of Tom's episodes on DVD. I wish he was here now. He'd rescue me. We could travel through time and the galaxies, away from here.

My baddie said I must be brave. I think it's a baddie but my head is messy. My baddie wants to be a hero too. Not even Doctor Who could make this baddie good.

I swallow my boo hoos. Now I'm six, I need to be brave. Hayden laughs when I say tears are in our throats. Sometimes boo hoos come out, like when I'm sick. Sometimes I swallow them, like my dinner.

Hayden says boo hoos come from your eyes. When he was sad, after our puppy, Joy, went missing, I rubbed Hayden's throat. I tried to make his boo hoos go down. I must have done it wrong. Hayden cried lots after that.

I rub my throat. Boo hoos come out.

I forgot. My baddie hates crying. It's for weak people. I don't know what that means.

My baddie grabs me. I hold my scarf. Where is the T.A.R.D.I.S.? Doctor Who, I need you.

I want Mummy.

8

RED

R ed harbours grudges like a territorial bird, nesting resentment. Before, she enjoyed witnessing the fracturing of Hayden's family. Now, Red will finish it.

Destruction awaits the Lawsons. Sarah must be taken down too. She should have stayed away from Hayden. Red's waited for years. She can wait a while longer.

Red observes Hayden moving around the kitchen, talking about something no doubt tedious. He's become a bore in his older years. Instead, Red chooses to remember him as a youngster. Sarah's eyes follow Hayden, staking her claim. The overgrown ivy trailing along the top of the window has been tamed. Red, the watcher, is grateful for the viewing space.

A thrill tingles throughout Red's body as she considers their ignorance of how close she is. Fireworks explode in Red's nerve endings: passion, revenge, and murder. It's coming.

Nothing will give Red greater pleasure than ending Hayden and Sarah's happiness. Death is as final as it gets.

9

SARAH

Hayden grips the steering wheel, swearing at other drivers. He battles cars conspiring against us getting to his mum. The younger sibling Hayden doted on is dead. After Mags' phone call I've hardly spoken. Words won't make this easier.

Since we reunited, Hayden has been reticent in talking about Tamsin. When he mentions her, his grief is visible. On our first date, Hayden shared how Tamsin disappeared in 2002 and hadn't been found. Mags severed contact with me not long after I left. Hearing about Tamsin was a shock. She was the younger sister I'd always wanted. Whenever Hayden discusses his relationship with Tamsin, I regret missing out on seeing her grow. Despite being the youngest and an accident – which Mags told me never to share – Tamsin was the adored baby of the family.

Hayden was incensed at the police for not finding Tamsin. He believes they didn't do enough and the trauma killed his dad, Paul.

'Tamsin's disappearance wrenched the centre from the family.' Hayden stares at the road ahead as he speaks. 'When a loved one disappears, you exist rather than live. Every day is spent wondering if they'll return. Everything stands still until you force yourself to carry on. It was so hard to do. Despite being the youngest, Tamsin was the heart of us. I didn't want to give up on seeing her alive.'

It's taking an enormous effort not to make Hayden stop the car so I can hold him. The trembling in his voice betrays attempts at stoicism. I remain silent. This isn't about me. Hayden needs to unleash some demons.

'A month after Tamsin disappeared, I returned to college,' Hayden continues. 'I didn't want to but Mum insisted, saying I mustn't throw away my career prospects although she always found it hard, me choosing to study in Leeds and live with my uncle. I was so bored of living in Great Parston. When I began my degree, she was so proud. I cringed whenever Mum told random people about her son, the trainee teacher.'

I'm proud of Hayden too. The boy who wanted to be an English teacher realised his dream. He's head of English and his department is the school's success story.

'I'll never forget the afternoon Mum phoned to say Tamsin had... gone.' Hayden falters on the last word. 'Trying to convince myself she'd walked off and was lost had helped at first. I needed to believe the searchers would find Tamsin, giving a cheeky smile, with an apology for being naughty.'

Tamsin had a smile for everyone. I fight against tears, remembering her gummy grin. She was only a baby when I last saw her. I'm no use to Hayden if I fall apart.

'I couldn't get back from Leeds fast enough.' Hayden's voice is so quiet I have to lean in to hear. 'I hadn't been home in months because I enjoyed living away. The contrast between the city and the claustrophobia of village life in Great Parston was weird. Not as strange as Tamsin not being there when I returned though. Dad played it cool, repeating how Tamsin would come home. He didn't give up searching. The guilt never ended.'

Paul had taken his daughter to the park in Great Parston that day. He was buying ice creams from a van, parked by the playground. When Paul turned back, Tamsin had vanished. The rest of the family never blamed Paul but he wouldn't accept mercy. Months later, he died from an overdose. He will never know the search for his child is over.

'Dad was broken and always picking fights with Mum,' Hayden says. 'I'm sure you remember how they'd never argue in front of us. After Tamsin disappeared, they gave up all pretences. Dad refused to accept Tamsin's disappearance wasn't his fault. Killing himself was senseless. It was another loss to deal with. I still miss him so much.'

When Hayden originally told me about Paul's death, I wasn't sure how to react. Despite being my foster father, Paul and I didn't bond. He was likeable enough but I felt he fostered for Mags' sake. Where she would treat us as her own, Paul was detached. His attention and love was reserved for his offspring.

'I'm amazed after all the searching how Tamsin was so near to your old house,' I say. The thought of Tamsin's bones lying close to the Lawsons' home twists my stomach. My medical mind imagines the state of decay. For the first time I regret my vocation.

'Mum swore Tamsin was nearby,' Hayden replies. 'We had to stay put because Mum believed Tamsin would return. Mum never imagined it like this though. She refused to consider death as an option. No one dared mention it around her.'

I've avoided asking Hayden the circumstances behind the discovery of Tamsin's body. Hayden needs to talk at his own pace. I'm hoping Tamsin had an accident and died peacefully. It seems the least painful of the possible scenarios. Hope can be foolish but where would we be without it?

Hayden thumps the centre of the steering wheel and the horn sounds. I startle at the blast. Hayden swerves the car into a

LISA SELL

lay-by and parks. He rubs his forehead, hunching over the dashboard. When he looks up at me, my insides clench. The storm
isn't over yet.

'Tamsin's body was inside a suitcase, buried in the earth.'

18

SARAH

'Don't be shy, sweetheart.' Mags gave Sarah a gentle nudge forward. 'This is your new home, for a while.'

Sarah regarded her foster mother. Mags Lawson summed up the mothers Sarah had read about: affectionate, firm in her parenting, and jovial. When she heard Mags insisted on collecting her from the police station, Sarah decided she already liked the woman. An adult who put Sarah first was an alien concept.

Paul gave Sarah a nod and words resembling a welcome when she'd entered his house. After giving Mags a peck on the cheek, Paul left. Sarah paid it no attention. Absent disinterested fathers were standard.

Dreading meeting the rest of the family, Sarah took a breath before she stepped into the lounge. She wasn't sure how to behave around other children. Sarah had spent her life with adults, packed into cramped spaces and neglectful of how their actions affected a minor. Her maturity made Sarah an outcast to her peers. They wanted to have fun, not sit and reflect.

A pretty blonde girl thrust out a hand to shake. She dropped a book she was holding, a manual on landscaping gardens. 'Hi,

Sarah, I'm Lily. I'm not part of the Lawson clan though. I live next door.' She pointed, in case it mattered.

'She might as well be, the amount of time she spends here,' a young man added. Sarah noted his wink to the blonde, as if staking a claim. In Sarah's experience, boys trying to be macho men never had good intentions.

Lily swatted the young boy across the head. 'Don't mind Steve. He's lacking in manners and thinks he's God's gift to girls, despite his age.'

'I can't help it if I'm irresistible. You'll succumb to my charms eventually, Lil.' They laughed at a seemingly old running joke. 'Is that your latest venture?' Steve asked Lily, pointing at the book.

'I think I'd be great at landscaping,' Lily replied. 'Can I start on your hedge, Mags?'

Mags gave a wry smile. 'Best not to handle sharp implements, Lil. You know what happened when you thought you could be a hairdresser.'

Steve pointed to his ear. 'I'm lucky to still have two of these after what you did with the scissors. Excuse my bad manners.' Steve turned to Sarah. 'Welcome to our home, Sarah. It's good to have you here.'

Sarah startled in response to an arm reaching around her shoulders.

'Sorry, my love. I should've thought,' Mags said, giving Sarah a knowing look.

Sarah despised the pity in Mags' eyes. Mags was the opposite of Kayleigh. Sarah's birth mother tried to be nurturing but heroin created a distance between mother and daughter. Kayleigh's idea of parenting was to tell Sarah to go to school, to give Kayleigh some peace and keep the authorities off their backs.

'Hayden, say hello to Sarah.' Mags grabbed a controller from a boy's hands.

'I was winning, Mum!' The youngster's fringe flopped over his eyes as he reached for the device.

'I bought you up better than that,' Mags said to the boy, placing the controller on a top shelf.

Mags' stern voice made the teenager comply. 'Hello, Sarah. Nice to see you and all that.' Hayden's sulky tone matched his pout.

Sarah knew they'd never get along. At least Hayden's flirty brother was polite. Hayden Lawson was a sullen boy Sarah wanted no part in knowing.

'Can I play my game again?' Hayden asked his mum.

Mags sighed. 'Do it upstairs. The noise might wake Tamsin.'

As Hayden huffed out of the room, Sarah glanced into the playpen. A cherubic baby slept an innocent sleep Sarah had never known. In squats you always had one eye open. Sarah learned to move within minutes. Police raids, addicts taking over, and rowdy drunks looking for a fight, demanded it.

Sarah found her voice. 'She's like an angel.'

'That's our Tamsin.' Lily spoke with discernible pride, despite the lack of family connection. 'We call her the accident because of the massive age gap between her and Hayden. Mags insists Tamsin's not.'

Mags blushed. 'Lil, don't share every thought that comes to mind. How many times has your mum told you? Right, Sarah, you've met the rabble. Let's go to your bedroom.'

'Have you got a sleeping bag?' Sarah asked. 'I left mine behind.'

Mags' upset dominated her face. It was probably shocking to hear how a thirteen-year-old girl went into a police station, with a note from her mother, stating she couldn't look after her child. Sarah only had the clothes she was wearing.

'You don't need a sleeping bag,' Mags said.

'It's okay.' Sarah stretched out on the rug. 'There's plenty of space and it's quite cosy down here.'

'Goodness me, no!' Mags rushed to pull Sarah up from the floor. 'You're sleeping in the bed. This room is all yours.'

'The whole thing?' Sarah couldn't conceal her astonishment. The bedroom was bigger than some of the places her parents had broken into. The Lawsons' house was bordering on a mansion.

Sarah assessed her surroundings. A pink paradise created for a princess. Sarah wouldn't confess to Mags how she was far removed from perfection. Sarah was more of a reluctant villain.

Mags led Sarah over to the bed. 'You're part of this family now. We'll never turn our backs on you.'

Mags broke her promise a few years later when she cut off contact.

11

SARAH

Since Mags and I fell out, I can't let go of my resentment towards her. I've tried, remembering the loving substitute mother who showed me kindness. All I can focus on is how Mags had offered security. Her absence cut deep. Once more I was abandoned.

Mags doesn't know where to draw the line regarding family business. It's confusing for someone who has birth, foster, and adoptive parents. I loved Mags and I confess I wondered if she'd adopt me. I wouldn't swap Denise, who's my "real" mother, for anything though. Denise and Zeke Jessop loved me without condition, despite knowing everything of my past. I told them. Mum is the only sharer of my secrets since Dad died.

I was lucky to be adopted by the Jessops. Their kindness was shown in wanting an older child, with an awareness babies were a more popular choice. Dad said he was glad to miss out on changing nappies and sleepless nights. The funny thing is he always soothed me after I had nightmares. I miss Dad intensely. Sometimes, when I catch a waft of Old Spice aftershave on my older patients, time freezes. Dad is with me again.

Mum and Dad were my world but it seemed like a part of me was missing. Kayleigh is out there somewhere, I hope.

In the months I'd lived with Mags we'd formed a bond. I still don't understand why she broke it. Mags views the world according to her rules. It's almost impossible to make her budge. Hayden has inherited his mother's stubbornness. Sometimes it's like I'm dealing with a mini Mags, although Hayden's more amenable. Give him a packet of Jelly Babies and you'll have a friend for life.

My nerves kick in as we enter Hayden's former home of Great Parston. We're on Mags' patch. This is a Buckinghamshire village I've heard of but hadn't visited until a few weeks ago. I lived with the Lawsons in Oxford. They moved to Great Parston soon after I left them. Hayden says I didn't miss much. When he set off to Leeds for college, Hayden couldn't get out of Great Parston fast enough. It's a utopia for adults seeking the quiet life. For youngsters who want entertainment, it's hell. I bet the villagers' faces were a picture when the Lawson family arrived with their menagerie of children and animals.

Hayden parks alongside the terraced houses on Oak Road. Each building has its own individual character, signified by cladding, different-coloured doors, and garden arrangements. It's the kind of place where neighbours try to be unique but are conflicted in wanting to outdo each other. Solar panels spread across the line. Salesmen must be rubbing their hands in glee.

The neat lawn and immaculate flower beds outside Mags' home are unexpected. Mags hated gardening. It was Paul's territory. I guess her second husband, Damien, has taken over the mantle. The Hell's Angel gnomes are a rebellious Mags thing. It's reassuring she hasn't become a Stepford wife. Despite the animosity between us, I wouldn't want Mags to lose her personality and purpose again.

Hayden says Mags shut down for a while after Tamsin went

missing and Paul died. Mags ate little and refused to move from her chair, repeating nursery rhymes she'd sung to Tamsin. I remember how those songs travelled to my room, helping me to drift into safe sleep.

After Tamsin disappeared, Hayden cared for his mum. He shared with me the hurt of spoon-feeding Mags and putting her into bed. Hayden's loyal to Mags. He tries not to cast her in a negative light, although he's realistic about her formidable nature.

Despite his disintegrating family, Hayden held on to his ambition. He needed to become a teacher. Without it, the future seemed pointless. Having a career meant being able to support Mags too. Paul's life insurance helped but he left a lot of debts behind. Hayden has always been a mummy's boy, no matter how much he denies it. He continued studying for Mags, as well as himself.

Hayden pats his coat pockets, cursing at forgetting the key. The doorbell plays *I Will Survive* while we wait. Under the circumstances of Hayden having a dead sister, I hope someone answers soon.

Before the door opens, I prepare to face a grieving woman who cast me out.

12

SARAH

One look at Hayden and Mags' tears flow. I follow them into the house, feeling like a snooper on their mourning, despite grieving for Tamsin too. A black Labrador puppy almost trips me over as it dances between my feet.

'Come here, Gus,' Hayden says to the dog and cradles it in his arms.

Signs on the walls share how love conquers all, we should dance in the rain, and home is where the heart is. In different circumstances, Hayden and I would mock the twee statements we love to hate. Winter sunlight spills from the upstairs window, bathing the hallway in an eerie glow. The welcoming atmosphere jars against the reason for being here.

Mags' husband, Damien, enters the lounge where we congregate. 'Can I get anyone a cuppa?'

Hayden thinks Damien is perfect for Mags. When Paul died, Mags told Hayden she couldn't consider marrying again. Time worked its healing magic. Damien treats Mags with respect and gentleness. Hayden's happy to call him a stepfather. I think Hayden's needed a father figure, not that anyone could replace Paul.

Hayden and Paul were inseparable. Father passed a love of literature to son. They often went to the library together and spent hours immersed in books. On Saturdays, Mags sent me to fetch them when lunch was nearly ready. She knew I wanted to go with them but they never invited me. It was a strictly male book-bonding event.

Damien's more receptive to me than Paul was. Whenever Damien goes to football matches with Hayden, we have dinner together afterwards at Hayden's flat. Damien's someone you can't help but like. He always defends Mags, and I wouldn't dream of saying anything derogatory about her in his company. Damien's tried to convince me to make amends with Mags. I was working up to it. Circumstances have moved it forward.

Having noted our drinks requirements, Damien goes into the kitchen. Mags grips the arms of a wingback chair. She's marked her territory with hand cream on one side and nail files on the other. Mags' one vanity is her nails and hands. I wish I could hold them again and feel their softness.

Hayden sits on the floor, placing Gus next to him, both near Mags' feet. As Mags strokes his hair, Hayden fiddles with loops in the rug. Tragedy reduces him to a child.

To avoid being near to Steve on the sofa, I take a chair from the dining room. Steve is everything Hayden isn't: flirty, extrovert, and mouthy. Despite my initial impression of the boys, my discomfort around Steve heightened when I lived in their house. Steve had plenty to say about the opposite sex and his eye for them.

Steve doesn't acknowledge me now. He's inevitably taking Mags' side in our argument. I hold back a snide remark about how Steve still lives with his mum. He's grieving for the sister he doted on.

'Thank you for coming along with our Hayden.'

Realising Mags is talking to me, a blush creeps into my

cheeks. Blending into the background was never going to happen under Mags' watchful eye.

'Of course I'd be here.' I'm starting wrong, sounding defensive. 'What I mean is, I...'

Mags smiles. It seems genuine. 'Don't worry, Sarah. I understand what you meant.'

Damien places mugs on the smoked glass coffee table, the same one the family had in Oxford. Hayden used to lie underneath, pressing his mouth against it to make faces, guaranteeing Tamsin's giggles. I turn away from the memory.

'You tell them what's happened, Damien.' Mags holds a hand against her chest. 'I can't. It's too horrific.'

TAMSIN

28TH JUNE 2002

Since I was tiny, Mummy reads our favourite poem, "Now We Are Six".

Whenever it's my birthday, Mummy wakes me up with a kiss and whispers how old I am. It tickles my ear and makes me laugh when she says where I am in our poem. It's not my birthday today but I like remembering the poem.

I don't remember being one, when I began. Mummy says it doesn't matter. It's enough I begun and that's brilliant.

I can't remember two. I was too new to have a brain to do the remember stuff.

Three, four, and five were the best. I pretended to be asleep when Mummy came into my room on those birthdays. She was surprised when I opened my eyes and said what age I was.

Mummy is lovely. She smells of flowers and cake. Mummy likes baking. I help her. Fairy cakes are my favourite.

I'm six now. Hayden says I'm clever. He tests me on *Doctor Who* and I never get it wrong. Daddy says I'm going to change the world.

I'm six now. My baddie doesn't like flowers, fairy cakes or *Doctor Who*.

I'm six now. I scream for Mummy.
I'm six now. A hand covers my mouth.
I'm six now. Forever.

14

SARAH

Mags is transfixed by a photograph of Tamsin. I take a glimpse at the image. Tamsin was two when I last saw her. The six-year-old version had white-blonde hair and a wide grin guaranteed a returned smile. Realising Tamsin's a pile of bones and not the girl in the photo is tough. I can't shift the vision in my head. Dissecting bodies at med school leaves an impression. I don't want to imagine Tamsin's decayed body. Yet my mind still goes there.

Frown lines settle into Damien's usually open face. The first time I met him it wasn't hard to figure out what attracted Mags. Damien is a handsome man with an indefinable twinkle in his eye. Now he's a muted version, preparing to deliver difficult news.

'I want to say how sorry I am for your loss, Hayden,' Damien says.

'Thank you.' Hayden continues fiddling with the rug. His nostrils flare whenever he fights against tears.

Damien clears his throat. 'Work's been going on at the old allotments, up the road. The land was sold to build flats. Absolute travesty. Why can't they build them in Aylesbury? There's far more space there. There was a waiting list as long as my arm for the allotment plots. Recently a digger struck something in the ground. As per procedure, they stopped work. It was a suitcase, like the family-sized ones or what Mags has to herself when we go on holiday.' Damien slaps a hand over his mouth, realising his usual quips are ill-timed.

I offer him a smile to acknowledge his efforts under difficult circumstances. Giving bad news is the worst part of my job. It doesn't get any easier. I don't envy Damien this task.

He takes a sip of tea. 'The foreman opened the case and found, well, er, he found... bones inside. The police got involved, of course. They checked missing children reports, based on the size of the...' Damien glances at Mags. 'As we all know, Tamsin is still listed as missing. Mags had to provide DNA.'

I wonder when Hayden will figure out how long Mags has known Tamsin might be dead. Hayden's focusing on Damien. The realisation is coming though.

'They considered if it was Benny Morgan,' Damien added. 'You may not have heard about him. He was a boy who went missing, ten years before Tamsin, in Little Parston.'

'Did he disappear from a park too?' I ask.

'Not that I know of.' Damien reddens. The task of bearing bad news isn't easy.

'Two children disappearing in neighbouring villages,' I say, 'didn't the police think it was suspicious?'

'No,' Steve replies. 'When Tamsin disappeared from the park, the police said there wasn't a discernible link with Benny. People around here believe Benny's dad might have had something to do with it. They did exactly the same to Dad, the bastards.'

'The remains discovered at the allotments were soon identified as female,' Damien adds.

'Tamsin's scarf was in there too,' Mags says. 'Do you

remember how you said she could be Doctor Who, wearing the same multi-coloured scarf?' Mags asks Hayden.

Hayden shared his *Doctor Who* obsession with Tamsin. They had posters above their beds and pored over *Doctor Who* annuals together. Tamsin challenged others to ask her questions on any of the Doctors. A proud Hayden said the answers were always correct. Hayden cried when he related how Tamsin said wearing the scarf meant she would keep people safe from the baddies. If only someone had protected Tamsin.

'Oh yes, the ridiculously long scarf you knitted because you forgot how to cast off,' Hayden says. 'With the badges pinned on it.'

'That's the one,' Mags replies.

'Wait a minute. Damien said you had to provide DNA. You knew then it might have been Tamsin. Why didn't you say anything?'

'Mum didn't tell me either.' Steve's rapid reply displays his annoyance.

'I couldn't.' Mags twists a silver stud around in her ear. 'If it wasn't Tamsin, I didn't want you to go through the heartache too. I was looking out for my children. Obviously not well enough. Tamsin would still be here if I'd done a better job.'

Damien moves Mags' nail files aside to sit by her. 'You're a wonderful mother. You weren't at the park, darling.' Damien takes a breath. 'Please don't keep blaming yourself.'

'Carry on telling them,' Mags says through her sobs.

'The DNA, dentist's records, and scarf matched to Tamsin,' Damien continues, trying to soothe his wife. 'We were informed today.'

'I swear if I find who did this, I'll kill them with my bare hands.' Hayden grabs the rug, snapping loops between his fingers.

'I'll be right beside you,' Steve adds. I notice he's lost weight.

It makes his buzz cut harsher. I'm surprised he's allowed it to happen. Steve wouldn't want to put ladies off.

Mags folds her arms. 'We've had a DI here, saying he'll do all he can to find Tamsin's killer. I'll believe it when I see it.'

'Let them do their job,' Damien says.

Mags gives him a hard stare.

The doorbell sounds. No one moves. I'm not sure who or what we're expecting. More devastation, I guess.

'Shall I get it?' I ask for Mags' permission and leave the room in response to her nod.

Escaping allows me time to process. The lounge is heavy with past and present grief and regrets.

I swing the door open to see a friendly face. Her timing is impeccable. My "thoughts twin" knew I needed her.

'Hello, Sarah. So, what's happening then?'

15

RED

Red is enjoying the unexpected gathering at Oak Road. When she followed Hayden and Sarah from the house, Red didn't expect they'd come here together. She knows about Sarah's spat with Mags.

Red makes it her business to know everything about Hayden and Sarah. Looking at the itinerary on her phone, Red performs her daily checks.

Dismember another bird and leave it as a gift. Check.

Replace broken knife sharpener. Check.

Taunt the Lawsons with the discovery of Tamsin's body. In progress.

Kill Hayden and Sarah. To be arranged.

16

RED

G reat Parston is a small place full of narrow minds and flapping mouths. The mechanic at the local garage told his apprentice about the discovery of a body at the former allotments. Fortunately for Red, the foreman overseeing the flats often gossiped over a pint with his drinking companion, the mechanic.

The men at the garage offered opinions on the identity of the corpse in the suitcase. It didn't take a genius to figure out it was a child, due to the size of the burial vessel. Most of the residents of Great Parston had heard of Tamsin Lawson's disappearance. It became legend. Children spooked each other with tales of Tamsin's ghost haunting the park, seeking her abductor.

Red didn't need to be at the garage. She knew how to corrode her car's spark plugs and play the dopey female with zero knowledge of vehicles. Allowing men to think they're superior amuses her. When their defences are lowered, Red exposes their weaknesses. Sometimes people get injured in the process.

Red learned maintenance on her first car. She deals with everything herself. No one else cares enough to help, even the

family for which she seeks revenge. Some bonds aren't recip-
rocated.

Red went to the garage on a whim. The past often draws her
in, with a challenge to tackle difficult memories. Red always
wins the tussle. Waiting in the reception area, she tried not to
laugh at being in the place Paul Lawson was often found. After
delivering spare parts, he stuck around for a cup of tea and a
chat. If Paul had been alive, he would have lost it, seeing Red
there. Paul was dead though and the thought, as ever, pleased
her.

This week has been a buzz. Red is thriving on the Lawsons'
renewed grief. It couldn't have happened to a more deserving
family.

SARAH

'Get down, Yellow!' Lily shouts at her golden retriever, resting his paws on my shoulders. Lily's daughter, Freya, pulls Yellow's lead to bring him to heel.

'This is a surprise,' I say, wiping dog drool off my jumper.

'I like to be spontaneous.' Lily pushes through into the house. Anyone else would be offended. When you've known Lily as long as I have, it's normal behaviour without a hint of rudeness. Those closest to her call it the "Lily Bubble" because she exists in her own world.

Yellow leads the way into the lounge, followed by his puppy shadow, Gus. Freya is in pursuit. Their chasing reminds me of a Tom and Jerry cartoon.

Although I've kept in contact since they moved to London, Freya's recent growth spurt is staggering. She's no longer a gawky little girl. Living with a moody teenager is one of Lily's favourite rants. She conveniently forgets she was similar at fourteen when we first met. Lily's adolescent emotions weren't so much mood swings as temperamental bungee jumps. Unfortunately, Lily didn't keep her grotty moods in the "Lily Bubble". We had to endure it with her.

I give Freya a hug. 'Good to see you, lovely girl.'

'Missed you, Sarah.'

The dogs slobber over Hayden and the earlier tension drops from his shoulders.

Mags assesses the visitors. 'For a second, Lily, I thought I'd gone back in time. Freya is the spit of you when you were a teenager.'

Freya rolls her eyes at the familiar statement. In everything but height, she's the image of her mum. Lily is unnaturally tall. No one can figure out why. Everyone else in the family is average, some are even short. The milkman's paternity is a regular wisecrack.

Freya no longer dresses like a "chav high on polyester" as Lily puts it. Freya's discovered her own brand of geek chic. Lily's impressed Freya's finding her own way but isn't so keen on Freya's natural beauty. It's not because of jealousy. Lily often threatens a slow painful death to any boy who expresses an interest in Freya. Unfortunately, Lily still hasn't got over a boy from the road we lived on in Oxford breaking her teenage heart. She wants to spare Freya the same.

'Hi, Mags,' Lily says. 'Sorry for dropping in unannounced, under the circumstances. We came to offer support.'

'Good to see you, love, as always.'

I try not to show my hurt at Lily and Mags being in regular contact. I miss Mags. I want to chat with her on the phone and visit. Why am I being punished when I've not done anything to deserve it?

'You got here quickly from Camden,' I say to Lily. 'I only sent you a text a short while ago.'

'We were in the area.' Lily picks up the dog's lead and gives it to Freya. 'Take Yellow into the garden, love. He could do with stretching his legs.'

'I'll go with you,' Damien says. 'Gus needs to go out too.'

Hayden hugs Lily. 'It's good to see your ugly mug, Lil.' He grins as she playfully swats at him. I love them for trying to keep some kind of normality. We all need it.

'Tamsin was a great kid,' Lily says. 'This is awful.' She throws her denim jacket on top of Steve and sits next to Hayden on the floor.

Steve hurls Lily's jacket at her. 'Use a coat hook. You're such a lazy cow.'

Lily replies with her middle finger and then turns to Mags. 'How are you holding up, Mags?'

Mags startles, disrupted from staring at Tamsin in the photograph. 'I haven't slept well since Tamsin disappeared. Can you imagine having years of insomnia?' Mags rubs her eyes. 'Knowing Tamsin's never coming home, I'm afraid to sleep, scared of what I'll dream. All I can think about is how she was found. I daren't let my mind wander any further.'

'Are you feeling all right, Mags?' I ask, noticing concerning signs.

Mags wipes her sweaty forehead with her sleeve. 'I'm fine. Don't fuss.'

Despite the harsh reply, I won't be quiet and watch Mags getting ill. 'When did you last eat?' I ask.

'I've eaten. Lay off it.' Mags is snappier than usual.

'Can I check you over please?' Professional responsibility trumps animosity.

'I'm okay,' Mags says, rolling up her shirt sleeves.

This conversation is over but my monitoring isn't. I'll speak to Damien and check Mags is looking after herself.

'How about a lie down, Mum?' Hayden helps Mags from the chair. 'Even if you don't sleep, at least you'll be resting.'

'I'm not an invalid.' Mags pulls away from Hayden's grasp. She looks at Hayden who appears close to tears. 'Maybe a rest is a good idea,' Mags concedes.

Hayden steps back, following his mum's lead. He glances at me and I nod, realising he wants me to keep an eye on Mags' health.

'Let's join your daughter and dog,' I say to Lily. 'We have a lot to discuss.'

18

SARAH

I n the garden, Freya throws a stick for Yellow to retrieve. The dog doesn't move. He's not giving up the only sliver of sun. Gus is busy digging up plants.

Damien grabs the puppy. 'This little pest could do with a walk.'

'Why don't you take Yellow along too?' I say to Freya.

Freya gives a dramatic sigh. 'It's not fair. People always send me away when they want to talk about interesting stuff. I'm not a child.' She glares at me above fake black-rimmed glasses.

Teenagers who wear non-prescription glasses baffle me. It's great this generation understand wearing specs isn't an affliction, even if they've taken it too far. What next? Fashionable hearing aids? Wow, I'm getting old. I couldn't tell you what's in fashion even if it bit me on the arse.

Freya scurries away in response to my death stare, reluctant dog in tow. Lily said I could discipline her daughter when she's being a pain in the backside. I rarely fall out with Freya and I'm proud of how we've formed a close relationship. Lily wishes I was Freya's godmother but Lily doesn't do religion, couldn't be bothered with a christening, and says it's too late for a dunking.

Lily and I sit on a bench in a shaded corner. Sun-seeking Yellow had the right idea. Regretting not wearing a coat, I cover my hands with my sleeves.

'What's happened?' I ask Lily.

'Nothing.'

'I can tell when you're lying, Lil. You concentrate.'

It's true. Usually, Lily gets distracted by every minor thing she sees. She's been staring at her feet for five minutes. Lily releases her hair from a bun. The usual bright blonde is more murky brown. She never misses a visit to the hairdresser.

'I left Gareth.' Lily speaks with the flatness of a defeated woman.

Bringing Freya along to witness the Lawsons' grief seemed odd. Lily tries to shield her daughter from the worst of human nature. It's proving more difficult with Freya's increasing determination to join the police force. She devours true crime books and serial killer documentaries. Lily insists on watching them with Freya, trying to be a decent parent. It's somewhat unnerving hearing mother and daughter discuss the best killing methods. Although Lily always wimps out when the conversation involves gore.

'What happened?' I hide my confusion at Lily leaving her husband.

I thought the Osbornes had it made, with their Camden pad and city lifestyle. Lily claimed to be living the dream of world-cuisine restaurants, theatres, and swanky shops, only a Tube ride away.

Lily fiddles with a bare rose bush until a thorn pierces her finger. 'Damn it.' She sucks the wound.

'Let me see.' I check the cut. 'You'll live. Here, press this tissue down on it.'

Lily winces as she wraps her finger. 'Gareth's been having an affair with one of his clients.'

Lily's husband runs his own marketing business. He left the security of an executive role in a successful Oxfordshire company to go out on his own. Lily didn't want to move to London but she values family. Gareth thrives on risk and danger. Affairs too, it seems.

Gareth's polite but has a habit of assessing me as lacking with a single look. Lily said not to take it personally because Gareth likes to get the measure of people. Whenever a new client walks in, he figures out if they're worth his time or not. As a GP, I understand reading others – you wouldn't believe how many patients expect me to work it out instead of sharing their symptoms – but I hope I never make them feel judged.

Gareth's like the popular kids at school; the gorgeous, confident, sporty high-achievers. I wasn't athletic and I'm still not. Yoga is as far as it goes. If there was a reason to get out of PE lessons, I had it. My teacher got wise after a series of faked notes from Dad, citing multiple injuries and ailments. My punishment was the public humiliation of showing the class how gymnastics *wasn't* done. Being around Gareth reminds me of making a clumsy attempt at the vaulting horse by crawling over it. I can still hear the cool kids jeering.

'I'd been keeping tabs on Gareth for a while,' Lily says. 'I used methods of detection and my suspicions were confirmed when I came home early after sneaking out of work. Well, I got the sack but that's another story. Gareth was banging some bint, who's older than me, and has saggy boobs. They were in our bed. I burned the mattress afterwards.'

I wouldn't expect anything less of Lily. Gareth's lucky she didn't add him to the bonfire.

Lily sits. 'I said it was over and I was leaving with Freya and Yellow. Gareth begged and pleaded. I didn't cave in. He's not getting away with it again.'

'Again? Gareth's cheated before? You never told me.'

Since Lily and I met when I moved in with the Lawsons in Oxford, next door to Lily's family, we've kept in touch. Despite me moving around the country, our friendship has strengthened. I thought we told each other everything. Then I remember I haven't shared with Lily my most shameful secrets. She wouldn't still be my friend if I had.

As Lily opens the cut in her finger, she sucks air through her teeth. 'I'm the pathetic woman who forgives a man after he's done the dirty. In my defence, I was young. We were at university. Gareth was a bit of a tart when we met. I believed I was "The One" and he'd settle down for me. I sound like a slushy romance novel.'

'A smidge.'

Lily continues. 'Gossip flew around campus about Gareth having a one-night stand. I broke into his room, coated the crotch of his boxers with itching powder, and then dumped him. The pleasure of watching Gareth furiously scratching his nuts when pleading for forgiveness was glorious. He spent weeks trying to make me take him back. I gave in. I loved him but I kept an eye on him throughout the rest of my course.

'Mum was livid when I told her what Gareth had done back then. She said I shouldn't have let him off. I thought I couldn't be without him. Mum promised to stay out of it but her expressions in our wedding photos say it all. It's a good thing Photoshop was invented so I didn't have to keep looking at her sour chops. For a laugh, I added extra teeth. She looks slightly unhinged. Mum won't let me put it up on the wall, the spoilsport.'

'Does Imogen know you're back?' I ask.

'No. I can't tell Mum I've failed again.' Lily begins to howl. She wipes away snot with the tissue still attached to her finger. I pass her the rest of the packet.

'I can't tell Mum,' Lily wails. 'You know what a radical feminist she is. Freya and I have been staying in a grotty hotel. They make Yellow sleep outside in a shed. There's no heating in our room, the man next door is keen on noisy self-love, and a chip fat stench from the kitchen seeps through the walls.'

I hold Lily tight. Despite her being a year older and thinking she's more mature, I'm the mothering one in our relationship. Lily loves a hug. She's a softy who makes no apologies for showing her emotions. It's why I love her.

'Stay with me while you get sorted out,' I say.

I'd do anything for Lily and Freya. I try not to imagine how Hayden will react considering I've put him off moving in. Lily's his friend too. He'll understand, I hope.

Lily moves away from being pressed into my neck. 'Give me some oxygen, will you? Thanks though. You're a star.'

'What happened with your job?'

'I told my boss to shove the photocopying up his rectum.'

'Nice to hear you're using medical terms but you can't always say what you think. You need to work on your brain-to-mouth filter. How many jobs have you had in Camden?'

Lily pretends to count on her fingers. She's walked out of, or been sacked from, six jobs in as many months. Lily's boredom threshold is low and her desire for new experiences high. The only thing she applies herself to for a prolonged length of time is study. Knowledge grounds her.

Hayden flings open the patio door. 'Quick, Sarah! Mum's in a bad way. She needs your help.'

19

RED

A hole in the garden fence is like a gift to Red. She's learned the woman visiting is Sarah's friend, Lily. It's good to put a face to the name.

Red thought she was tall but Lily is a giant in comparison. Red feels superior in being more confident in her height than Lily. The unassured woman appears set to fall over her feet at any moment.

Hayden used to talk about Lily, the goofy attention-deficit neighbour from when the Lawsons previously lived in Oxford. From what Red can hear, Lily hasn't changed much.

Mags and Damien's garden backs onto an alleyway. Red already knew. She could find her way around Great Parston blindfolded. Red leans against the fencing panel, grateful there isn't a gate. She cannot be seen. Glimpses through the spyhole are limited. Someone spotting a watcher's eye would ruin everything.

Lily is admirable and annoying. Red likes Lily's determination but not her weakness. Lily reminds Red of a frustrating girl she witnessed evolving into a complex woman. Trying to be positive, Red focuses on Lily's ballsiness for leaving her husband, rather than forgiving his first indiscretion. Gareth's no doubt cheated more often than Lily knows. She needs to toughen up. Red's already showed another woman how to be strong and deceitful. Now Lily is a candidate for Red's instruction.

If Lily is to be a match for Red, Lily must strive for perfection. Red will make sure of it.

20

RED

Red places her hand against the fence as Lily continues crying. The choice between wanting to soothe Lily and batter her is intense.

Men never dupe Red. They flock to her, challenged by her frostiness, hinting at a blaze within. Her flame-red hair is the main draw. They stroke it as if bewitched, asking if it's natural. She reassures them there's nothing fake about her.

Red is so much more than a hair colour. Red is a state of being. She is passion and love. Red ignites, catches hold of others' lives, and watches them burn.

21

SARAH

A damp patch on the pillow circles around Mags' head. Tendrils of sweat-soaked hair stick to her face. As I check Mags' pulse, her arm shakes.

'Look at me, Mags,' I say with my doctor voice. Mags will not focus. Incoherent mumbling spills from her mouth.

'Does she have a glucagon kit?' I ask Hayden, who's hovering in the doorway.

Hayden slaps the side of his head. 'Damn, yes. I forgot.' He runs downstairs.

Lily paces on the landing. I made her stay outside. She's not always the best person to have around in a crisis. Lily freaks out and reacts to every fight-or-flight thought that enters her mind.

Hayden appears. 'Here you go.' He gives me the essential glucose to tackle Mags' low blood sugar.

My hands tremble more than Mags' as I hold the vial and syringe. They're only medical equipment. I'm trained. I can do this. I must. Mags' skin is clammy and she's losing consciousness. Everyone is depending on me.

The syringe lays heavy in my palm. I drift away to a place I don't want to go.

A needle.
Drowsiness.
A leer.
Forbidden touch.
Screams.
Escape.

22

RED

Red paces the alleyway, waiting for the end of Mags' life.

Steve was in the garden. His panicked voice on the phone demanded Damien return to be with his wife. Red's pulse quickens in celebration of another Lawson death. She checks her watch, etching Mags' demise in her mind.

Red didn't have to lift a finger. Good. She'll save her energy for killing Sarah and Hayden.

23

SARAH

'Do something!' Steve shouts as he bursts in, smacking the bedroom door against the wall.

'Sarah, hurry up!' Hayden grasps my shoulder, pulling me to the present. 'Give Mum the injection.'

'I'll do it,' Damien says, calmly entering the room. 'I'm used to it.'

Sets of accusing and confused eyes follow me as I leave. The bathroom is a refuge where I can compose myself and formulate another lie.

I lean away from Mags on the bed, finishing checking her over. 'I don't think you need to go to hospital. The injection is working and you're already perking up.'

Mags gives a weak smile.

'All thanks to Damien,' Steve says. 'Good thing I phoned and told him to come back, seeing as no one else was helping Mum.'

Lily punches Steve's arm, aware he's making a dig at me.

'Get Mags some water please, Steve.' With the need for him

to leave, I rediscover my authority. I won't be scrutinised for my ability to do my job.

'I'm okay. It's only a blip,' Mags says. She has more colour in her face but is visibly drained.

'Haven't you been eating?' Damien asks, stroking a thumb across Mags' forehead. 'I should've kept an eye on you. Mags stops eating when she's stressed,' Damien tells me. 'I'll make a sandwich.'

'Thanks, Damien,' I reply. He looks at me, no doubt understanding I'm thanking him for more than making a snack.

'I need to change out of these sweaty clothes,' Mags says. 'If you wouldn't mind leaving the room for a minute.'

We can hear Lily downstairs, bossing Steve and Damien with how to prepare a drink and a sandwich. I lean against the banisters, facing Hayden sitting on the top stair.

'What happened?' he asks.

'Mags isn't managing her diabetes.'

'You know what I mean. Why did you freeze at giving Mum the injection?' There's no accusation in his question, only confusion.

Truth or lie? Which will it be? Keep your partner or lose him?

'I panicked. Mags was like a mum to me. There's a reason doctors don't treat their own family. Let's not make a big thing of it. I'm embarrassed enough as it is.'

Hayden sits next to me and laces his fingers through mine. 'Don't be embarrassed. I lost it too. Thankfully, Damien's done it before.'

I'm grateful to Lily for walking up the stairs with a tray, interrupting further conversation. How can I explain I'm a GP who's wary of needles? I've blagged it so far. Patients are referred to hospital for blood tests. Training was tricky though. I learned mind techniques to see me through whenever sharps appeared. Now I'm out of practise.

When I held the needle and prepared to inject Mags, I visualised a different adult there; one greedy for the next fix. I saw my sordid past.

24

SARAH

In one day so much has changed. I haven't been thrown out of Mags' house, Tamsin is dead, Lily has left her cheating husband, and my deepest fear defeated me.

The intimacy of being in Mags' bedroom is awkward. Being flanked by people who are aware of our row helps. Hayden holds my hand while Lily rubs my back.

A stack of pillows bolsters Mags. At least I'm still able to assess patients even if I have difficulty injecting them. Mags has made a quick recovery. As she seeks a comfortable position, I check out the room. It's unusually bland. I expected explosions of colour, signifying the confident woman who lives here. Instead, beige curtains match a plain duvet set. The pine wardrobes and drawers are tasteful and the cream wallpaper is decorated with a delicate floral pattern. Lily steals a glance at me, after performing a similar search, and shrugs. Maybe aliens abducted the real Mags. I can but hope. Perhaps alien Mags doesn't know she's supposed to be annoyed with me.

Mags' bedroom in Oxford was a riot of colour. The walls were painted in the primary shades. Busy patterns dominated the carpet, duvet, and curtains. We named it the Rainbow

Room. Paul complained it gave him a headache as soon as he woke. Mags called him a miserable git who needed more brightness in his life. I enjoyed their banter once I got used to it.

After fighting through a mountain of cushions, Hayden finds a spot next to Mags. I'm standing at the foot of the bed, waiting for a rollicking. Mags won't forget our argument.

Lily's nibbling her cut finger, making it bleed again. The drips on Mags' carpet deserve a bravery award for spoiling her sanctuary. I try to point it out to Lily, who's too busy practically nibbling her fingertips off. I know she's nervous for me. We've had many conversations about the row Mags and I had. Lily said she'd tell Mags what she thought of her next time they met. My best friend is often brave in theory.

'You both doted on Tamsin,' Mags says to Lily and me. 'You cared for her as if she was your sister. I'm grateful to you for it and for being here. I expect being around me is the last thing you want, Sarah.'

'Not now, Mum.' Hayden's protective instinct kicks in. 'Let's not dredge it up. You haven't been fair on Sarah and I'm not letting you have a go at her again.'

'Sarah and I will sort it out in a bit,' Mags replies. 'Calm down.'

I ruffle Hayden's hair. 'It's fine. Don't worry.' I don't add how I'm doing the worrying for him.

'We have more pressing matters to discuss,' Mags begins. 'The detective says they'll be on the case, finding out what happened to Tamsin. Will they do all they can though? Will they not rest until the murdering scumbag is found? Will they be driven by memories of a precious girl who brought so much joy? For them it's a job and not one they've done well. Yes, the police have training and forensics but do they have the drive to keep going until Tamsin has justice?'

'I can't believe how long it's taken them to find her,' Hayden adds. He looks at Mags and I note their mutual grief.

'I'm considering getting a private investigator,' Mags says. 'I'll rustle up the money from somewhere, even if I have to get a mortgage on the house. Luckily, Paul's debt didn't result in me having to sell it.'

No one replies. Hayden told me it's always been a sore subject. Paul took out a few loans he kept secret from Mags. He said he was getting pay rises and promotions as a cover for his spending. After Paul's death, Mags dealt with the money sharks, telling them they could go whistle, trying to extract money from a widow.

Mags continues. 'A PI will do a thorough job. My girl needs their determination so she can rest in peace. I need to go to my grave assured my child's killer is banged up.'

'You're not dying, are you?'

Hayden and I wince at Lily's habit of placing a foot firmly in her mouth.

Mags' laugh has a sharp edge. 'No, you daft cow, although believe me, sometimes I wished I *was* dead. When Tamsin went missing I wanted to disappear too. Living without her was unbearable. I kept going for my boys and because I had to be here when Tamsin came home. I always believed she'd return. Wishing myself dead isn't an option. While someone's out there, thinking they've got away with it, I won't give up.'

Lily chews her lip. She's engaged her thinking face. This often spells disaster. 'I'll do it.'

'Do what?' Hayden asks.

'I'll investigate Tamsin's death.'

25

RED

Mothers are a strange breed. Red's mother defines definition.

Mags however was always an earth mother, nurturing extraordinaire. Red was never sure if she liked or loathed it.

'Mum said to welcome you to the road.' Hayden stood on Red's doorstep. He couldn't have looked less like a welcoming party if he tried. He thrust a cake tin at Red and turned to leave.

'Stop a minute,' Red said. 'At least wait while I see what it is.' Aromas of spiced fruit and marzipan tickled her nostrils as she removed the lid. 'Fruit cake's my favourite. Thank you.'

'Thank Mum, not me.' Hayden shoved his hands in his pockets.

As he shifted from foot to foot, Red understood he was waiting to be dismissed. She wouldn't allow it. They were finally talking. Red's usual confidence around the opposite sex eluded her around Hayden, despite her being older.

'Why don't you want to talk to me?' Red couldn't hide her frustration. Hayden was ruining the perfect moment created in her mind. 'Am I not good enough for you?'

Red didn't realise she'd seized Hayden until he shook her off.

'Calm down,' Hayden said, rubbing his wrist. 'You've got some serious issues.'

Red stepped towards Hayden, refusing to acknowledge his alarm. 'I'm sorry. So sorry. Please forget that happened. We don't get many visitors.'

Hayden held up his hands and backed away. 'Yeah, okay. Whatever. What's that noise?'

The grating sound of violin practice, taking place in the lounge, jangled Red's frayed nerves. Once again her moment was ruined by the interloper.

'What's happening here then?' Red's mother stepped into the doorway. Her hair was in curlers, ready for an evening of showing off her auburn locks to any man who took notice. The woman assessed the teenagers.

'I was dropping off a cake my mum made,' Hayden replied. 'It's a welcome-to-the-road present.' Hayden sounded bored. He looked behind him, probably waiting for the cue to leave.

'How lovely.' Red's mother stroked the back of her daughter's neck. Red flinched at the vulgar touch. 'Let's have a slice while it's fresh, shall we?' Red's mother added.

Hayden left. Red's mother had a habit of making people disappear. A look was enough. She'd learned it from her own mother. Red considered a suitable punishment to inflict upon her mother ruining the opportunity to connect with Hayden.

The house reverberated as Red's mother slammed the door. The cat strangling sounds of the violin ceased. Red's mother marched into the kitchen and tipped the cake in the bin. 'I'm sick and tired of receiving others' pity and cast-offs. They wouldn't be so smug if I told them I was first. Never forget it, girl.'

How could Red forget? It was all her mother talked about; the one that got away. Hayden had got away too. Red wasn't a quitter like her mother though. Hayden and Red would be together, no matter how long it took for Red to make it happen.

26

SARAH

I consider my words carefully, knowing Lily will be disappointed with my reaction. 'In case you're forgetting, Lil, you're not a private investigator.'

'I've always wanted to be in the police.'

'You're mixing up your ambitions with Freya's,' I reply. 'Remember your daughter, the one who wants to be a PC?'

Lily puffs out her cheeks. 'I aspired to be a copper too.'

'Since when?' Hayden asks, not even trying to hide his amusement.

'Since forever.' This translates as Lily watched a crime series recently and thinks it's an exciting vocation. Lily changes jobs more often than some people change their undies.

'Lil, no,' I say as gently as possible. 'You're not trained to investigate.'

Lily scratches her eyebrow. The thinking face is engaged again. 'I kind of am actually. The rest of you might as well know that my husband has been cheating on me. I learned how to catch him out.'

'Sorry to hear about Gareth,' Hayden replies, 'but stalking an unfaithful husband isn't the same as tracking down a killer.'

Hayden addresses Mags. 'I'll find a private investigator and help you with the cost.'

'No!' Lily's outburst startles us. 'Stop treating me like a child. I *can* do this. I know I'm ditsy and sometimes away with the fairies but I want to help Mags. You can't dispute I'm clever.'

'No one said you're not. We're aware your IQ is off the charts.' Hayden understands Lily needs his belief. It's also true she's a genius. Lily's mum sprouted premature grey hairs dealing with her demanding child prodigy.

'It's not something you can automatically do,' I say to Lily, reaching for her.

She moves away. 'This is what I'm trying to explain. I've been doing online courses in profiling and private investigation. When Gareth started acting weird almost a year ago, I decided to learn how to investigate. Much as I hate that I was right about Gareth, he was a good case study. The best way to learn is on the job. A teacher and a doctor should understand.

'I've done some jobs for friends too, to test out my skills. I provided evidence to my boss of the bloke in accounts who was helping himself to money, found a pedigree dog stolen for breeding, and I was working on a fraud before I left London. If you want me to, Mags, I'll do it. I'll find justice for Tamsin.'

Mags sits up higher. 'Would you do that for me?'

Lily blushes. 'Of course. I'd do anything for you, Mags. You're my second mum. Sarah and I will find Tamsin's killer.'

'Er, no we won't,' I reply. 'Have you forgotten some of us have real jobs? Besides, you're not an actual investigator, Lil.'

'I've passed every single module with distinctions.' Lily presses a few options on her phone and shows me an email, detailing her qualifications. It's an impressive list.

'How come you never told us about this?' Hayden asks. 'You're usually shouting to the world about your latest course.'

Lily winks at him. 'Shows how good I am at being an investigator, doesn't it? Even my best friends and family didn't know.'

In her defence, Lily can pick up anything she sets her mind to within hours. It's a strange quirk of someone who has the attention span of a goldfish. Give her a textbook, though, and you've lost her. Lily will immerse herself in knowledge until she comes out the other end, hopefully wiser.

'You can help investigate outside surgery hours or get in a locum,' Lily says to me.

Hayden laughs. 'Lil, you can't expect people to drop everything. Sarah isn't trained in private investigation. I admire you for wanting to help but it's a killer you're dealing with. You could get hurt.'

Lily screws up her face. 'Nah. I'll be fine. Sarah'll have my back.'

I don't bother replying. We'll have this conversation later when it's not so awkward and doesn't appear I'm letting Mags down.

Mags slumps. 'I understand it's a lot to expect of you both. Discuss it. If you were to help, I'd be grateful. Now, I could do with a nap.'

I follow Hayden and Lily as they leave. Mags takes my hand as I trail behind.

'You and I need to have a chat first,' Mags says.

27

SARAH

Mags pats the side of her bed. I sit, desperate for the closeness but scared of the outcome.

'I was hard on you,' Mags says. 'Truly, I'm sorry, and not because Lily is offering your help.'

'Thank you. I bet it took a lot to say that.'

Mags laughs. 'For a stubborn old harpy? Don't look so shocked. I'm aware of what a handful I can be. Never make apologies for who you are, Sarah. Move on from your mistakes. Stop dwelling on the past.'

'I would if you'd give me half a chance.' The words are blunter than I intended but they're the truth. 'Hayden and I aren't brother and sister, you have to accept it.'

'I know.' Mags lies back and focuses on the ceiling. 'In the time you were with us, you became like a daughter to me. I was shocked when Hayden said you're together. I've always viewed you as one of mine.'

I won't get into how she abandoned me. Mags is tiring and not ready to deal with years of suppressed hurt. For now she'll have the facts to reflect on. 'Hayden and I aren't related. You tried to make us feel our relationship is wrong. Foster siblings

LISA SELL

can be together. As a foster mother, you should be aware of how it works.'

'I was stupid,' Mags replies, finally looking at me. 'I said some hurtful things and I regret every word.'

'When you stopped talking to me, I was gutted. You never fell out with Hayden though.'

'He's my son.' Mags' tone is snappier.

'And apparently I'm your daughter, even though I'm not.' My tone is equally harsh.

'I'm a foolish old woman who isn't great at admitting when she's wrong. I'm doing it now. Please forgive me. It's great you're with Hayden. You're good for him. Anyone can see it. In loving Hayden, we have something in common and we should recognise it. I accept you're what he wants and needs.'

I can't keep fighting with Mags. I've been waiting for this moment. It's sad it took Tamsin's death to bring us back together but I'll take it. 'I'm sorry too for the horrible things I said.'

'Let's move on. Don't stand in Lily's way with the investigation. She needs a purpose. Maybe this is it. If you'll consider helping, to keep an eye on her, I'd appreciate it. Give it some thought. I need you to shake this world up and down until you find who killed Tamsin. Please, do this for me, for us all.'

'You should sleep.' I let go of Mags' hand, substituting her iron clasp for the door handle.

Mags won't get the answer she wants. I'm not investigating. For once, Lily is going it alone, without her best friend.

28

SARAH

I join Hayden and Lily in the garden. Knowing Mags' lack of green fingers, Damien must have created this oriental oasis. Miniature bridges, lanterns, pagodas, and snaking gravel paths cover the area. Traces of bamboo, hiding their leaves until spring, line every edge.

Freya is still out with Yellow. The ten-pound note Lily slipped in her pocket was a message to make it a long walk. Where Freya can spend the money, out here in the sticks, is another matter.

'How's Mum?' Hayden asks.

'She's fine. Almost back to her usual self,' I reply.

'Bossing you around then?'

'Something like that. Well, I never. Lily Osborne smoking?'

Lily stubs out a cigarette on a terracotta soldier's head.

'Why are you letting her smoke?' I ask Hayden.

'Last time I tried to tell Lily what to do, my ears were ringing for days.'

'Don't judge me,' Lily says. 'My husband is a cheat and I'm stressed beyond belief. If it helps, every puff was disgusting. I can't believe I enjoyed smoking.' She crumples the cigarette pack.

'Steve'll take them off you,' Hayden says.

Lily smooths out the box. 'Ciggies are stupidly expensive. I handed over a fiver for twenty cigarettes and the newsagent asked what decade I was in.'

I spot an engraved plaque on the wall behind Hayden. The dedication is supposed to read "For Tamsin, who loved to play here". Weathered letters make it incomplete. It's pitiful not even this remains of her.

'Are we investigating Tamsin's death?' Lily won't give up. She has an opportunity to feel useful, and focus on something other than her dead marriage.

I sit next to Hayden on the bench. He faces me. 'It's hard to refuse her, eh? You have to though. It's risky. Neither of you should do it.'

Lily exhales hard enough to blow her fringe off her forehead. 'Stop being so macho. We can take care of ourselves.'

'Chill out, Lil,' I reply. 'I understand you're anti-men and Hayden falls into the category but don't forget he's your friend.'

Lily sticks her tongue out at Hayden.

He does the same back before replying. 'You might be hurt or worse if you get too close to Tamsin's killer. I couldn't bear someone else I care about being treated like that.'

I expect we're all thinking how only a calculated evil mind kills a child and disposes of them in a suitcase. It would be a small consolation if Tamsin was dead before being captured in a dark prison.

Lily flips the cigarette packet lid open and closed. She throws them into the water feature. The fountain's boy statue does its thing and pees on them.

'Better fish those out,' Hayden says. 'You know how much Mum hates littering.'

'I'm more than capable of looking after myself, with your mum and when investigating.' Lily marches across the patio. 'I'm an expert at swerving trouble.'

'Is that right?' Hayden raises an eyebrow. 'So, the stint you did as an acrobat was your idea of keeping safe?'

Lily cracks her knuckles. 'Given a few more weeks I'd have improved.'

'You broke your legs,' Hayden adds. 'What about when you were a nightclub bouncer and that bloke sued you?'

Lily plays with her phone. 'It's not my fault he was so short I didn't see him.'

'You knocked him out,' I say. 'Poor man was only standing in the queue. You're very expressive with your arms. Investigating can be dangerous, Lil.'

Lily holds out her mobile. 'The 1950s called for you two. They want their sexist attitudes back. Women can be investigators too. In fact, I took a module on just that and passed.'

'Really? You think I'm sexist?' Hayden slumps like a deflated balloon. 'I would *never* hold you back. Your bravery is astounding. Offering to do this for Tamsin is so generous. If anything happened to either of you though, I couldn't bear it.'

Lily grabs Hayden's face and plants a kiss on his nose. 'I never knew you cared so much. Okay, we won't investigate, seeing as you're being so nice and all.'

'I wasn't doing it anyway,' I add.

'Do you promise?' Hayden asks.

'I promise,' I say, without hesitation.

'Suppose so.' Lily's pout could outshine a catwalk model.

29

RED

Red embraces the roughness of the fencing panels. Splinters pierce into her. The pain replaces rage. It is a prudent move. Her temper often creates trouble, usually for Red.

Mags survived. The Lawsons always prosper. Sure, Tamsin died but that's so 2002. Mags' death would have been a bonus. Red deserves a reward. The Lawsons will pay for what they took from Red. They broke her family. It's time for the Lawsons to shatter.

Red splays her fingers, pushing the splinters in deep, while chanting the names of her intended victims. Blood trickles into her palms. She imagines it as their blood and smiles.

30

SARAH

Hayden leaves to check on Mags. I prepare for Lily's inevitable outburst as she sits next to me. She's probably ready to mouth off about Hayden asking her not to investigate. Instead, we focus on the spurting, rather than flowing, waterfall. ' enjoy the peace within a tumultuous day.

'Who the hell does Hayden think he is, telling us what to
Lily's silence never lasts long.

've you forgotten who Hayden is?' I'm trying to hold in my
ce. 'He's not a cheating husband or a threat to femi-
den's the most decent bloke you'll ever meet, Lily

my hip. 'Sorry, you're right. Hayden is a keeper,
one. I can't understand why you don't want to
Tamsin.'

as I unclench my fists. 'I want her killer
'ustice as much as you. I'm not the person
'h. I respect how you've been studying
'ey're trained to do.'

'er thighs. 'I need this. My life's in
'ul. We both know how crap I am

71

at holding down a job. My last one was dire. The corporate life is a drip feed of death; hours chained to a desk, in an office reeking of BO, and failed dreams. Taking instructions was torture. I want to be in charge for once and I'm certain I can do this. I'm so ashamed I'm in my thirties and I've still not got a career. All my friends on Facebook do.'

'Don't believe everything you see on social media. People present their best faces and filtered lives there. At least you've had the courage to try different things. I wish I were as brave as you.'

Lily gives my arm an affectionate squeeze. 'You're the most courageous person I've ever met, Sarah. After what you went through, you've come out of it strong. I wish I was as together as you.'

'Keep being you. We love you for who you are. You're fabulous, Lily Osborne.'

Lily hugs me. 'Thank you. I'll be a great investigator, I can feel it. My module leader on tracing and surveillance said my skills were amazing. I followed her around London once. She almost had a heart attack when I cornered her in the toilets. I think she was a little proud of me too, although she reminded me about boundaries.'

I check the patio door is closed. 'You're determined to do this, aren't you?'

'Yes. I understand you don't want in but I need you to kee this a secret from Hayden. He'll go spare if he finds out I' broken my promise.'

'What about me lying to him? It's just as bad.'

'I'm helping Hayden and his family. He'll understand w tell him later on. A little white lie hurt no one.'

It's what my birth father used to say. It *did* hurt. It di damage than he or I expected. Lily's puppy-dog eyes rep memory of an enraged James.

'I'll keep your secret, for the moment,' I say, 'although I'm already regretting it. You must tell Hayden soon.'

Lily performs a celebration dance, adding a series of whoops.

I clamp a hand over her mouth.

I've broken my promise to Hayden within minutes of giving it.

Damn you, Lily.

31

RED

On the other side of the fencing panel, Red celebrates with Lily, only in her head. Red is too disciplined for such childish displays. The narrow alleyway offers privacy but still she won't let go. Nothing disrupts Red's attention, although the sound of the water fountain threatened to break her bladder. Listening to Lily and Sarah plotting helped Red focus.

It's going better than planned. Before, Red was prepared to sit back and savour the Lawsons' misery, after the discovery of Tamsin's body. Now it's game on.

With Lily working on finding Tamsin's killer, Red has more reason to stick around. Sarah will have no choice but to investigate too. Red will make it happen. These women aren't pushovers and they offer the challenge Red craves. Too bad for them Red's already won.

32

RED

R ed's prizes are often hard won. She learned from an early age to fight for what she wanted and never give up.

When Red was younger, other children teased her for not having a dad and being the product of teenage parents. Not only did Red have to suffer, knowing her father didn't want her, she was judged by others for being born too.

Back then, youngsters relished learning the literal meaning of *bastard* and using it as an insult. They picked the wrong girl. Red punched her way out of it. Each thump was in retaliation against an absent father. Her mother's irritation increased, not difficult considering the resentment she harboured for her daughter. Red learned her mother's affections weren't always equal.

Red landed on the teachers' radar. She learned from her mistakes. Red had to be smarter when exacting revenge.

Aged six, Red began a life of subterfuge and abuse. Young Red offered fake sympathy as a fellow pupil, Olivia, wept over a smashed clay pot, torn exercise books, and a slashed school bag. The staff expressed horror at the cycle of disturbing events happening to such a sweet child. Their blindness to Olivia's bullying of the other children infuriated Red. Only beautiful girls could be victims.

From there, Red ramped it up. With every slight, things happened she ensured she couldn't be linked to: pigtails cut from sleeping girls at story time, unscrewing bolts on play equipment for "accidents" to happen, tyres slashed, windscreens smashed, hate mail, blackmail, burglaries, fraud, affairs, deceit, and death. There was no line to draw. Red did it all and will now take it further.

There is only one thing left; prolonged torture.

33

SARAH

I've lost track of how many cups of coffee I've had. Today is a slow starter. Getting out of bed was a mission. It went downhill from there.

Ditching an Ashtanga session shows things aren't good. Yoga sets me up for the day. My muscles screaming in protest makes me feel alive. It's a relaxing form of torture. Lily says I'm a sadist who should lift weights instead. She's certainly got a great set of guns on her. Never take up Lily on an arm wrestling challenge.

The guilt of lying to Hayden haunts me, demanding attention. I hardly slept last night, trying to find the right words to explain to Hayden about Lily investigating Tamsin's death. My relationship with Hayden seems solid but agreeing not to tell him what Lily's doing could have consequences.

Lily had a habit of leading me astray when we were younger. I looked up to her back then. When you're thirteen, a girl a year older than you borders on an adult. I was seduced by Lily's casual air. Before we met I was uptight; looking for danger so I could avoid it. I mistook Lily's nonchalance for coolness. Over the years I realised she's scatty.

Despite my dark background, I'd never been in trouble of

my own doing. When I met Lily, she got me into quite a few scrapes, always without intent. I remember how we were chased by an irate man for stealing his apples. Lily said any fruit growing naturally was free. It was only stealing if you took apples from the supermarket. I believed her.

There was also a "shoplifting" incident. As we sat in the police station, waiting for our parents to arrive, I was convinced Mags and Paul would send me back to social services as a problem child. Thankfully, the police believed Lily was an idiot. She had a habit of putting things in her pockets instead of a basket. Lily forgot to do the paying part. Her mum, Imogen, explained Lily's distractedness and we were set free.

The first sip of coffee scalds my tongue but I knock it back. Lily says my asbestos mouth is a biological phenomenon. When I became a practice partner, I upgraded the kettle to a swanky coffee machine. It was a congratulatory present to myself. Years of study and moving around the country was demanding. Settling into my house in Oxfordshire was a relief. I'd longed for my home county and to be closer to Mum.

Before I was accepted for med school, I knew I wanted to be a GP and practice partner. I never allowed my troubled childhood to hold me back. In fact, it's motivated me. I wouldn't be another casualty of addict parents, become an addict myself or a sob story.

I hear Lily's voice before seeing her. In reception, Lily's showing my practice partner, Phoebe, something on her phone. They're giggling like flighty schoolgirls. Lily holds up the screen, playing a video of a naked man exiting a lift while shaking his attributes. I recognise the television presenter.

'Can you believe Lily recorded this when she was in London?' Phoebe says. 'She heard he likes to run around in the buff in fancy hotels after getting high.'

'I staked him out,' Lily adds, pride on her face. She's trying to prove she has investigative skills.

Kevin, our other practice partner, comes over to see what the fuss is about. He peers over Lily's shoulder at her phone. 'Are you okay with this, Sarah?' His voice is sorrowful because he knows about my birth parents.

'Damn it.' Lily switches off her mobile. 'I wasn't bashing drug addicts.'

Phoebe looks equally mortified.

Lowering my head, I respond. 'I'm gutted you'd use addiction for a cheap laugh. I expected better of you both.'

'Please accept my apology. It's inexcusable.' Phoebe shifts from one foot to the other.

'I thought you were more compassionate, Phoebe,' Kevin adds.

I point at Phoebe and Lily. 'Got ya. Chill out, will you? I can take a joke.'

Kevin and I are in hysterics at their reactions. I hold on to him, trying to compose myself.

'Not cool, Captain Kirk.' Phoebe punches Kevin's arm.

Kevin gives a dramatic eye roll at a joke that began when his full name was read from the class register.

'Kevin Kirk!' Lily exclaims. 'So, you're like the man in *Star Wars*?'

Lily waits for a response from a baffled Kevin. Phoebe and I laugh. Lily's often late to punchlines and not a fan of sci-fi.

'You two are such wind-up merchants,' Phoebe says to Kevin and me. 'Good to see you have a sense of humour sometimes.'

'Stop being so cheeky,' I reply. 'I have some corking stories about you at med school I could share.'

Phoebe blushes. 'Don't you dare. What happens at med school stays at med school.'

Phoebe oozes class and sophistication until she opens her

mouth. In friendly company, she swears like a trooper. I told her it astounded me how such words come from a former boarding-school girl. She laughed at my naivety in believing Malory Towers is real. Boarding school is where she picked up most of her profane language.

'My work here is done.' Kevin gives me a wink and leaves.

Lily waits for Kevin to shut his door. 'I'm here to share some ideas I've got for the investigation,' she says.

'What investigation?' Phoebe asks.

Lily tells her about Tamsin's death and how she's helping Mags. I move them to a quiet corner where Nina, our reception-ist, can't eavesdrop. She develops bat ears whenever gossip takes place. Nina hasn't gone for her break, probably because she's dying to know what we're talking about. We're closed for lunch so at least the patients won't overhear.

After Lily shares the details, Phoebe taps the side of her nose. 'I'll keep it hush hush. Better go. I've got a fungal toenail to prepare for.'

Lily gags.

'What happened to keeping your investigation secret?' I ask her. 'Your mouth is wider than the Eurotunnel.'

'I got carried away.' Lily looks down at her feet.

'Fancy some lunch?' I know socialising always lightens her mood.

'Yes please,' Lily replies, looking back up and rubbing her tummy in appreciation.

I have a feeling the bounce in Lily's step is not at being fed but putting her investigation into action. I'm already getting sucked in. Where will it end?

34

RED

R ed could kill Sarah for being terribly British, apologising for what's obviously Red's fault. Sarah needs to get her priorities right. She has more to apologise for than a spilled drink.

Red accepts she's taking risks but it was too good an opportunity to miss. The little devil on her shoulder whispered to follow Lily and Sarah to the pub. Who is Red kidding? *Red* is the devil pulling her own strings.

Tied-back hair makes Red more ordinary. She can't attract Sarah's attention. Red will stay in the background for as long as possible. Being out of the spotlight is torture. If Red had her way, others would always notice her.

Red sniffs her top, satisfied a squirt of perfume covers the aromas from her job. There wasn't time to change. Her sense of smell is unsurpassed. People create a saturation of odours. Their stench sheds, leaving a part of themselves behind. Before bed, Red exfoliates her body, sloughing off the tainted layer of skin. After being here, she will scour for longer than usual.

The pub is part of a chain. Red loathes these places, with the same faded sticky carpet. Head Office directs their staff to add personal touches with pictures of local interest. Amateur sketches of 1900s Oxford humiliate the walls. A waft of stale urine and sickly air freshener from the toilets launch a nasal assault.

Why Sarah and Lily want to eat here is confusing. Maybe it's because it's near the surgery. It can't be for the food. Red sneers at the menu of a never-ending list of burgers. Basic recipes are passed off as culinary delights, named after British actors.

Red expects Sarah and Lily are "keeping it real"; women from middle-class rural villages hobnobbing with the peasants. Red thrives on recognition of a different kind. When she doesn't have to hide, all eyes are on her. Her mother said it was wearing. What did the hypocrite know? Red's mother hunted men and wore them down, trying to get their attention. She claims to be celibate but Red isn't fooled. Her mother would still drop her drawers in a heartbeat for any man who gave her the eye. Thankfully, Red's mother can't have any more children. The consequences are always complicated when she does.

As they wait at the bar, Red sneaks glances to study Sarah's face. From previous observation, Red has figured Sarah doesn't acknowledge her attractiveness. Sarah never gives a sly glance to the mirrors or windows she passes. She only bothers with her appearance for work. The GP must wear her armour. Red can't understand why Sarah doesn't capitalise on her looks. The warm brown eyes, curly hair, and smooth skin could get her further ahead.

The urge to touch Sarah threatens Red's plan. She focuses on Sarah's hands, seeking the dreaded confirmation of taking the next step with Hayden. Red sneers at the gaudy purple ring on Sarah's middle finger. It must have sentimental value. No one would choose such an ugly item willingly. Red covets beauty: trinkets, clothes, men, and sweet beautiful revenge.

Red and Sarah stand achingly close. A sliver separates them. One touch and a connection will begin. Red leans away. The static between them intensifies. It is too much. Red reaches towards Sarah.

35

RED

Red's hand advances, uncertain of whether to strike or retreat. She picks up a menu. Her elbow hovers. A drink spills. The liquid seeps into Sarah's white shirt. Red is mesmerised by the pale skin showing through. Underneath lies a pulse. Red imagines the fading drum of Sarah's heart as Red takes her life. Not yet.

Instead, Red endures Sarah's embarrassment. The insincere apologies grate on Red's nerves. She mumbles, 'It's fine,' and finds a booth on the other side of where Lily is seated.

'I saw what the clumsy cow did at the bar,' Lily says, as Sarah returns to the table.

'It was an accident. No harm done. Stop being so gobby.'

Sarah's passivity disgusts Red. She needs a more equal adversary. It's a good thing Lily has promise. Red feels a link forming. Lily reminds her of herself. They're both determined and stubborn.

Fixating on Lily is dangerous. Red obsesses over people she admires. Stoking up a new interest would be a distraction.

Red has much to do but Lily could help complete the

mission. Not that Lily would know. Red adds Lily to the players in her game.

36

SARAH

'I spoke to Mum on the phone today,' Lily garbles around a mouthful of food.

'It's like watching a chimp eat.' I pick up pieces of chewed meat from the table into a napkin.

'I'm multi-tasking. I've got a lot to say and I'm starving.'

'Clearly.'

'As I was saying, before I was so rudely interrupted,' Lily says, 'I told Mum that Freya and I are here for a break. I can't tell Mum about Gareth's cheating yet. Hearing how I shouldn't have taken him back before would piss me off.' Lily stabs her knife into a slab of beef.

'Imogen will find out soon,' I reply. 'I reckon she won't judge. She's an advocate of free love and all that hippy crap.'

'She doesn't agree with having affairs though. Neither do I.'

I touch Lily's hand. 'Me neither. Gareth is a Grade A bastard. I think your mum will be supportive.'

I'm trying to help Lily but I want to live alone again. Freya and Lily constantly argue. Milk is always sour because Lily forgets to put it back in the fridge, Freya is a sullen teenager extraordinaire, and my cat picks on Yellow. It's carnage.

'I'll tell Mum in my own time.' Lily's bottom lip protrudes, confirming who's teaching Freya how to be grumpy.

'Did you mention your investigation to Imogen, considering you've already told Phoebe?'

'I slipped up. I won't tell anyone else.'

'You told Imogen, didn't you?'

'Sometimes I hate you knowing me so well,' Lily says, chewing a potato. 'I needed Mum to know, despite my failed marriage, that I've been studying and doing well. Mum says it's exciting, in a sad way, of course. She was devastated to learn about Tamsin. Mum loved having cuddles with her when they lived next door. By the way, Mum's being weird at the moment.'

'Weirder than usual?' It's a fair comment. Imogen is an outspoken feminist, eco-warrior extrovert. Being around her for longer than an hour saps the energy out of me.

'When I mentioned going to see Mum she said she'd have to check her diary.' Lily sniffs. 'I remarked on how she's retired and doesn't have to prepare lecture notes or do any marking. She got narky and said she has a life, and it's none of my business. She's up to something.'

'I expect you'll investigate it too.' I can't resist teasing Lily.

'Yes, I think I will.'

I berate myself for planting the idea in Lily's head. I forget how suggestible she can be.

'Talking of investigations, I've had an idea,' Lily says.

'You don't have to discuss it with me. In fact, I'd rather you didn't.' I want as few reasons as possible to be linked to Lily's amateur sleuthing.

'I need you to hear my ideas. You tell me if I'm being a bit out there. Uncomfortable as it is, I have to consider how Paul features in Tamsin's disappearance. I'm not keen on making a dead man a suspect. Hopefully, I can eliminate him quickly.'

'You can't believe Paul had anything to do with Tamsin's death.' Appetite gone, I put down my Judi Dench burger.

'I don't think he killed her. Paul adored that girl,' Lily replies. 'Tamsin sat on Paul's shoulders so often I wondered if she was glued on. I need to consider what Paul was doing at the ice cream van though. Look at this.' Lily hands over a copy of an original police report on Tamsin's disappearance.

'Where did you get this?'

'Best you don't know. It's not exactly ethical.' Lily points at a paragraph in the document. 'This article details how Paul lingered at the van for around thirty minutes. From what witnesses say, no ice cream was produced. I have to find out what Paul was doing. Maybe he was involved in stuff leading to Tamsin's death.'

'I wouldn't tell Mags about it until you have some evidence.'

'Good point.' Lily soaks up gravy on her plate with a bread roll. 'Steve's being sneaky too, more than usual. He's too polite. When I rocked up at their house, I expected rude comments about my height, boobs, or a request for a date.'

'Steve's always been guarded.' He was impossible to work out when I was living with him. I got the feeling it was intentional.

'I'm checking out where Steve was when Tamsin disappeared. This is where I need a favour.'

'No.'

Lily places her hands in a prayer position. 'Please, please come with me to talk to Steve. He's such a lech sometimes and I'd rather have you there. You're great at making him behave.'

'Lil, I said I wasn't getting involved. Anyway, if you want to be a PI, you need to get used to dealing with difficult people.'

'For Tamsin?' Lily pleads.

'Don't emotionally blackmail me.'

'For me then, please? I've got to do this right.' Lily lays down her cutlery and stares at me.

'Stop it.'

'Stop what?'

'Okay. Just this once. You owe me.'

'Thanks so much. Lucky us.' Lily groans. 'We get to spend quality time chatting with Steve.'

I groan too, but not at the prospect of being around Steve. How can I do this without Hayden finding out?

37

SARAH

The path outside the pub is forming an icy sheen. I take cautious steps.

'I think you've downed one too many gins,' I say to Lily as she trips over the step. 'Be careful, Bambi.'

'I only had one drink and it was as weak as piss. It's slippery.' Lily inspects her feet. 'Maybe these heels weren't such a good idea.'

'Considering how much my neck is aching looking up at you, I agree. Why someone as clumsy and tall as you chooses to wear stilettos is beyond me.'

Lily links her arm with mine. 'You're jealous because you resemble a constipated giraffe whenever you wear anything higher than a kitten heel.' She mimics my posture in silly shoes. To be fair, it's pretty close.

As we reach the kerb to cross the road, we're still laughing. A speeding car swerves towards us. I try to pull Lily back but she's so focused on walking carefully she doesn't see the threat.

My hip strikes a parked car. Lily tumbles into the road. The other car's tyres screech as it races off.

I rush to Lily who's holding a shoe without a heel. She staggers to stand on one foot and falls against my painful hip.

'My shoe's broken!' Lily shouts, waving it around. 'What the hell happened?'

'Some tosser in a BMW took the corner too fast.' As I say it I'm not certain it's true. I hope it is. Intention is worrying.

'Did you get the number plate?' Lily asks.

'No. I was busy scraping myself off the car I fell on. Are you okay?'

'My bum is sore but I'll survive.' Lily brandishes her damaged shoe. 'I'm more annoyed about these. They cost a fortune.'

I escort Lily away from the kerb. 'Perhaps it's a sign you shouldn't wear silly footwear.'

'Never. A thoughtless driver won't stop me wearing these bad boys.'

Thoughtless? Careless driver? Maybe.

The flick of red hair as they sped by seemed more like defiance.

38

RED

There's nothing like scaring people to make them aware of who's in charge. Red couldn't resist. Sarah and Lily were asking to be run over, clambering into the road.

It's an unexpected pleasure how Lily is proving to be useful. Not only is she investigating Tamsin's death but she's making it entertaining. Paul Lawson as a suspect. Brilliant. He deserves it. Paul claimed to be an attentive dad but Red knows the truth.

Paul deserved to die. Red knows why.

39

RED

Paul Lawson's parenting skills bordered on non-existent. Red hopes Paul was so wracked with guilt for his misdeeds he didn't sleep at night.

Paul's aftermath didn't give Red any peace either. Her mind drifts to a memory of a heartless father.

Red sat at the back of the bus, alone. The other passengers shunned the coveted seats. They'd seen her at the bus stop. The glares showed those who knew of her reputation. As soon as you did something wrong, you became the village pariah. Red wore it like a medal, flashing her credentials with pride.

If she'd discovered what her daughter had done, Red's mother would have lost it. The concern wouldn't have been for her young daughter's safety. Red proved she could take care of herself and was often called "a handful" for it. Gran said Red's mother had the patience of a sinner rather than a saint.

"The Man" was her mother's secret. By making him an enigma, her mother created a mystery Red needed to solve. She wanted to do something right and good. Years of listening to private conversations led to this moment.

A few days before, Red's mother finally named him. An argument with Gran ended in loose tongues. Red's mother slammed the door but the knowledge had already reached her daughter. Armed with the secret, Red decided to find "The Man". The father had shirked his responsibilities for too long.

The motion of the bus stirred Red's travel sickness. She swallowed the acid biting her throat and pinched the web between her thumb and finger. Gran had taught her the trick. Red wasn't sure if it was a cure or a distraction. It always worked.

Women nattered. A baby's cries pierced Red's calm. The man coughing on the back of her neck almost broke her. Red could hurt them. Why didn't they understand? They were lucky love kept her focused. Love was good and bad. That day it was rotten. A father should never withhold affection from his child.

40

RED

Red's adolescent legs twinged in protest at walking the rest of the route. She kicked a discarded bottle, unleashing annoyance at herself for getting off the bus too early.

Red checked her map of Oxford, stolen from the local library. She smiled at her bravado. The librarian had opened her mouth, given a look of recognition, and remained silent. Red walked out, giving a jubilant wave. No one who knew her challenged Red.

Red negotiated a maze of roads and lines of houses. On the street where "The Man" lived, children played Bulldog. It was an unremarkable suburban road, flanked by enormous houses. Red heard "The Man" had inherited it from his wife's family. It seemed he *was* living the charmed life Red's mother despised him for.

Red sat on the kerb opposite his house. She drew her legs close to her chest, trying to decrease. It was his fault. Without "The Man", Red might have received her mother's love. Without "The Man" it would have been just Red and her mother. Red had wished a life away. She wasn't sure how she felt about it. Love and hate were constant bedfellows in Red's heart.

"The Man" had a habit of making people feel insignificant. Red's mother said he could fell you with a look. The thought of him challenged Red's courage.

When he opened the back door, Red wondered if she was lucky or cursed. She didn't plan that far and loathed him for highlighting her lack of preparation. After, Red would never act without a complete plan again.

"The Man" held a baby, a girl wearing a pink dress. Red hadn't known he'd replaced his other daughter. Father and daughter connected in laughter as "The Man" threw the baby up and down. Red waited for the girl to drop, relishing the thought of a baby's brain splattered on the concrete. Instead, the child was rewarded with an embrace.

Heart heavy, vengeance ignited, Red returned home. "The Man" didn't want his first-born child. He may not have been aware of his other daughter but Red saw there wasn't space for two children. It seemed to be the norm. Paul would pay for his narrow heart. Red would see to it.

41
———

SARAH

'Missed again!' I shout as a peanut flies past my ear.

Hayden's aim is way off target. We're rubbish at throwing them into each other's mouths but our competitive spirits won't let us stop. Hayden hinders the game by getting up regularly to pick up the debris. Mess makes him twitchy. I remind him of this whenever he proposes living together.

We're at Hayden's place rather than facing the Armageddon at mine, courtesy of Lily and Freya. The quiet here is a miracle considering Hayden's neighbours. Above his ground-floor flat they may as well be jiving. The occupants on the right blast dance music from evening until the early hours. Hayden tries to make them stop. They promise to turn it down only to whack the volume up as soon as he leaves. I wouldn't be surprised to hear about a murder in Wheatley if Hayden's neighbours keep it up. Maybe Lily can investigate that too.

Hayden's stereo plays calming music in the lounge's gloom. The grey and blue décor makes it drab but Hayden says as a divorcée, he needed to put his own mark on it. It's a man cave, groaning with high-tech sound equipment, cinema screen TV, and games consoles.

Silence between us is never awkward. We don't need to compensate by engaging in pointless chatter. I must speak soon though. As usual Lily has talked me into doing something for her; asking Hayden about Paul. Lily owes me a lot of friendship points.

'Paul thought the world of Tamsin, didn't he?'

Hayden spirals my hair around his finger. 'Dad would've done anything for Tamsin. Even though she was unexpected, Dad adored her. He often looked at Tamsin as if he couldn't believe she was his. I think he secretly wanted a daughter as well as sons. When Tamsin went missing, Dad spent hours searching. He printed posters and put them up everywhere. He'd knock on doors, asking people to check their garages and sheds. It became an obsession.'

'How so?' I try to keep my tone light and vaguely interested.

'Dad was convinced certain blokes in the village had taken Tamsin. The police had a word with him for hounding innocent men.'

'Paul must have been desperate.'

'The bloke in charge of the case said Dad wouldn't be any good to Tamsin if she returned and her father was banged up. Dad calmed down but he was broken. He needed to be active and responsive. Sitting and waiting for an outcome did Dad in. It's probably why he killed himself.' Hayden stops playing with my hair. 'Why are you asking questions about Dad?'

'Just making conversation.'

'Your eyes are shifting all over the place.'

Damn it. 'My eyes are tired. I must book an eye test.'

'Are you investigating Tamsin's death?'

I'll offer my life, riches, and anything else they want, to whoever's calling Hayden's mobile at this moment.

He frowns at the screen. 'I'll take this in the kitchen while I make a start on dinner.'

Hayden's been doing this more often. Not making dinner. It's a Hayden thing. He enjoys cooking and can rustle up amazing meals with a small amount of ingredients. Taking calls in different rooms is what's worrying me. It can't be Mags as we've begun to settle our differences. This secrecy does nothing for my trust issues. I'm aware of my hypocrisy, considering I'm covering for Lily. I try not to be a people pleaser. Those I love always get the best of me.

Curiosity leads me to the kitchen door. If Hayden opens it, I'll look a right numpty with my ear pressed against it.

'It's not a problem. I said before I won't let anything happen.' Hayden's voice is soothing. 'Call me anytime. I'm here for you, like I've always been. Do you want me to come over?'

My jealousy simmers. Oh no, he bloody well isn't going to see you, whoever you are. He's with me.

'I'll tell Sarah it's an emergency.'

Is Hayden deciding to lie to me?

'Let's stick to the plan then. We've come this far.'

I won't believe Hayden's having an affair. I'm not a woman who doesn't trust her partner. Yet, I won't move in with him and I'm snooping. I'm also lying to Hayden. The deceit has already begun.

No. Hayden wouldn't cheat. He loves me. What do I know of the missing years though? We've covered a lot but there are still things I haven't told him. What's Hayden hiding?

'Me too,' he says, ending the call.

Two simple words threaten our future. Did Hayden declare his love to someone else?

42

RED

What a naughty boy Hayden is, lying to his partner. Red could have warned Sarah to never trust a Lawson. However, Red resents Sarah too much to want to help her. Let the whore find out for herself.

Red knows *all* of Hayden's secrets.

43

SARAH

Using overdue admin as an excuse, I left Hayden's soon after the phone call. He knows how crap I am with paperwork and didn't question my sudden departure. Pretending I hadn't heard what resembled a declaration of love was unbearable. I had to leave before saying something I'd regret. I need space to consider what to do.

Before Lily and Freya returned to Oxfordshire, Hayden often stayed over at mine. My guests in a cramped two-bedroom house are his excuses for leaving early. After hearing the phone conversation, I'm not convinced. I should have asked who Hayden was talking to but I don't want to hear lies spilling out of his awkward mouth. Hayden is a terrible liar. He stumbles and stutters over falsehoods. The churning in my stomach punishes me for lying to Hayden too.

'Here you go.' Lily hands me a hot chocolate. It's her speciality. I can hardly balance the mug for the overflowing cream and marshmallows on top.

'This is the least you can do.' I didn't intend to sound as annoyed as it comes out.

Lily curls her legs underneath her and sips her drink.

Chocolate marks her nose. I'm too pissed off with Lily to point it out.

'I've said I'm sorry a trillion times,' Lily says. 'I'm aware I've asked a lot from you recently.'

'My house–'

'You offered.'

'Most of my groceries, my cat's sanity while she adapts to Yellow, my patience with your tantruming daughter, asking me to lie to Hayden...' I count each one on my fingers.

'All right, I get your point.' Lily puts down her chocolate. 'I am grateful. I love you, Sarah. You're the best person in the world.'

I lay a blanket over us. 'You've got chocolate on your nose. Ignore me. I'm pissed off with Hayden. I like having you and Freya around. The lying part I'm not so keen on.'

Freya sashays into the room. 'Can either of you wing eyeliner?' Her own attempts are obvious. Freya resembles a crazed panda. Lily looks at me and we descend into hysterics.

'You're so mean!' Freya shouts, leaving in a diva strop.

I catch my breath. 'I almost peed my pants.'

'I actually did,' Lily replies. 'Having kids wrecks your pelvic floor. In all seriousness, Hayden wouldn't have an affair.'

'I agree.' Freya's head appears around the door frame.

'Sort your face out, Shakespears Sister,' Lily says.

'Who?' Freya asks but doesn't wait for an answer. The need for the perfect face lures her back to the bathroom mirror.

I pick up the conversation with Lily. 'We've spent years apart. Maybe I don't know him as well as I think. He's changed from the sulky boy we knew. I've changed too.'

'Not as much as you think,' Lily says, stroking Yellow's ears. He's taking advantage of the warmth from the fire. 'You're still incredibly untidy but the most loving person ever.'

'Thanks, I think.'

'What were you like before you lived with the Lawsons?' Lily asks. 'You don't often talk about it.'

I push the blanket away. 'There's not much to say. It was awful. End of.'

'Stop being so defensive whenever I ask about your past. I'm only being caring.'

'You're trying to get in my head. Haven't you moved on from wanting to be a psychologist?'

'Couldn't be bothered to train. It takes years. I would have been brilliant at it though.'

'Not everyone wants to keep going over things, Lil. It's done. I'm in a great place. I don't want to talk about *them*.'

Lily doesn't press any further. She knows I'm referring to Kayleigh and James. It still hurts, wondering where Kayleigh is and if she ever thinks of me.

'So, you're looking into Paul and Steve at the moment,' I continue, glad to push disturbing thoughts away. 'You can't possibly believe either of them killed Tamsin. Paul adored her. Steve's a bit of a lad, but murder?'

'I've got to start somewhere. They may not have killed Tamsin but both were, and, in Steve's case, still are, up to something. He's being cagey. We'll find out what.'

'*You* will, not *we*.'

'Yeah, yeah.'

I peer at her over my cup. 'I don't need the aggravation.'

'Can I talk to you about my investigation though?' Lily uses her whiny pleading voice. 'I don't want to discuss it with the course leaders as they'll tell me off for doing such a big case when I'm not fully trained.'

'If you must,' I reply, not bothering to suppress the accompanying sigh.

Lily bounces in her seat. 'I've come up trumps. You may shower praise and adoration upon me.'

'Have you cleared your hair out of the bath plughole? I could knit a jumper with it.'

'No, but I will. Anyway, you can't knit. I've been in touch with Paul's mum, Queenie. We're seeing her tomorrow. If anyone knows a person, it's their mother. Well, most do, unlike Kayleigh.'

I don't contest it. My loyalty to Kayleigh is confused. For every memory I have of her giving me a hug, other memories of her leaving me unsupervised in squats replace them.

'Back up a bit,' I wind my hand in a circle. 'You said we're seeing Queenie tomorrow. No way am I going to her house.'

'Still scared of her? Me too.' Lily's eyes widen. 'Don't make me go there alone. I'll never get out alive.'

'Lil, you'll be the death of me. You owe me big time, starting with making another hot chocolate, accompanied by a Crunchie.'

'We don't have any Crunchies.'

'Better go to the shop then.'

'Yes, ma'am.' Lily gives a salute. 'Let's see what I can unearth on Paul. I'm convinced he was up to something when Tamsin disappeared. I *will* find out the truth.'

44

RED

In Red's defence, she tried to get by without Hayden. She invented ways to keep him in her life without Hayden's actual presence. It was never quite the same as the real thing but it was always fun.

'You stabbed me, you crazy bitch!' He cuffed a hand around his arm.

Red watched the blood running. The desire to lick it from his skin was overwhelming.

He dug his heels into the mattress, levering himself away from Red. The scurrying sewer rat amused her. He was surplus to requirements. It was a shame. The relationship had potential. If only he'd learned to behave.

Red reached for him. The headboard thumped against the wall. His prostrate body flattened the pillows. Red trailed a finger under his chin and despised him for recoiling. She thought he was made of stronger stuff. When it came to sex, he had no boundaries.

'It's only a scratch,' Red said. 'Count yourself lucky. I could have finished the job.'

She tore a strip from the sheet and tied a tourniquet around his forearm. He foolishly smiled at the gesture. Red tightened the hold.

'Shit, that hurts!' he yelled. 'Get the hell away from me!' He pushed Red aside to pick up his clothes from the floor.

Strike One. Red abhorred carelessness. He knew to fold his clothes and place them on the chair, no matter which hotel they met in.

Strike Two. She'd only had dinner with him earlier because a woman's got to eat. The intimacy of candlelight and soft jazz music placed her on edge. Despite the excellent food, it wouldn't do. They didn't date. They sparred.

Strike Three. He refused to role play. He tried to be himself. Red didn't care who he was and what he did. She never asked. Over dinner, he wanted them to share more of each other and connect. He said he was bored with playing the part of Hayden, whoever he was. The man insisted upon using his own name.

He'd known from the start Red had picked him because he resembled the one that got away. His hair, eyes, and manner reminded her of Hayden. If the replacement kept his mouth shut, she imagined it was Hayden placing his hands over her body.

Strike Four. The replacement pushed her away when she called him Hayden at the height of ecstasy. The man rejected her and the fantasy. Red's rage exploded. She stabbed him with the corkscrew lying on the bedside cabinet.

No more strikes. The man was out. He should have considered himself lucky he raised his arm when she attacked. Red was aiming for his heart.

'I'm going to the police,' he said, buttoning his shirt. 'You won't get away with this.'

Red laid on the bed, fingers laced behind her head. 'Don't be so rash. Do you want your family to find out what you've been doing?'

He fumbled with his tie. 'You wouldn't dare.'

Red admired his attempt at bravery. At least he tried. Those before him had cowered at that point.

Red pulled his tie. 'Don't ever offer me a dare. I'll never decline.' She tightened the tie and enjoyed the tussle as he fought to breathe. 'Besides, I know where your wife works and where your children go to school. I could make them have an accident in seconds.'

She drank in his fear.

'Scoot, Hayden,' Red said, patting the man on the backside. 'You've got a class to teach, darling.'

45

SARAH

The sign for Chinnor resurrects my fear of Queenie Lawson. We're on her patch. After negotiating around parked cars like she's on a racing track, Lily pulls up in the only space, on a bend. The road is narrow and she'll be lucky to keep her wing mirrors. Her Clio already has missing parts so a few less won't matter.

I've never known Queenie's real name. Being the matriarch in a family of men, she took the title for herself and insisted everyone used it. Queenie visited when I lived with the Lawsons. Hayden wasn't keen on her as she regularly started arguments with Mags. It became a sport where the women waited it out for a while. Then subtle digs escalated to slammed doors and Queenie marching out of the house.

Queenie was a menacing Morticia Addams parody, with a widow's peak, white powdered face, and floaty black dresses. As the door opens, I can't resist mimicking a creaking coffin lid. In deference to Queenie's deathly style, Hayden and I made the noise when she was nearby, never to her face.

'Do you have something stuck in your throat?' Lily asks. I forgot she wasn't in on the joke.

Queenie stares and then holds out a hand, inviting us to lead the way. She doesn't speak. I scuttle into the hallway, glancing back at the aged undead. Didn't Hansel and Gretel make a mistake by entering the witch's lair? I expect Lily's hoping Queenie offers more than gingerbread for our troubles.

Queenie makes tea while we wait in the lounge. The cork-tiled wall is similar to the one the Lawsons had in their dining room. Mags hated the eighties feature wall but money was tight and decorating low on the list. Steve, Hayden, Lily and I used it as a dartboard. It's the only occasion I can remember Paul having fun with me as he showed me how to aim. He seemed more relaxed. Paul was often delivering car parts or going out for the evening, leaving Mags behind. She said she'd rather be with her children in any case.

Queenie's tiled coffee table is the same as those we made in woodwork lessons. I never finished mine. I'm useless at making things. Flat pack furniture is my nemesis. I expect one of Queenie's six sons made this table at school. The grout is crumbling and a wedge of cardboard props a wobbly leg.

Lily stands by a collection of Pierrot dolls, placed next to the television. She rubs her eyes and makes fake crying sounds, aping the clowns' tears. I try to signal Queenie is returning. Lily doesn't notice.

'They're my pride and joy.' Queenie raises her voice as she moves behind Lily.

Lily gasps.

Queenie addresses Lily. 'Every Christmas and birthday my boys bought me a Pierrot. Eric, my husband, said I should sell them on eBay. They might be worth a fortune but I'd never part with my lovelies.' She picks up the largest doll and sways it within her arms.

Lily mouths, "What the hell?"

I sip from the mug to hide my grin. Clowns freak me out.

When I was five, a clown in a shopping centre bent down to offer me a balloon. I bit him. I remember James wrenching me off the howling clown's nose.

'Thanks for agreeing to see us, Queenie, or should I say, Mrs Lawson?' Lily asks.

'Don't stand on ceremony here.' Queenie nibbles a biscuit from a selection box.

I expect she was waiting for an occasion to crack open the tin, seeing as it's a Christmas edition. Lily rams custard creams in her mouth like they're going on ration.

'I don't get many visitors nowadays,' Queenie says. 'The boys are busy. This house is so quiet since Eric passed away.'

Lily groans. I kick her ankle. Lily's not great with chatty people. She can't keep up with them. Patience is not Lily's best virtue.

'My Paul, bless him, came here as much as he could,' Queenie says. 'He always brought Tamsin with him. She was an absolute treasure.' Queenie pulls a tissue from under her cuff and blows her nose.

Queenie sparks up a cigarette. I decline her offer. I shoot Lily a disapproving look when she grabs one. Lily takes a short sharp drag and then places it in the ashtray. A layer of smoke lingers above our heads. Previously cream walls have browned with nicotine. A rectangular stain, edged with a filigree pattern, hints at the mirror that hung there. I wish I could confirm with Hayden how Queenie *is* a vampire who can't reveal her lack of reflection.

Queenie displays mother bear teeth. My hand flies to my neck for protection. 'Before we start, I won't have you girls accusing my Paul of anything,' Queenie says. 'Paul paid for his part in Tamsin's death.'

46

RED

Red wasn't aware of where Queenie Lawson lives. Lily's snooping is proving to be useful. It's highly likely Queenie's home is social housing. Such people never aspire to more than they are given. They are the type to demand the world takes them as they are. Sheer laziness.

Red found Queenie's mistress-of-the-night look ridiculous. It didn't scare Red. When Queenie dropped in at Great Parston, she respected Red's bravery, acknowledging a fellow strong spirit.

Queenie wouldn't recognise Red. She's glad. Red can't risk engaging in a conversation about Paul as she'd offend Queenie and reveal secrets not ready to be shared. Most mothers defend their offspring. Red has never known motherly protection. She knows better than to blame mothers for all their children's actions. When mothers fail, children must step up and take responsibility, sometimes for other children too.

Queenie was once kind to Red when she needed it. The giving of sweets and a gentle embrace remained. No one touched her. They worried their fingers might get burned. Red recalls the musty smell of cigarettes and Tramp perfume, trapped in the weave of Queenie's coat. The odours made Red nauseous but she stayed close. Someone had hugged her.

Red wishes she could hear what Queenie has to say. Then again, Red probably knows. If Queenie is sharing the details of Paul's role in Tamsin's death, Red doesn't need to be a fly on the wall. She practically wrote the script.

47

SARAH

Queenie settles after her outburst to continue telling us about Paul. 'There were so many accusations flying about when Tamsin disappeared,' she says. 'Some blighter sprayed graffiti on my door, calling Paul a murderer. They were too chicken to do it at his house. Paul was crushed when he saw it. I told him I'd clean up but he insisted on doing it. He cried as he scrubbed away the filth. It was more than vandalism that upset him. He felt awful about Tamsin and his part in her disappearance. Excuse me, ladies, I could do with a piddle. This chilly weather plays havoc with my waterworks.' Queenie leaves the room, swishing her cloak-like cardigan.

'Damn it,' Lily says. 'She was opening up.'

'What the hell are you doing, smoking again?' I ask.

'I'm not.' Lily points at the cigarette, almost burned to ash. 'It's a PI trick to do as your interviewee does. It makes them believe you have something in common. They open up more.'

'What if your interviewee is taking hard-core drugs or is into kinky sex?'

Lily grins.

'Or they're the bride of Dracula?' I whisper and nod towards the door.

Lily doesn't get a chance to respond. Queenie returns. She straightens the armchair covers and picks up her burning cigarette. Lily follows her lead.

'Where was I?' Queenie asks. 'How's Mags doing, by the way?'

'She's not great,' I reply. 'Hayden and Damien are looking after her though.'

'I notice you didn't mention Steve.' Queenie gives us a knowing look. 'He's a bit of a playboy. There's more to him than people think. Steve's a sensitive lad. I saw it in his aura.'

'Right.' I've never been a fan of spiritual codswallop.

'Scrape the surface of Steve and you'll discover why he's so defensive.'

I consider asking Queenie to explain but Lily shuts it down. 'Mags asked us to investigate Tamsin's death. She reckons we have a better chance of finding out what happened because we're family friends.'

'Lily's confused,' I add. 'She's the one who's investigating. I'm here for a catch up, after all these years.' I add an exaggerated smile for effect.

Queenie scowls in response. 'The coppers will do their bit, I'm sure. Some of my sons aren't fans of the police. Let's say they've been naughty boys. Personally, I don't mind coppers. I've never been on the wrong side of the law and intend for it to stay that way.'

'I'll tell the police anything significant I discover,' Lily interjects. 'I want to work with them, not against them. You're so kind, speaking to me.'

Queenie frowns. 'This is the second visit about Tamsin in as many days. Had a policeman here recently. He's high up as he had a *D* in his title. On the telly they're always important when the rank begins with *D*.'

I make a mental note to find out who's working on Tamsin's case for Lily's sake. If she can avoid them, it will keep her out of trouble. I don't want to annoy the local constabulary either. My job would be threatened and after a childhood of running away from the police, alongside reprobate parents, I'd rather leave it behind.

Queenie's tongue flicks over her top lip. I wonder if she's feasted on someone and going to the toilet was an excuse. 'That copper was a bit of a looker,' she says. 'Lots of charm and swagger. If I was thirty years younger, he'd have been all mine.'

Lily and I flatter her by laughing along.

'He had such kind eyes,' Queenie adds. 'I had to tell him what Paul did. You can't lie to a decent man. God rest my boy's tortured soul but Paul was guilty. It was time the police knew the real story.'

48

RED

Red recalls Paul playing the doting dad before Tamsin disappeared. Paul acted like the sun shone out of his daughter's proverbial.

Tamsin wasn't as annoying as most children. She could be outspoken but had good manners. Small and spritely, she was a fairy-tale imp of a girl. Tamsin never stood still until the moment when she had no choice.

When Paul took his daughter to the park, Tamsin's end was inevitable. Red knows who is to blame. She will enjoy watching Lily and Sarah trying to work it out.

49

SARAH

'Paul couldn't live with the remorse he felt at Tamsin's disappearance,' Queenie says. 'His overdose broke my heart.'

Lily and I are silent. Paul's death demands reverence.

'Not long before Paul died, he told me everything.' Queenie wipes her eyes with a crusty tissue.

Avoiding the snot rag Queenie's holding, I risk touching her arm. Queenie's lost her son, granddaughter, and husband. She's also part of Hayden's family. I try not to react at the grimace forming on Queenie's face as she seizes my hand.

'Paul got himself into some financial trouble. You probably know a little about it already.' Queenie releases her grip on me. 'From the moment Paul met Mags, he tried to impress her. He never felt good enough because her parents were quite well off. I told him he was as good as her, if not better, being from working-class grafting stock. When Mags' grandmother left her the house in Oxford, I warned Paul it wasn't a gift horse. The place was falling apart and needed a lot of work.'

I remember leaks pouring through the roof whenever it

rained. It became a game, racing to catch the drips with buckets. Mags tried to make everything fun.

Queenie continues. 'My stupid son started gambling. Paul thought he'd keep up his lifestyle by betting. You'll remember how he wore the best clothes, drank the finest wines, and often had nights out. I haven't got a clue where he got the taste for it from. Certainly not from me. In her defence, Mags didn't want anything fancy.'

'Hayden said Paul left them with some debts,' I say. 'Surely Mags knew about Paul's gambling.'

'My son got lucky, if you call killing yourself luck.' Queenie sniffs. 'Most of the loan sharks and casinos were astute enough to understand you can't get money out of the deceased. Mags only had to deal with the official stuff. She believed Paul had overextended himself, borrowing to do the house up. Silly cow should have figured out not much was mended or improved.'

'I wondered where Paul got the money he flashed about,' Lily says. 'Mum joked he was a secret drug dealer.'

'Lil, think things, don't say them, remember?' As I speak, Queenie's mouth drops.

'Paul nearly landed up dealing drugs.' Queenie blows her nose so hard I fear for its attachment to her face. 'The gambling got out of control. Paul had loan sharks on his back. They were men you didn't mess with. Paul thought he'd invest in drugs and make money. When he told me he'd considered it, I said it's not what a responsible father does. Paul tried to palm me off with how the money would have been for Tamsin. Turns out he never had the chance to spend it on her anyway.'

'Did Mags know about the drugs?' Lily asks.

'Of course not,' Queenie replies. 'Mags isn't aware of the extent of Paul's debt or him considering dealing. She'd have left him in a heartbeat.'

'How is this related to Tamsin's death?' Lily asks.

'I'm getting to it. You're an impatient one, aren't you, dear?'

Lily bunches her fists.

'I expect you heard Paul was buying ice creams at the park,' Queenie says. 'What you don't know is the van owner was a supplier. Still is. Nick was a little scrote who grew up to be a thug. Paul was considering doing business with him.' Queenie grinds the cigarette into the ashtray, killing it under her thumb. 'Paul and Nick argued. Nick asked for ridiculous prices, aware of Paul's desperation. They haggled for a while. Paul was so ashamed when he told me. While knocking down the price of coke, someone took Tamsin.'

'What a dick,' Lily says. 'Pardon me.' She moves behind the jungle of a spider plant.

'Don't worry.' Queenie cackles. 'With a house full of blokes, the air turned blue in here years ago. Yes, Paul was a dick, as you put it, for what he did. He paid the price. Paul obviously didn't tell the police about trying to do a deal. He said he was buying Tamsin an ice cream. The sad part is, Paul backed out.' Queenie looks at me. 'He couldn't sell drugs, knowing what you'd been through with your parents. Paul didn't want you having drugs in your life again.'

'Right.' I don't have all the words to reply. I'm stunned to hear Paul considered me at all.

Queenie continues. 'It took some persuasion to get Nick to give Paul an alibi, saying they were old friends catching up. He didn't want to be involved as the coppers would start sniffing around. There's no way I'd allow Paul to be pegged as a sicko who'd done something to his child. The rumours gained ground. The woman who owned the Post Office refused to serve me. When Paul died, she came here to offer condolences. I told her to stick them where the sun doesn't shine.

'My men had a word with Nick. After an unfortunate accident and a few nights in hospital, Nick told the police Paul was with him when Tamsin disappeared. He said they were having a chat. It got Paul off the hook but he refused to forgive himself.'

'It explains why Paul took his own life, I guess.' I try to keep my tone soft. 'I wondered why he didn't leave a note. Paul probably wanted to spare Mags the truth of his debt and considering drug dealing. She had enough to contend with.'

'Paul seemed so defeated the last time he visited.' Queenie glances at her beloved Pierrots. 'He brought me a doll which he hadn't done in years. I told him my silence wasn't easily bought. Paul said he wanted to treat me. Before Paul met Mags, he'd bring a new doll whenever he came here. Then he started spending his money and effort on her. I realised something was up when Paul gave me the Pierrot. He insisted he was fine. I wish I'd trusted my instincts. I might have stopped him.'

'Don't torture yourself,' I say. 'If Paul killed himself, it was his decision. I'm not blaming him. He must have been in a bad way to think it was the only option. Nothing you did or didn't do led to Paul's suicide.'

'You're a kind girl,' Queenie replies. 'It's obvious why Hayden's so keen on you.'

I smile and then it drops. Is Hayden as keen on me as he might be on someone else? I paste the smile back on for Queenie's sake.

'Thank you, Queenie.' Lily stands. 'I expect it was hard to share all that. We're grateful.'

'You're welcome.' Queenie rises from the chair. The imprint of her body remains in the cushions. I search for the shape of bat wings.

'Don't worry about seeing us out,' Lily says.

'Right you are,' Queenie replies. 'By the way, Lily, don't pretend to smoke to look cool. I'm way beyond the age of being impressed and I hate to see a ciggie go to waste.'

We flee from the vampire's lair.

50

RED

Red lowers the sun visor, using it as a partial shield. When Lily tried to high-five Sarah outside Queenie's house, Sarah gave her a disdainful look. Despite herself, Red laughed. She waits for Lily and Sarah to drive away before following at a distance.

Queenie's obviously fed them juicy information. Paul must have confessed to his mum how he was haggling over drugs instead of looking after Tamsin. Good old Queenie has a knack for extracting the truth.

Tamsin's disappearance was justified. If drugs were more important, then Paul didn't deserve to have children. Paul never had his priorities right. Only once had he almost convinced Red he wouldn't let Tamsin down.

Red watched Tamsin waiting for her dad at the school gate. The girl's expressions alternated between expectancy and sadness as parents arrived and left. Tamsin stood in the deserted playground. Motivated by a strange sense of compassion, Red considered taking her home.

Paul ran up the path, clutching a box under his arm. He handed it to a gleeful Tamsin. Red retreated to the shadow of a tree and listened to Paul's apologies. He'd spent the afternoon searching for the *Doctor Who* figure Tamsin wanted. Red had seen it circled in the Argos catalogue, which was always open on the family's dining room table. Whenever Red mentioned the toy, Tamsin said she knew it was just a dream. The figure had sold out. Tamsin shouldn't have underestimated Paul's contacts and seemingly unlimited finances.

For once, Red admired Paul and questioned if her assessment of his parenting was harsh.

Later, Paul would revert to type. Tamsin died because of her father's selfishness.

51

RED

Unlike his father, Hayden was attentive to Tamsin's needs. Wherever Hayden went, Tamsin tried to follow. It became an issue for someone who needed Hayden's full attention. Fortunately, Tamsin was easily persuaded to leave. Waving sweets under her nose soon pushed her out of the picture.

Tamsin was a compliant child. Good for Red. Not so great for Tamsin.

52

RED

R ed remembers how Tamsin had tried to show bravery despite her fear of Red.

'Come on, it will be fun.' Red's words sounded strangled. Coaxing the spoiled brat was tiresome.

'Mum says I have to go to bed at this time,' Tamsin garbled, around sucking her thumb. 'I don't like doing it either. It's scary.'

Red prised Tamsin's other hand from the door handle. The fragility of the girl's fingers tempted Red to break them.

'I'll tell Hayden and Steve you're a scaredy-cat.' Red knew which of Tamsin's buttons to press.

'I hate it when you do the light switch thing,' Tamsin said.

Red understood. Her moods changed in an instant, like the flicking of a switch. Tamsin never knew what she was getting with Red; friend or foe.

Red livened up babysitting sessions by exerting control over Tamsin. It served Tamsin right for stating she preferred the other babysitter. Red had enough of not matching up to "Little Miss Perfect".

Babysitting Tamsin was a ruse for Red get closer to Hayden. Red despised those younger than her. They demanded all the attention. The only reason Red would consider having children would be to mould them. No child of Red's would grow up to be a loveless coward.

Tamsin tightened her scarf, readying herself. 'Okay, I'll do it but only for a minute.'

Red seized Tamsin's hand, moving it away from touching a badge on her scarf. The talisman was useless. Tamsin's body contorted into the tight space. Before sliding the child lock in place, Red marvelled at Tamsin's skill.

Red took a seat and turned on the television. A music video drowned out the banging. Tamsin's cries dropped to a whimper. She had to toughen up. Red did Tamsin a favour.

Hayden hadn't taught his sister the more essential life skills. Red could have told him how it was done, if he bothered to pay her attention. Red showed Tamsin how to survive, at least on that occasion. Really, Hayden should have been grateful.

53

SARAH

Freya is cooking dinner. It's a welcome event because Lily's not doing it. She sets the smoke alarms off every time. Yesterday I had to rescue a tin of beans from the microwave before she pressed "Start".

Freya has impressive culinary skills although they're chaotic. Sauce is splattered over the hob and chopped vegetables cover most surfaces. She's worse than me for messiness. Lily dips a spoon into the chilli for a taste. Freya slaps her hand away.

'I was checking if it's edible.' Lily sounds more like a sulky teenager than her daughter.

'Cheek! I know you, Mum. There'll be nothing left if your nose gets in the trough.'

'Charming.' Lily roots around the cupboards. 'Why isn't there any chocolate in this house?'

'Because I've eaten it,' I reply.

'How are you doing?' Lily joins me at the kitchen table. 'I expect hearing what Queenie said about Paul has hit you hard.'

'Seems like my father figures wanted to be involved in drugs in one way or another.'

'At least Paul didn't go through with the deal. He was thinking of you. You'll break that pen if you're not careful.'

Too late; the Biro I'm gripping snaps in my hand. 'Let's hope Zeke wasn't partial to a toot of something on the sly.'

'No way! Zeke was a straight shooter. Oops, pardon the expression. The idea of Zeke taking anything stronger than coffee is hilarious.'

We laugh at the thought of my cuddly adoptive dad veering off his sensible path. I miss him so much. His advice would be useful. Dad was my moral compass. I sometimes wonder what kind of father James would have been if he'd never started taking drugs.

'Turn that frown upside down,' I say to Lily, aware of how much she hates the saying.

She clasps her hands to the side of her head. 'Aargh! Don't. Time to be serious. Are you going to tell Hayden about Paul?'

'I can't keep it from Hayden. Paul's his dad. I need to consider how to broach it. Sullying the memory of a man who took his own life is shitty.'

We sit and contemplate. When will the Lawsons catch a break from this flood of tragedy?

'Sarah, there's a package for you on the sideboard,' Freya says, ending the silence. She's become more sensitive to people's feelings, as long as they're not Lily. I know Freya's rescuing me from spiralling into sadness.

I inspect the item. The postmark is from Oxford. Something rattles inside. I rip into the brown paper, discovering it's only the top layer.

'This is like pass the parcel.' Lily claps her hands. 'Can I have a turn?'

Lily reaches for the package and I pull it towards me. I peel off the last sheet and open an envelope. A badge drops to the floor. Lily swipes it up, a habit formed from Yellow considering anything at ground level as a dog treat.

'No way.' Colour drains from Lily's face. She gives the badge to me, with a sleeve covering her fingers. 'Don't get more finger-prints on it.'

I grab a clean tea towel to hold and inspect the evidence. The black and white badge is edged with thick rust. Erosion hasn't obscured the writing, declaring "Tamsin is the Boss". I had the badge made, certain it was perfect for Tamsin. All the Lawsons did the bidding of the adored baby of the family.

I remember pinning the gift to Tamsin's scarf; the first of her badge collection. Hayden questioned if giving a small child items with pins was a good idea. I pointed at Tamsin's delighted expression, asking if Hayden could deny her. Hayden agreed he couldn't take the badge away from Tamsin but someone did: her killer.

54

SARAH

Hayden's phone keeps going through to voicemail. He sent a message earlier stating he's having a quiet night in after a full-on day at work. Trying to call Hayden too, Lily swears at her mobile. We need to tell him about Tamsin's badge. If he finds out Lily's investigating, so be it.

'I'm giving this to the police,' I say to Lily, who's taking photos of the packaging, address label, and badge.

'But if we...' Lily looks away.

'Lily, we have to. I'm not withholding evidence. If they find out, we'll be in serious trouble.'

'Mum.' Freya wields a wooden spoon. 'Behave yourself.'

Lily holds up her hands. 'Calm down. I'll give it to the police. Look, no crossed fingers behind my back.'

'Let me check you over,' Freya says, while trying to watch the bubbling pot of chilli.

'Step away, child of mine. What could I possibly cross?'

'Your legs,' I say, pointing to Lily's left leg placed in front of the right.

'Un-flipping-believable.' Freya turns away to continue with dinner.

'I need a pee.' Lily's excuses begin.

My phone rings. It's Hayden. I move to the bottom of the stairs to take the call. There's an argument brewing in the kitchen between Lily and Freya.

'Hi,' Hayden says. 'Sorry I didn't answer earlier. I was sorting some stuff. I'm having a soak in the bath. Are you okay? You and Lily called quite a few times.'

I wish I believed Hayden's edginess is concern and not deceit. After I tell him about the badge, he's silent.

'Hayden, are you still there? It's upsetting but I thought you should know.'

'I think I'm in shock,' he says, 'and worried the person who killed Tamsin knows where you live. Why would they send it to you and not the family?'

'Maybe they think it's less risky. The police are often at Mags' house, following up on stuff.'

'Make sure you pass the badge on to the police. Please stay safe. Don't let Lily use this as an excuse to meddle.'

'What are you up to this evening?' I cover my guilt with small talk.

'Chilling. I need it.'

The strain in Hayden's voice makes the statement believable. He works hard. Hayden performs the usual teaching duties: sorts out errant pupils, supports frazzled English teachers, plans lessons, and marks stacks of work. Hayden usually falls asleep on my shoulder in the evening when we're watching a film.

As a boy, he devoured books, even when other boys told him it wasn't cool. Hayden's always been content with who he is and makes no apologies for it. Although we often fell out when we were younger, I admired his confidence.

I was set to propose seeing Hayden this evening to talk about Paul. Hayden's tiredness makes me decide to leave it. I hear talking in the background of Hayden's call but I can't make out what's being said.

'What was that I heard?' I ask.

'What do you mean?'

'Someone's talking to you.'

'No... Nothing.' Hayden draws out the words. 'Oh yes, it's the television.'

'I hope you haven't set up a TV in the bathroom. Don't electrocute yourself.'

'Um, I meant a podcast, playing on my tablet.'

'Right, of course it is.' I refuse to hide my suspicion. 'For a moment I thought you had a woman there. Silly me.'

'Got to go. See you tomorrow.'

Hayden ends the call before I can reply. I swear a woman was talking to him. Hayden didn't deny it. I didn't get the opportunity to challenge the change of excuse from a television to a tablet.

I say goodbye to a disconnected call.

55

RED

Knowing Hayden is deceiving Sarah strengthens Red's hold over them. Hayden can't resist a damsel in distress. He's come to the rescue again with a female who needs his help and has jeopardised his relationship. Sarah and Hayden aren't as solid as they think. Naughty Sarah is a liar too. Red knows everything.

When he discovers Sarah's secrets, Hayden will be furious. Red knows honour is one of Hayden's motivations. She'd already tested it.

56

RED

R ed didn't want to ruin Hayden's birthday but matters were out of her control. If Hayden hadn't ignored her by fawning over another girl, Red wouldn't have chosen the drastic measure.

From a self-imposed exile in the corner of the village hall, Red observed the partygoers. Mags and Paul chatted with their many friends. Hayden's birthday was the perfect excuse for another Lawson social gathering. Red's gran commented on how they had more money than sense and she refused to attend. It was a blessing for Red as Gran wouldn't usually allow her to get so close to Hayden.

Hayden whispered in a pretty girl's ear. She gave a pathetic giggle. A woman remarked on how they made a perfect couple. Red wouldn't stand for it. The girl knew she was on dangerous ground, creating the wrong impression.

Red wasn't a wallflower, meant to blend into the background. Hayden belonged to her, not the girl who had already taken everything Red wanted. While their intentions towards Hayden differed, Red's claim upon him would ensure success for Red and her rival. It was complicated but necessary.

In the privacy of the toilets, Red considered her options. She splashed water on her face and slapped her cheeks, punishing the badness swirling inside. When Red behaved impulsively, dangerous things happened. Although Hayden hurt her, she wouldn't lash out. His approval meant everything. The girl would escape harm too. She would be reminded later, though, of her misdirected loyalties.

Red decided to play nice and offer Hayden a drink. If he went with Red to the bar, the other girl would fade away. Red exited the toilets, confident with the simple scheme.

A stumbling Steve crashed into her, struggling with his zip as he left the gents. 'Get out the way, you ugly scrag end.'

Red stopped. Impulse took over.

57

RED

I t was difficult, later, to state who was more confused; the crowd who rushed towards the toilets or Steve. Red's torn collar added to the drama of her screams.

Reliable Hayden got there first. He hugged Red and soothed away the hysterics. Steve's explosions at being accused of roughing up a girl played into Red's hands. She sobbed at Steve's "lies" as Hayden held her close.

Paul pulled Steve back from advancing upon Red, and ushered his son outside. As the main door opened, Red shivered. Hayden placed his jumper around her shoulders. She inhaled scents of deodorant and washing powder. Red stroked the wool as she wore Hayden next to her skin. She never wanted to take him off. The garment went home with Red. Hayden didn't.

Red ignored Mags' scrutinising glare. The woman was a protective mother and a threat. Mags blasted questions and challenged why Steve attacked Red. She glared at Red throughout the telling of how Red asked Steve for a cigarette and he'd reacted with aggressiveness. Red hammed up how she thought Steve was joking until he grabbed her dress and ripped the neckline. Enjoying the collective sympathy, Red drew out the story. Finally, people noticed her for the right reasons. Some offered kind words and commented on Steve's unacceptable behaviour.

Mags said Red must report it to the police, if that's what really happened. Red knew it was a test. She told Mags she'd never do that to the Lawsons; they were as good as family. Red ignored Mags' distrusting look.

Only Hayden's opinion mattered to Red. The girl who'd been glued to his side quit the competition and disappeared. Not for long but it was still a victory. Red won as Hayden stayed with her for the rest of the party. She wondered if this was love.

Steve was inconsequential. Sometimes there were casualties. Red always got what she wanted. Steve owed her for not reporting his "assault". Later, Red would recall the favour.

58

RED

Memories of Hayden's party lead Red to the memento under her bed. She allows herself the guilty pleasure of releasing Hayden's jumper from the vacuum-sealed bag. As the wool strokes her body, she imagines it's Hayden's fingers. The sleeves wrap her in an embrace, permeated with Hayden's fading scent.

Infiltrating her way back into Hayden's life is working. His protective instinct is still there. Such a shame for Hayden no one will be able to save him.

59

SARAH

'I'm freezing my nuts off here,' Lily mumbles. Most of her face is hidden inside her parka's hood.

'You don't have nuts,' I reply.

'It's so cold they've dropped off.'

'You set up this meeting in the park. Don't they teach you on your course to find more comfortable interrogation surroundings?' I refuse to hide my annoyance. It's early on a Sunday and I could be wrapped up in a duvet. I'm not even part of this investigation, in theory.

Lily's mouth pops up above the zipper of her coat. 'Steve insisted. I suggested going to the house but he wanted to talk here.' She plays a game on her phone, throwing off the gloves hindering her performance.

I take in the view, if that's what you call it. Great Parston's park lets down the rest of the area. The village is the type to enter Flower in Bloom and tidy village competitions and win. The park lurks on the edge; a dirty secret pushed aside. I expect the villagers often complain about it.

Misspelled graffiti covers every upright surface. Lily's already had a pen out of her bag to correct errors. The playground is an accident waiting to happen. Broken equipment, exposed nails, and flaking rust are everywhere. The path offers no less chance of stepping in dog crap than the grass.

Damaged bench slats challenge our balance. One wrong bum cheek placement will lead to injury. I sit on the end. My thighs take the strain. I'd be better off standing up but I'm so cold I can't move.

This is the park where Tamsin disappeared. Steve's choice to meet here feels macabre. Why would he want to be where his sister was taken? I look across at the forklifts, laying still from their usual activity of digging up the old allotments. My heart hurts for Tamsin that she was buried there.

'Can we not mention Paul's debt and attempt at a drugs deal please?' I ask Lily. 'I haven't told Hayden yet. It's best if he tells Mags and Steve.'

'Sure. I'd rather not be the one to break the news to Steve anyhow. Here he is.' Lily points at Steve approaching.

Steve's collar is pulled high. He resembles a crazed meerkat, checking out his surroundings. As he nears us, he reverts to type, affecting a grin and adding a wink.

Lily offers a space on the bench.

Steve shakes his head as he paces in front of us. 'Looking good, ladies.'

'Cut the crap, Steve. Let's get this over with so I can go back to bed.' I realise not having a second cup of coffee was a mistake.

'You're a ray of sunshine this morning. Whatever I tell you goes no further, right?' Steve's voice is pleading. I've never seen him so vulnerable. I regret being snappy with him.

'Anything you say stays with us,' Lily replies.

'I agreed to talk to you because you two are decent people, even if one of you picked the wrong brother.'

I don't reply. Feeding Steve's ego isn't wise. We'll be here all day listening to his cheesy chat-up lines, although Steve seems troubled underneath the machismo.

He walks the strip of concrete in front of the bench. 'Make no mistake, I loved Tamsin. I was an annoying brother and wound the kid up, but I loved the bones of her.' Steve recoils at the choice of phrase. 'I admit I was jealous of Tamsin sometimes. She came along when I thought my parents were done with children, despite the procession of foster kids. Mum doted on Tamsin. The youngest gets most of the attention. Tamsin was so cute. I regret how much I teased her.'

'What do you want to say, Steve?' I ask. 'I'm becoming an ice statue and it reeks of pee around here.' Yes, I definitely need more coffee.

'Calm your shit, Sarah.'

'Play nice, kids,' Lily says. 'Let's get to the point of being here. What would you like to tell us, Steve?'

As Steve looks at us, I can see he's falling apart.

'It's my fault Tamsin's dead.'

60

RED

D eath happens. Steve made it happen.
Red smirks as she remembers his reaction to taking a life.

~

'She's dead.'

'Check again!' Steve's voice wobbled.

Red savoured Steve's terror. How would he tell his parents about this? Their precious girl was dead and it was Steve's fault.

Red leaned against the oak tree. Luckily for Steve, the weather was foul. The gales and torrential rain kept most people indoors, except them.

'No matter how many times you check her pulse, she'll still be dead.' Red's statement was made with the emotion of reading a shopping list. 'Mags will lose it. She'll throw you out.'

Steve raked his hands down his face. Driving rain beat against him. He moved to the cover of the tree.

'How can you stand there, acting as if nothing happened?' Steve asked Red.

'The sooner you accept it, the better. It's her time to die. End of.'

'You're a callous wench. Don't you care about anything? Do you even have a heart?'

Red seized his neck. 'Don't judge me. I have more heart than your whole family put together. Never tell me I'm incapable of love.'

Steve's slippery hands gripped hers, seeking purchase. 'Let go. I can hardly breathe.'

Red enjoyed her newfound strength. Steve wasn't aware she'd started weight training. It was part of a long-term strategy. Her mental fortitude was at its peak. Emerging physical strength made her a double threat.

'This is the beginning of you paying me back.' Red released her hold.

As Steve fell away, coughing and rubbing his neck, Red assessed the pathetic display. There was pleasure in taking him down.

'I think you'll find it's me who's owed the favour, after what you did at Hayden's party,' Steve said.

As Red advanced towards him, she enjoyed watching Steve trying not to flinch.

'I didn't report it,' Red said, oozing calm. 'Therefore, you owe me.'

'I never touched you!' Steve shouted, stumbling over the corpse as he backed away.

'No one else knows that. Hurry up. I'm bored. Bury her.'

Steve held up his hands. 'No way! You can't make me do it!'

'I can, I will, and I am.' Red played with her hair. 'Do it or I'll tell your parents you killed her.'

Steve tiptoed towards the body. As he picked up the corpse, he gagged. Steve cradled her in his arms. Red smirked as a tear fell down his cheek.

61

RED

Steve had taken to performing stunts on a friend's motorbike around Great Parston. The locals protested, particularly as he was underage, but Steve took no notice. Many commented on how there would be an accident soon. There was, of sorts.

Red had offered to take Mags' Yorkshire terrier, Joy, for a walk, expecting Hayden to join them. He loved dog walks. Every day, Red watched from her window for Hayden to appear. He practically skipped along the pavement, with a dog at his heels.

When Mags said Hayden was out with friends, Red concealed her annoyance. Mags was busy with a pile of ironing, calling Red a treasure for offering. Red hoped the iron slipped and burned Mags' skin off.

Red dragged a reluctant Joy in the rain. The dog often sat instead of moving. She never misbehaved with Hayden. Red considered leaving Joy behind if the dog pulled the stunt again.

The pneumatic sound of Steve's bike announced his arrival. He passed, giving Red a wave. Steve's cockiness riled her. She knew he was mocking her, after the incident at Hayden's party.

Steve turned around for a victory lap, unaware Red had

already won. She'd cast him as a sex pest, next a killer. Joy strained against the lead. Red set the dog free.

62

RED

Steve wiped his brow as he lowered his head. His lips moved although Red couldn't hear the words.

'Are you seriously praying for a dog?' she asked.

'I'm showing respect, you heartless cow!'

Red let the comment about her lack of heart slide. Steve had done his part and buried the dog in the woods. The work was completed.

'Let this be a lesson.' Red scuffed her foot over Joy's grave. 'Never cross me. You can't comprehend the lengths I'll go to to get what I want. You'll owe me until the day you die. Prepare to get your hands dirty again, Steve.'

'I've carried this guilt for so long it's eating me up.' This contrite version of Steve is far removed from the egotistical boy and man.

Steve takes a breath and continues. 'The day Tamsin was taken I was meeting someone here. There's no way we could've gone to my house.'

'What were you up to?' Lily asks.

Steve punches the bench. The remaining slats reverberate. Under Mags' influence, I never believed Steve would hit a woman. Now I'm wondering if we've pushed him too far.

'That's right, assume I was up to no good,' Steve says. 'Everything is black and white with you, isn't it? Because you're playing at investigating, you think you can ask questions and instantly work people out.'

Lily taps her foot against the concrete. 'I may not be at Miss Marple standard yet but I'm having a good crack at this. Everything I'm doing is for your sister. You'd do well to remember it before you mouth off at me again.'

Steve slumps. The fight within him has evaporated. 'I'm

sorry I got wound up. It's exhausting living with a secret tearing you apart.'

I can't look at Steve. He'll see the guilt in my eyes.

Lily reclines on the bench. 'You're gay, aren't you?'

'Watch your mouth.' Steve's tear-stained cheeks betray his attempt at playing alpha male.

'Steve, give it up,' Lily says. 'No one's judging you.'

In moments like these I realise why I love Lily. Her compassion is endless.

'How did you work it out?' Steve wipes a sleeve across his face. 'Yes, I am. Going to make snide jokes?'

'Not at all,' Lily replies. 'About time you came out. How long's it been?'

'Years. Maybe I've always known. I can't tell my family.'

'Mags will be supportive,' I say. 'She loves you without question and won't tolerate homophobic crap. Hayden won't have an issue because it *isn't* an issue. Being gay is part of who you are. No one has the right to make you feel ashamed.'

As Steve smiles, I see a scared boy offered hope.

'I've tried telling Mum so many times but I'm afraid. If I speak the words, it becomes real. I've said it though, haven't I?'

'We're honoured you told us,' Lily replies. 'I expect it was hard, growing up and working out your sexuality. Kids can be absolute twats. Some of them would've had a field day with you being homosexual. You've always projected a lover boy image. Overcompensating by any chance?'

'Probably,' Steve mutters. 'Thank you for making me feel like I'm normal.'

'You are,' Lily says. 'Well, the being gay part anyway.'

'Get lost,' Steve replies, joining in with Lily's laughter.

'What were you doing at the park when Tamsin disappeared?' she asks.

Steve stops larking around. 'Not doing enough to protect my little sister. My selfishness killed Tamsin.'

64

RED

Hayden became Red's target when the Lawsons moved to Great Parston. Until then, Red stagnated in village life, sleeping with men she shouldn't and taunting her family with the information. Used to her outlandish ways, the villagers didn't react. Red needed a more interesting challenge.

She watched the couple she'd later know as Paul and Mags, regarding their brood from the doorstep of their new home. It was a sickeningly sweet family scene and one Red's family could never emulate. A procession of youngsters carried items into the Lawsons' new house. Red assessed them.

First in line was Tamsin. Clichéd as it sounded, she resembled an angel, with her blonde hair shining like a halo. Tamsin held her toys close as unsteady legs hurtled her along the path. When she tripped over an untied lace, Red fought the strange instinct to run to her aid.

Red's conflicting emotions were often confusing. She loved and hated in equal measure. No one could guess which she felt at any moment. Red might be reaching for an embrace or angling a knife towards your back.

Tamsin's rescuer charged in. Red later punished herself for the foolish notion of falling in love at first sight.

The knight swept up his sister. Red deplored romance as being for the gullible. How had an unremarkable boy seized her heart? It troubled her. Hayden had no right to take what wasn't his.

Hayden's caring captivated Red. Whenever she sought her family's care, they recoiled. As Hayden checked Tamsin's grazed elbow, Red wanted to swap places with Tamsin. The desperation repulsed Red.

She focused on the next Lawson boy as a distraction from the strange fluttering in her chest. Steve's bulky frame and swagger reignited her nastiness. He quashed the emotional fragility threatening to consume her. Steve wasn't someone she could ever like. They had a link though; an inner conflict, causing pain. It was etched on Steve like a tattoo.

SARAH

Steve sits, preparing to tell his story. 'I was meeting a bloke I'd started seeing. We weren't up to anything filthy, I was underage, so don't give me that look, Lily. We were getting to know each other. This park was our meeting place. Then we'd take a walk further afield, away from the nosey old biddies in the village.'

'Did you see Paul and Tamsin?' Lily asks.

'I did and I almost shat my pants. Reuben was due any minute and I didn't want to bump into Dad. I could have passed Reuben off as a mate but you know how Dad was about gay people. He had a gaydar and a habit of being insensitive. Reuben was early and I avoided Dad. He was chatting with Nick at the ice cream van. Tamsin waved to me from the roundabout. It was the last time I saw her. If I'd gone over, rather than hiding, Tamsin would still be alive.' Steve thumps his fists together.

'Don't blame yourself,' I say. 'The killer could have taken Tamsin at any moment. Was anyone near her who seemed like they shouldn't be there?'

'It's so long ago and I was standing far away. Sometimes I struggle to remember what Tamsin looked like. It does me in

151

whenever I try to picture her and I can't. From what I recall, Tamsin was alone. There were adults around who I think were parents. I need you two to keep it quiet about me being gay. Reuben and I are still together.'

'You've been with him all this time?' Lily says.

Steve gives a shy smile. 'Yes. I didn't want anyone else after I met Reuben. He puts up with my stupidity and talks me down when I try to be tough. This sounds soppy but I can be myself with him. Reuben likes me for who I really am. He finds it sad I flirt with women as a cover. Reuben wants to marry but I keep putting him off. How do I tell my family I'm marrying a man?'

I touch Steve's hand. 'I'll be there alongside you, if or when you do.'

'Thanks. I'm not ready to share with others yet. Can you keep it quiet?'

'Yes,' Lily and I reply.

'I'm done in after all that. See you soon.' Steve walks away. His steps are lighter than when he arrived.

'That was one hell of a revelation,' I say to Lily.

'I worked it out ages ago. The stud thing never fooled me. It's often the most homophobic people who are so far in the closet they're practically in Narnia camping it up with the fawns. Joking, Sarah, before you go politically correct. Nothing gets past me, apart from who killed Tamsin. I will find them though, watch me. I'm getting closer. I can feel it.'

66

RED

Today, Red is doing a good deed. At least it seems like it. She's taking a neighbour's dog for a walk. Gladys isn't getting around so well as she's riddled with arthritis. It's culled her energetic social life. Red admires the old lady's spirit but not her nosiness. It's not surprising Gladys was shocked at Red's offer. Red's neighbours hardly know her, much to Gladys' annoyance. It's important Red stays off people's radars. The dog is part of the disguise.

Gladys *will* get her dog back, unlike Mags. Years ago, Red returned from watching Joy's burial with a forced sombre expression. Mags was distraught at her puppy slipping the lead. Stoic as ever, Hayden tried to hide his upset. For effect, Red squeezed out a tear. Steve never told his family what really happened to their dog.

Red wishes Gladys had a more robust dog than a Pomeranian. A tiny ball of white fluff doesn't help when being inconspicuous. Red goes with it, cooing over her little princess while fighting the urge to batter the pooch. People may recall the idiot with the midget pooch but it's all they'll remember. Sometimes you can hide in plain sight.

Red follows Steve at a safe distance, after watching him with Lily and Sarah in the park. Not being close enough to hear their conversation was frustrating. She could see it was emotional. Taunting Steve with the dog, as a reminder of the death of Joy, was almost irresistible. Red reined herself, and the dog, in.

Red hates not knowing what Steve said to Lily and Sarah. As he makes a call, it's like he can read her thoughts. Steve shields the mouthpiece, trying to protect the person he's talking to.

Red is taking a risk being on this road. She's well disguised though, and the moving cotton wool ball at her feet demands the attention. She drags Snookums from sniffing every strip of pavement to keep up with Steve.

He ends the call at the front door. Red turns back, processing her new knowledge. Steve is gay. She should have figured it out.

Steve having a boyfriend, with a view to marriage, is solid-gold information. Hearing Steve confirming his certainty Sarah and Lily would keep his secret was hilarious. Lily and Sarah *can* be trusted. You can *never* trust Red.

67

LILY

'Since we left London, you've been a right royal pain in the bum,' Lily says to Freya.

'Because you're keeping me from Dad.' Freya's reply is surprisingly measured considering they've been yelling at each other for twenty minutes.

Lily gives a jaded laugh. 'You speak to Dad every day. I would never keep you from him.'

'When you left Dad, you separated us.' Freya places her hands on her hips.

In an attempt to extinguish the argument, Lily composes her thoughts before she replies. She must not erupt again and say what she thinks of her husband. Freya idolises Gareth. It would be wrong for Lily to shatter her daughter's illusions.

'You're old enough to understand why I had to leave,' Lily says. 'Mistakes were made. We have to move on.'

'Why can't we visit Nan?'

Lily won't confess it's because she's too ashamed to admit her marriage is over. Maybe Imogen won't judge but Lily can't deal with the inevitable pity.

'We'll go there soon,' Lily says.

'I'll believe it when I see it.' Freya marches out of the kitchen.

'Get ready for school!' Lily shouts, no longer caring about playing nice.

'I can hear you two yelling outside,' Sarah says from the hallway. She enters the kitchen. 'I forgot my wallet.'

'Here it is.' Lily hands the item to Sarah. 'Sorry about these rows Freya insists on having. I expect it's wearing on you too.'

As only a best friend does, Sarah sticks on the coffee machine and gets chocolate out of the cupboard; the friends' signal for a chat. Work can wait.

'You're doing your best, Lil,' Sarah says. 'It can't be easy being a single mum to a teenage girl.'

'I love my daughter more than life itself but it's debatable if Freya will make her next birthday.'

'You wouldn't be without her. Besides, you've basically raised a version of yourself. Your mum must find it hilarious how it all comes back around.'

Despite her upset, Lily smiles because it's true. 'Freya is incredible. Not that I'm letting her know it right now. Guess I got the strong-minded child I hoped for. When the pregnancy scan confirmed Freya was a girl, I planned to raise an Amazonian warrior woman. Gareth said he'd settle for a confident being, saying Amazonian females took up space and were often volatile.'

A disapproving sound comes from Sarah's mouth. 'Gareth isn't someone whose opinion I'd value anyway.'

'What you're politely not saying is my husband is an idiot. Even though we're separated, he continues to cause problems. It was his fault Freya and I argued.' Lily takes the coffee mug. 'When Freya and Gareth video called earlier, I couldn't bear to look. He tried to engage when he spotted me in the background. Freya said I was being mean to him. It hurt not to chat with Gareth like we used to. However, we stopped doing such simple things a long time ago. The rut crept in and created a gateway for Gareth to cheat.'

Sarah stands behind Lily to hug her. 'He doesn't deserve you, Lil. Gareth chose to have an affair. That's on him. Concentrate on making a better life for you and Freya.' Sarah plants a kiss on Lily's head. 'I've got to go. We'll talk more tonight. Love you, Lil.'

'Love you too.'

Lily watches Sarah leave. Their friendship helps Lily to keep going. She wonders how she ever coped without her. Being in the same room means so much more than phone calls or messages.

When Lily met Sarah, Lily knew they would be friends. Admittedly, Lily's bossy nature came out, wanting to nurture an abandoned girl. Sarah soon set her straight, showing Lily she was a confident and savvy person. Lily admired Sarah's fortitude, if not her guardedness. Sarah always steered the conversation elsewhere whenever Lily asked about Sarah's upbringing and her parents.

Lily enjoyed the months she spent getting to know Sarah. They hardly spent a day apart and formed a lifelong friendship. Meeting Sarah is one of Lily's favourite life events. She wishes she could say the same about this phase of her relationship with her daughter. Freya is slipping away. Of course, Freya is growing up. The sooner the better. Clingy mothers who seek validation in their children are monsters. Freya is part of Lily but also a separate being. Despite knowing this, Lily still mourns the bond she thought was unbreakable.

Weatherwax butts Lily's hands away from her lap, demanding a sleeping space.

'Bossy one, aren't you?' Lily says to the purring cat. 'I could learn a lot from you, Weatherwax, particularly about forging my own way. Let's hope I've got the courage to see it through.'

The cat replies with her usual disdainful glare. Still, Lily will take pet therapy over daring to speak to her daughter any day.

'My cheekiness fools people into thinking I've got it all together. It's bluster, Weatherwax. If you give me love and then take it away, I suffer. I hold on to those who love me without conditions or deceit. Shame my husband didn't.'

Weatherwax purrs her agreement as she settles in for a nap. It gives Lily time to consider how to channel the love she has for a murdered girl. Justice is coming for Tamsin. Lily will find it.

68

SARAH

'I can't believe you both lied.' Hayden hands the letter to me, the damning evidence.

'I didn't write it.' Lily focuses on her innocence instead of the domestic taking place in my lounge.

From the moment Hayden walked in, I knew we were busted. His face showed it. Unlike me, who simmers on things until I combust, Hayden unleashes his anger instantly. He says he'd rather tackle an issue head-on than let it fester. Lily says he doesn't appreciate the satisfaction of a good sulk.

I've read the letter sent to Mags, stating Steve's gay and in a long-term relationship. Malicious sentences show a bitter and vengeful writer.

'I was commanded to Mum's house to deal with the matter,' Hayden says, waving the paper in his hand. 'You can imagine how much fun that was, particularly as Steve thought you two blabbed to someone else.'

'Thank goodness Steve doesn't think we'd write and send it,' I reply, trying to look for the positives.

The fury on Hayden's face increases. 'Stop glossing over the main point. You both lied to me.'

'Is Steve okay?' Lily asks. 'He doesn't think I have anything to do with that letter, does he?'

'Mum comforted Steve and asserted his sexuality is his business, although he shouldn't have worried about telling us. As usual, Damien made endless cups of tea. I was gutted Steve felt he couldn't talk to me. However, I was more upset to hear Steve told you about Reuben because it's relevant to your investigation. Would this be the investigation you promised not to start?'

Stalling for time, I focus on Lily. Her knee is taking the brunt of her distress as she smacks her phone against it. 'No one thinks you'd write such hateful things, Lil.'

'Never mind who wrote it.' Hayden raises his voice. 'You lied to me, Sarah. What happened to the promise you made not to investigate?'

'I'm not investigating! I was there because Lily was too chicken to see Steve on her own.'

'Cheers, Sarah.' Lily puts her mobile aside. 'We're trying to help your family, Hayden, for crying out loud. Sarah wasn't doing anything wrong. Stop being so patriarchal.'

'Stop copying your mum and her rants.' Hayden adopts a similar sarcastic tone. 'Women can do what they want. Sarah is independent but she kept this from me. I love her and wanting to keep her safe is part of it. Playing detectives is dangerous.'

Aware an outburst is coming, I cover Lily's open mouth.

'I'll speak for myself, thank you, Lily. Go out and find something to do. Hayden and I need to talk.'

Lily sticks her middle finger up at Hayden. In response, he raises his two fingers in a *V*.

I wait for the front door to shut before talking. 'I wasn't investigating. Lily asked me to tag along because Steve makes her uncomfortable with his macho behaviour. Turns out it was a front anyway.'

'Why do you let Lily dominate you?'

'I don't.' The petulance in my voice isn't helping.

'Lily has a habit of getting you involved in things.'

The fight has left me as I take a seat. 'Someone has to keep Lily in order. Left unsupervised, she'd get herself into all kinds of scrapes. Past evidence shows it.'

Hayden sits with me. 'Like when she chained herself to the library railings in protest at it being closed down?'

'Only to be told it was the wrong library after she'd thrown away the key.' Hayden laughs despite his earlier annoyance. 'The photos of Lily being set free by the police are absolute gems.'

'You were such a knob for taking pictures of her.'

After our laughter dies, I accept I have to confront a truth I've recently realised. 'I want to help Lily investigate. I've been helping Lily because I needed to help Mags too. We'd made up and it felt like Mags was relying on me. Yes, my motivations were initially selfish. I had to please your mum. It's become so much more than doing this for Mags' approval though. This is about Tamsin. She deserves for her killer to be found and punished.'

'It's the police's job.' Hayden edges away from me.

'I agree with Mags. The police will do what they can but they won't be motivated by having known and cared for Tamsin. Lily and I are.'

'I understand but why you? Lily is sort of trained to do it but you're not. Besides, how are you going to do this with such a demanding job?'

I rub my jaw, trying to soothe my painful teeth from the grinding. 'I've managed so far and will investigate when I can. If Lil needs me more, I'll get cover. I often miss out on annual leave because I'm so wrapped up in work.'

Hayden shuffles closer. 'Don't burn yourself out. I care, despite how it may seem. The lying upsets me more than the investigation.'

'That's rich, coming from you.' I push his approaching hand away. 'I'm not the only one who's been lying.'

69
RED

Hayden is a liar. He said he was a friend but his friendship has always wavered.

Red made the mistake of trusting Hayden with her heart. He trod all over it. It's only fair Red seizes his heart too and drains the life out of it.

70

RED

Red sometimes wonders what her life would have been like if she'd never met Hayden Lawson. She can't visualise it. Hayden is part of her and always will be, for better or worse.

'This obsession with the Lawson boy stops right now!' Red's gran threw the damning evidence on the floor.

Red gathered the notebooks, not daring to look at Gran. Every fantasy, dream, illicit thought, and observation were scrawled within the books. For once, Red was grateful for the violin strains coming from upstairs. At least she had been spared one humiliation. Not everyone needed to participate in her audience of shame.

Spotting the open page where she practised signing her married Lawson name, Red stifled a sob. She should have known. Gran was an expert truth-seeker. The old woman knew every hiding place. It was her house, after all. The sooner Red's mother stood up to Gran and moved her family out, the better.

There were many notebooks, filled within months of meeting Hayden. Every word became a humiliating stick for Gran to beat Red with. Gran threw one into the fire before she left. Red watched it burn and pictured Gran's funeral pyre.

Red's mother placed her legs on the table. Her mini skirt rode up, revealing her underwear. Red looked away. Why couldn't her mother behave like the other mothers and show some decency? The woman thought because she was young when she got pregnant, she could continue behaving like a rampant teenager.

'You're a dark horse,' Red's mother said, blowing on wet nail varnish. 'Got a crush on Hayden Lawson?'

Red imagined her mother's scarlet fingernails as bleeding fingertips. Pulling each nail off and witnessing her tormentor's suffering would be exquisite.

'Don't be embarrassed,' Red's mother said, sitting on the sofa next to her daughter.

Red moved away. The proximity was stifling and unknown. Red would only deal in certainties.

'We all have fixations sometimes,' Red's mother said, crossing her legs.

Red was likely to fill the woman's mouth with her fist if she didn't stop talking or flashing her knickers.

Red's mother continued. 'Who knows? Hayden might be your greatest love. Never let go. You'll regret it.'

Red's mother reached for the nail polish, preparing to apply a second coat. Red knew she wasn't giving motherly advice. The slut was mocking her.

Red grasped her mother's hands. The surprise on the woman's face at the physical contact amused Red.

Red stroked her mother's fingers. The woman's fearful eyes didn't match her confused smile. Red's nails scratched into the manicure; marking the red.

'Tend to your own problems,' Red said as her mother inspected the gouges in her talons. 'You've certainly created enough of them and they're all under your own roof.'

'When have I lied?' Hayden asks me.

He's either being honest or has gained superb acting skills. His face doesn't carry a hint of shame.

'Who are you talking to when you leave the room to take a call? Who's the woman I heard in the background when I phoned last night and you were allegedly in the bath? I swear if you lie to me, I'll lose it.'

'She's a friend.' Hayden goes over to the fireplace and leans against the mantelpiece. 'An old friend, Anna Hart. She's fallen on hard times and needs my help.'

'Why the secrecy? Why not tell me about her?'

'I wanted to but she asked me not to say anything to anyone.' Hayden steps away from the heat of the fire. 'Anna isn't comfortable around new people and takes a while to open up. She's taken a lot of knocks and it's had a huge impact. I wasn't there for Anna when she needed me. Recently, I've helped her get back on her feet. She lived with me for a few months, before you and I met again.'

My judging eyebrow darts upwards.

'No, Sarah. It's not like that. Anna and I weren't in a relationship and we're certainly not now. When I was younger, I got really drunk and kissed Anna. It was such a stupid thing to do and felt like I was kissing a sister. You're the only woman I want. No one could match up to you. I hated not telling you about Anna but she begged me. We've had a rocky friendship in the past. I let her down and I'm trying to make up for it. It was stupid to put her needs before you though.'

I try not to show surprise at hearing he kissed this Anna person. It was years ago and I can't expect Hayden to have avoided females before we reunited. I will focus on Anna as a person rather than a threat. 'It's strange how she doesn't want you to mention her. Is Anna in trouble with the police?'

'Already an investigator, aren't you?' Hayden's tone borders on scathing. 'Anna isn't a criminal. She's a childhood friend who's having problems with her family. Anna's a private person and she doesn't want people knowing about her background.'

Anna makes me uneasy. It's not jealousy. It was ridiculous to even consider Hayden cheating on me. I know him. Anna is the stranger. What are her intentions towards Hayden? Why has she reappeared? I understand reunions happen. Hayden and I are proof of it. I hope Anna doesn't expect more from Hayden than friendship. She'll have a fight on her hands if she does.

Hayden kneels in front of me. 'We've both been out of order. I don't want a relationship where we hide things from each other. I'm sorry I didn't mention Anna. Not being able to tell you was difficult but she was so desperate.'

'I'm sorry too. I should've said I wanted to investigate and we'd have discussed it. You accept I'd still have done it though, right?'

'I don't doubt it. It's one of the many reasons why I love you. You stand up for what you believe in. Do what you need to do.' Hayden looks into my eyes. I can see what it's costing him. 'Be careful. I'm keen on having you and the infuriating Lily around for a lot longer.'

'I'm set on being around for a while too.'

As I draw him in for a kiss, I hope we're secure because I'm about to drop another bombshell.

RED

G ran said letter writing was a dying art form. She was a stickler for tradition. Red could almost hear Gran's praise as she wrote the letter to Mags. If she was alive, Gran would tell Red what a good girl she was for practising her handwriting on "that heathen" Mags.

As soon as Gran heard about the family moving into Great Parston, she made it her business to check them out. Gran returned from her visit, assessing Mags as too brash, "that one thinks she's something special". Red's mother agreed. Of course she did.

It's Steve's turn to learn what happens when he doesn't do as he's told. He forgot to behave. Steve stopped doing the favours he owed for Red not reporting his "attack" on her at Hayden's party or killing Mags' dog.

Steve thought he'd got away with it. Silly boy.

RED

Red has been off the scene for years. Now she's back. Bad luck, Steve.

Bad luck, Sarah. Hayden knows you've been lying to him. It hurts when he's angry with you, doesn't it?

'Are you following me?'

Red stumbled as she stopped walking. Finally, Hayden noticed her. She wasn't prepared.

'Not at all,' Red replied, affecting a carefree tone, despite rising fear. Whenever Hayden looked at her, which wasn't often, she felt like oxygen was in short supply.

Hayden walked towards her.

This is it, Red thought, *this is our moment*. They would connect. The love affair would begin. He would forget about the other girl and understand Red was the more suitable choice.

Hayden retrieved a notebook from inside his jacket. He flicked through its pages. Red imagined it full of his poetry. She waited for a sonnet, declaring hidden feelings for her.

Hayden wrinkled his nose as he perused the contents. Reaching into his back pocket, he pulled out a pen and began writing.

Red leaned against a fence, scared to speak, afraid of ruining the moment. What words had she inspired him to write? Red was a muse, Hayden's muse!

'See this?' Hayden held the notebook towards Red. 'This is evidence. I've recorded every time you've stood outside our house, staring up at my window, turned up at my Saturday job or appeared wherever I am. If you don't stop following me, I'm taking this to the police.'

Red's vision swam. Air left her lungs. Hayden *had* noticed her but not the way she wanted.

'You're not right in the head!' Hayden shouted, his cheeks turning scarlet. 'Everyone says it but I gave you a chance. Enough. Leave me alone or you'll regret it.'

For the first time, someone's anger, apart from her gran's, terrified Red. Hayden advanced upon her, pounding out his annoyance. She stepped away, not recognising the coward she'd become. Hayden reduced her to nothing.

'Stay away from me.' Hayden's face neared Red's. 'I'll be at college in Leeds next week. I'm sure you can manage it until then. Stop hanging around my family too. Mum says to be nice because no one talks to you. Dad says you're a slut. Even Steve wouldn't touch you with a bargepole. You're a freak. Stick with your messed-up family.'

The final word brought Red to her senses. No one was allowed involvement in her family business. It was Red's turn to barrel towards Hayden. His astonishment made Red's steps focused and brave.

'I advise you to stay away from my family,' Red said, gripping his shoulder. 'It would be a huge mistake for you to stir that particular pot. I could bring the Lawsons down with a few words. I won't forget this.'

Hayden brushed Red off with the flick of a hand. 'Whatever, ginger. Get over it and go back to your psycho gran. I'm done with you.'

But I'm not done with you, Red thought, as Hayden walked away.

Red's now glad Hayden is the forgiving sort. The plan would have failed without his recent kindness. Hayden's caring is Red's route to killing.

74

LILY

On the drive to Imogen's house, Lily has increased Freya's knowledge of expletives. Lily doesn't often swear in front of Freya. Since Gareth did the dirty, Lily's mouth has become filthy too.

'If you shake that thing at me once more, I won't be responsible for my actions.' Lily pushes away the swear tin Freya's holding.

'Stop swearing then.'

'You're not my bloody mother.'

'A pound, please.' Freya holds out her open palm. 'I bet you can't make it through the rest of this journey without swearing.'

'I sodding well can. Oh, shit.' Lily rummages in her pocket for money. 'I'm broke. Bugger off.'

'Three quid.' Freya rattles the tin.

Lily has a headache. She seizes the tin and throws it out her open window.

After a slight delay in retrieving the tin, due to Freya stating how much was in it, they arrive at Imogen's house. Lily's stress lessens. Being here soothes her.

Moving to London was the beginning of the end of her marriage. Gareth was the city boy to Lily's rural girl. Where she felt at home in Buckinghamshire and Oxfordshire, with roads she could negotiate in her sleep, Gareth craved the anonymity of a metropolitan environment.

How Gareth's heart wasn't captured by Ickford is beyond Lily. Stone houses radiate the buttery afternoon sun. Thatched roofs hug buildings. This is Lily's world, not getting black bogeys from waiting in the Underground or speeding through a concrete landscape.

Walking ahead, Freya opens Imogen's door with their key. After seeing Imogen isn't around, Freya races up the stairs. Lily is grateful for the closeness between grandmother and grand-daughter. Leaving Imogen behind was a wrench.

Screams travel. Running to the source, Lily imagines Imogen is dead, tied up by burglars or having her organs harvested. Lily's clumsiness will come back to haunt her as she trips over a rug and lands on Imogen's bed. It's occupied by Imogen and a "friend". Fleshy parts are swiftly covered.

Lily wobbles as she stands. 'Well, Mother, I'd never have guessed you're a cougar.'

Imogen hides behind a pillow.

'Nice to meet you, and all that.' Imogen's younger lover has impeccable manners. 'Would you two mind going outside while we make ourselves more presentable?'

'You saucy minx,' Lily says to a fully clothed Imogen. 'I clocked you snogging that boy's face off when he left.'

'Do you have to make everything sound so tawdry?' Imogen asks. 'He's a man, not a boy.'

'He's certainly spritely. Not a sag or wrinkle in sight.'

'You're not too old for a smack across the head.'

Freya sniggers at the chastisement.

'My computer's playing up again,' Imogen says to Freya. 'Take a look at it, please.'

Freya leaves, as any self-respecting teen does when there's a conversation taking place about their nan's sex life.

Lily shuts the lounge door. 'What's his name?'

'Myles.'

'How long have you been getting it on with the nubile Myles?'

'Stop making it sound so illicit. We've been together a while. We kept it quiet because we want to see where it's going.'

'Pretty well, I'd say.'

Imogen slaps the chair arm. 'Grow up. Older people still have relationships. I'm not dead yet.'

'I'm happy for you.' Lily is more serious. 'How did you meet?'

'He was one of my students, although not great at Sociology. He got a 2.2. We bumped into each other in a café recently and the rest is history.'

'Retirement's doing you wonders. Does he ask you to lecture him in bed to remind him of uni?'

'Think it, don't say it, remember, Lil?'

Lily slaps her own hand, a learned response to loved ones reminding her of her runaway mouth. 'You deserve someone nice, Mum. It looks like he makes you happy.' Lily enjoys Imogen's soppy smile. 'Don't forget to make me Matron of Honour.'

'Behave yourself.' Imogen blushes. 'I'll never get married

again. It oppresses women and frankly, your dad was a total shit. On that note, we need to talk about Gareth. I heard you've left him and what the unimaginable cock did.'

Lily would laugh if it wasn't so mortifying Imogen knowing about Gareth's affair.

'Spare me the lecture on taking Gareth back before and how I set myself up for this. How did you find out?'

'Gareth phoned yesterday, believing I'd convince you to forgive him. He thought I knew everything and you'd come to your mum. I'm hurt you didn't.'

Lily gravitates towards the woman who always makes it better. 'I was embarrassed.'

'It's not for you to feel ashamed.' Imogen kisses Lily's head. 'By the way, I told Gareth to piss off.'

The dam bursts. Lily sobs. Mother and daughter connect. Lily moves her cheek away from the damp patch on Imogen's shoulder.

'This house is too big for one person,' Imogen says. 'Move in with me. I'd love to have you both here.'

'Thank you.' Lily wipes snot away with her hand. 'Sarah will be pleased to have her place back, much as she's been an absolute legend.'

Freya darts into the room. 'Yay, we're coming home!'

Lily doesn't reprimand her daughter for listening at closed doors. Freya has got it right. This is home. It always has been.

Red understands she won't learn much being outside Sarah's house. Still, she waits. Stalking is addictive. Red is accomplished at it. Being on the outside is where she belongs.

Red tried to fit in with her family. Her intensity and intelligence scared them. Mystified by her child, Red's mother usually regarded her with contempt.

Red stood outside the kitchen, listening at the door. Many secrets were shared this way. Even though she was only eight, Red already used them to her advantage.

Through the crack in the doorway, Red watched her mother's face emerge from behind her hands. Streaked make-up marked her cheeks. 'I don't know what to do with her anymore.'

'Nonsense,' Gran replied. 'All the girl needs is a firm hand and direction. Sort yourself out. You're more devious than that girl could ever be. She learned her wickedness from you. Heaven knows, you never learn from your sordid mistakes. Ever since you were sixteen, you've brought trouble for this family.'

Gran's authority and solidness filled the room. She was Red's role model and great fear. With Gran's praise, Red felt she could conquer anything. It made up for when the matriarch showed Red the error of her ways. Red accepted it was for her own good. She had to be better, cleverer, and stronger than everyone else.

Checking her reflection in a compact mirror, Red's mother scrubbed her face with a baby wipe.

'If you weren't so self-absorbed, the child wouldn't cause trouble.' The formidable matriarch swiped the tool of vanity from her daughter's hand. Red didn't flinch. The sound of glass crashing against stone tiles was mesmerising.

'She isn't normal! Why can't she be like other children?' Red's mother shouted. Her eyes flitted to the partially open doorway. 'We both know little girls can be absolute angels. *That* girl breaks my things, trips me up, and laughs when I fall. Sometimes I catch her staring at me and it's like, like...'

'Spit it out,' Gran commanded.

'I think she wants to kill me.'

Red slinked away, enjoying her gran's laughter. Good. Red's mother finally got the message. She deserved it.

76

SARAH

Lily sits on the bed, folding clothes into a suitcase. My spare room is unrecognisable. It's rammed with Lily and Freya's belongings. Having them in one room was a tight fit, not helped by the crap I've been storing in there. Isn't that what a second room is for?

I feel a twist of future loneliness realising Weatherwax and I will be going solo again. Then I get over it. No more queuing for the bathroom every morning. No more getting up at the crack of sparrows to have a pee.

'Hayden's all right with us investigating?' Lily asks. Although Hayden and Lily annoy each other, she'd never hurt him.

'He accepts it. He's not comfortable with it but he understands why we're continuing.'

'I'm so pleased you're helping me. It wouldn't be the same without you. How's Hayden doing since you told him about Paul's debt and the drugs thing?'

'He's devastated. It tore me apart to see how crushed he was. What's most worrying is how quiet he became. You know how vocal he gets when he's upset.'

'Don't I just. He'll bounce back. He's got us. What about this Anna?'

Lily wasn't impressed to hear of Hayden's secret friend and him kissing her, when they were younger. Even though I've told Lily I'm okay with it, she's jealous on my behalf.

'There's not much to say.' I fling Lily's socks into a holdall. 'Anna's lucky to have Hayden on her side.'

Lily teeters above a heap of jeans, balancing on the bed. 'Saint Sarah, admit you're a teensy bit ticked off.'

'I'm not happy Hayden didn't mention Anna, and I'm wondering what her motives are. I trust Hayden though. He loves me, not her.'

'Right answer. Hayden's one of the good ones.' Lily winces as she removes hair straighteners from under her backside. 'I'll check Anna out.'

'I was hoping you'd say that. She's far too mysterious for my liking.'

We're interrupted by the doorbell.

'The police are here!' Freya shouts. I won't miss the not-so-dulcet tones of my teenage butler.

'What have you done?' I ask Lily.

'Nothing. Honestly. Stop looking at me like that.'

Our guest, DI Chris Watts, is a handsome gazelle of a man. He's full of energy, legs bouncing in front of him as he sits. His height is complimented by muscles lining a slim-fit shirt, topped with a patterned waistcoat. Lily has noticed DI Watts' charms. I've never seen her so flirty. Freya was captivated by him too, grilling him on his career and how she can join the police. Freya's gone out after Lily's instruction to do so.

'I'm not one to beat around the bush,' DI Watts says and then grins at Lily's snort-laugh. 'I'm aware you two have been looking into Tamsin's death.'

'What gives you that impression?' I ask, giving a blank stare.

'Queenie Lawson.' Watts grimaces. 'She's been on the phone saying we should pull our fingers out. Apparently you're running rings around us.'

Damn you, Queenie, and your no-nonsense ways.

'We were only visiting an old friend.' Lily tries out her posh voice. Whoever told her it's seductive was having a laugh. Lily sounds like she's choking on a plum.

'Lily, may I call you Lily?' Watts asks. Lily simpers in response. 'While off the record I find it commendable you want to help Mags, you're putting yourselves in potential danger.'

'We can handle it.' Lily forgets the snobby persona and reverts to stubbornness.

'Not that we need to,' I add. 'We're supporting the family, not investigating.'

'Here's my position so you understand. I'm not here to tell you off.' Watts lays his forearms on his thighs. I catch Lily focusing on his biceps. 'My dad was on the original team dealing with Tamsin's disappearance. He regretted not finding the killer. Between us, they believed Tamsin was murdered but there was no definitive proof. I have a vested interest in finding Tamsin's killer and begged to work on this case. I'm not only doing my job. This is for my old man too. Usually I'd send a sergeant to have a word with you but I need you to know how invested I am in this case.'

Lily tears herself away from idol worshipping to get the bag out of a drawer. 'Someone sent this to Sarah. I touched it because it fell on the floor and my dog would have nabbed it.'

Watts inspects the badge through the clear plastic. I explain how I originally gave it to Tamsin.

'Thank you for handing this over,' Watts says. 'Anything like this in the future, tell me immediately.' The hint he accepts we'll continue to investigate is there.

'We intended to give it to the police, Chris.' Lily is practically purring.

'DI Watts.' I keep it professional as a message to Lily. 'We'll let you know if we learn anything about Tamsin. Of course, we will leave the police to do their work.' I make sure not to add how we're doing our part too.

Watts smirks. 'I have a feeling it's difficult to get one over on you, Sarah.'

Lily leans forward, blocking my view. 'Would you like a drink, Chris?'

'No thanks. Got to get back to it. Consider yourselves visited and warned. I'll see myself out. It was a pleasure meeting you.' He's speaking to Lily.

'You too, Chris.' Lily drapes herself against the door frame.

After he leaves, I can't resist launching at her. 'You too, Chris. Anything you say, Chris. How obvious were you?'

'I don't know what you mean.' Lily reddens.

'Lily and Chris, sitting in a tree. K.I.S.S.I.N.G.'

'Are you twelve because you're acting like it?'

'Says the person who cooed over a bloke like she was back at school.'

'I did not! Even if the silver fox is charming, nothing's stopping us from finding Tamsin's killer.'

'That's my girl.' I lead Lily upstairs to finish packing. 'Silver fox, eh? Someone's got a crush.'

The doorbell sounds again.

'I'll get it,' Lily says. 'Chris might have forgotten something.'

I follow, ready to tease her some more.

The door swings open to reveal a woman. She ignores Lily, looking behind her at me. 'You must be Sarah.'

'Yes.' I step forward.

'It's great to meet at last.' The woman's broad smile and exuberant handshake seem forced.

'And you are?' Lily scans the visitor.

'I'm Anna Hart, Hayden's friend.'

RED

Complacency is a killer. When people are contented, they're disturbed by shocking events. Lily and Sarah have had it too easy. They think they're leading the investigation.

Red doesn't mind people believing they're autonomous. It makes it so much sweeter when she cuts their strings. The puppet master watches her puppets fall.

A new stage has been set. Red is taking it to the next level with a blast from the past.

SARAH

Anna twists a ring around her finger. Lily and I are on the other side of the breakfast bar, creating an interrogation atmosphere.

I assess the woman of mystery. Anna's cornered bird movements are jerky. Her eyes skitter across the room. I wonder if she hates her freckles. The attempt to cover them with foundation isn't successful. It's clear Anna's unsure of herself. As she fusses with her hair, I consider how the constant flicking must be giving her a headache. I'm always casting an observing eye over people, especially when we first meet. Being a GP demands it.

'How come you're here?' Lily asks. 'Did Hayden tell you where Sarah lives? Does he know you're visiting?'

Anna's uncertain laugh betrays her nerves. 'Hayden said you're inquisitive.'

'I bet he didn't say *inquisitive*,' I reply.

'I expect it was ruder,' Lily says, grinning.

Anna glares at Lily and frowns.

'Don't mind us,' I say.

Anna's too preoccupied with surveying the kitchen to respond. She seems to be memorising everything. I'm not sure if

I should be offended. Her scrutiny is more than assessing my taste.

'Earth to Anna,' Lily says.

'Sorry. I zoned out. To answer your questions, I found out where Sarah lives from Hayden's address book. He doesn't know I'm here.'

I'm sure Hayden doesn't have an address book. It's archaic for a technology geek. Perhaps it's something I'm yet to discover about him since we met again. If he has one, what the hell is Anna doing, rifling through Hayden's belongings?

'Sneaky manoeuvre,' Lily says. 'Why didn't you tell Hayden you're coming here? Anyhow, Sarah's heard about you already.' If there was a nearby lamp, Lily would shine it in Anna's eyes.

Anna addresses me. 'I'm sorry I asked Hayden not to mention me. For my safety, I couldn't have people knowing where I am. I didn't realise it would cause problems for you and Hayden. Therefore, I thought it best to meet you.'

'Our relationship is fine, thank you.' I refuse to curb my snarkiness, while wondering why Anna needs protection.

'Oh dear, I'm offending you.' Anna sticks out her bottom lip, revealing teeth marks embedded in the skin.

'Anyway,' Lily interrupts, 'why are you here?'

'I want to clear things up and meet Sarah. Now I have the pleasure of meeting you too.' Anna's stretched mouth wouldn't fool anyone it's a genuine smile.

'How do you know Hayden?'

I'm glad Lily's asking the questions. It saves me from coming across as the scorned woman.

'I met Hayden when the Lawsons moved from Oxford. We hung around the same places and became friends.'

'Were you interested in him?' Lily asks.

'That's a suspicious mind you've got there,' Anna replies. 'We worked on the school newspaper, although we were in different years, and bonded through our shared love of books.'

I won't show my hurt at Hayden not warming to me when I was younger. I thought it was because I was a girl. I wrestle with feelings of betrayal. Hayden owed me nothing. I'm an adult in a relationship with him, not a teenager who didn't even care if he noticed me.

Anna continues. 'Hayden took me under his wing. My family life was, let's say, difficult. He helped me escape from it sometimes. I'd rather not talk about it.'

'Did you keep in contact with Hayden all this time?' Lily leans over the counter.

Anna edges back. 'No. I've moved house a lot. We lost touch. When I returned to the area, I contacted Hayden. He's been amazing and even helped me get a job.'

'What do you do?' I decide to take a more active part in talking to Anna.

'I'm a ward clerk at the John Radcliffe. A friend of Hayden's told him about the position. The trek from Haddenham is annoying but it pays the bills.'

'I work in Oxford too,' I say. 'It sounds like you've got a true friend in Hayden.' I keep my tone light. Anna doesn't need an extra grilling. Lily's doing well enough.

'Do you have any brothers or sisters?' Lily asks.

'No.'

'Same for me,' Lily replies. 'I always wished I had siblings. How about you?'

'I'm happy with it being only me.' Anna looks away. 'Brothers usually find their sisters to be a nuisance. I've heard having a sister can be hard work too.'

Anna fusses over Weatherwax, who's jumped up on the breakfast bar. No matter how many times I tell her to get off it, she's taken it as a challenge. Anna scowls as I remove the cat.

'I'd love to have had a sister, although we're as good as, right, Lil?' I give her a wink.

'Damn straight.'

Anna gathers her coat and bag. She seems in a hurry to leave.

'Going already?' I ask.

'Thanks for seeing me. I've been looking forward to meeting you properly, rather than from afar.'

'What do you mean?' Lily asks. 'Have you been following us?'

79

SARAH

Anna looks everywhere but at Lily and me. 'I'm not a stalker. I meant I've heard so much from Hayden it feels like I know you already.'

'Have you ever snogged Hayden?' Before Anna leaves, Lily gets the more brutal questions in, even though she knows the answer.

Anna's blushing matches her coat. 'Wow, you really are inquisitive. Hayden tried to kiss me, a long time ago. I pushed him away. It shouldn't have happened. We hardly spoke afterwards.' Although Anna's brushing it off, I can sense her pain.

'Was it definitely a one-off?' Lily asks.

'I'm not a liar. My relationship with Hayden is platonic.'

I refuse to be upset by Hayden's inebriated youthful error. Envying Anna is futile. Hayden is with me.

'I understand why you're suspicious of my motives,' Anna says. 'I'm only here to smooth things over and get to know you better.'

'It might be difficult,' Lily replies, nostrils flaring as she sniffs. 'We're extremely busy.'

'Oh yes. You're investigating Tamsin's death.' Anna's no

longer intent on leaving. 'I was devastated when she went missing. She was such a good kid. The fact Tamsin was murdered is unbelievable. Have you found out much so far?'

'It's confidential.' Lily's abrasiveness could scour a burned saucepan.

'Of course it is.'

Is Anna taunting Lily?

'I've got packing to do and Sarah's helping,' Lily says. Attention span stretched, she goes upstairs without saying goodbye.

Anna grabs the front door handle. 'Right. I mustn't keep you.'

'Thanks for coming here,' I say. 'I expect it took a lot of courage.'

'More than you could ever understand.'

For Hayden's sake, I want to like Anna. Her intensity makes getting close difficult.

After she leaves, I lean against the door, relieved Anna's gone.

'She's got secrets,' Lily says, appearing at the top of the stairs.

'And you'll find out what they are.'

'Too right.' Lily punches a fist into her other open hand. 'Anna's not duping me with the scared little girl act. There's something else she's rubbish at hiding.'

'What?'

'Didn't you see?' Lily asks. 'Anna needs to get to the hairdresser, pronto. Those roots need doing. Why she's covering her natural colour is beyond me. I quite fancy being a redhead.'

RED

The plan is gaining momentum. Anna has paid a visit. She's proved to be useful. Anna will always be a part of Red.

Red mulls over Anna's meeting with Sarah and Lily. Seeds of suspicion were planted. Anna was nervous and inquisitive. Sarah was edgy. Lily didn't let up. The game is on and Red is warming to the firecracker. Lily's a worthy adversary. It's a shame she'll be extinguished.

Sarah tried to cover her jealousy. She hadn't expected timid Anna to be forthright about Hayden's kiss. Consuming Sarah with doubts regarding Anna and Hayden's relationship will render her a less-effective investigator.

Anna is quite the actress but it's time to put her back in the box. It's Red's turn now.

RED

Red tried to teach Tamsin the importance of being centre stage when they were together.

Painting a "whore's mask", as Gran called it, was one of Red's favourite babysitting pastimes. It wasn't something Tamsin enjoyed, which made the task even better.

'I don't like lipstick,' Tamsin whined. 'It tastes funny.' She slid her hand across her mouth. Bright pink streaks marked Tamsin's cheek.

'You're not supposed to lick it, stupid.' Red squeezed Tamsin's cheeks, making the girl's lips form a pout. 'We're having fun, remember?'

'I want to read my book,' Tamsin garbled as lipstick lined her mouth.

Red threw the lipstick onto the dressing table. For someone who wore little make-up, Mags had a lot of it. She was one of those women who let themselves go as they aged. Red never would.

Red admired the wall. If she focused on the red paint, she could almost forgive Mags for the colours on the other walls. Mags' bedroom resembled a primary school classroom: garish, bright, and lacking artistic merit. The woman had no taste. Among other things, Mags and Red's mother had that in common.

Red turned Tamsin towards the mirror above the table. 'Look,' Red said to the girl.

Squeezing her eyes shut tight, Tamsin refused. Red wasn't sure if she admired the girl's determination or wanted to end it.

Red pulled Tamsin forward. The girl fell on the dresser, whimpering as her nose squashed against the glass.

'Do as you're told!' Red shouted. 'Look!'

'I'm looking! I'm looking!'

Satisfied of Tamsin's compliance, Red let go. Tamsin stayed in place.

'Make-up is a mask,' Red began. 'It's part of the act. You can be whoever you want to be, Tamsin. Learn from me.'

Tamsin nodded vigorously, daring to retreat.

Red saw Hayden in the mirror. She checked her reflection. Perfect.

'What's going on in here?' Hayden asked. 'I heard shouting.'

Tamsin didn't speak.

'Are you okay?' Hayden kneeled in front of Tamsin and placed his hands on her shoulders. 'Why do you look like a clown?'

'We're having girls' time, trying out some looks, isn't that right?' Red gave the girl a stare.

'Yes,' Tamsin muttered around sucking her thumb. Pink lipstick coated the digit.

'Tamsin wants to be an actress when she grows up,' Red said, monopolising Hayden's attention. 'Don't you, dearest?'

Tamsin gave a brief nod.

'I thought you wanted to be Doctor Who or an astronaut?' Hayden addressed Tamsin.

'She's changed her mind,' Red replied on Tamsin's behalf. 'Tamsin's decided adopting different roles is best.'

'Whatever,' Hayden said, already leaving the room.

Because Tamsin forgot how to play her part, she is now a pile of bones.

82

SARAH

Lily and I were teenagers the last time we were in the Unity Café. It hasn't changed much. The same checked plastic tablecloths cover the tables. I swear they're glued on with grease.

It's comforting being near to the Lawsons' and Lily's old houses in Oxford. Tamsin's death is making Lily and me nostalgic.

Lily and I felt so grown up when we came into this café alone. We always had cheese rolls and enormous chocolate milkshakes. Grated cheese sprinkled down our fronts and brown moustaches decorated our top lips. Once our tummies were full, we'd sit outside. As people passed by, we concocted stories for them. I could do it for hours. Lily was bored within minutes.

'Is it good to be back in the hood?' Lily asks.

'I haven't visited this part of Oxford since I left the Lawsons' house.'

'Are you eating that?' Lily reaches for my chocolate caramel slice.

I pull my plate away from her pincer hand. 'Do I need to check your gut? You're constantly stuffing your face.'

'I'm comfort eating and doing my bit for the planet. No waste.'

'You'll have a heart attack at the rate you're going.'

'Says you who's on her second cake.'

'Do as I say not as I do.'

'What do you know about Damien, by the way?' Lily asks.

'Swift change of subject.' I nibble the slice before Lily gets her mitts on it. 'Damien seems down-to-earth and kind. Why are you asking?'

A commotion takes place at another table. A waitress dashes away. The irate customer is probably embarrassed, considering they're hiding under the table.

'Damien's on my radar,' Lily says. 'No one's ever that nice and he was being strange when I last saw him. I had to check him out.'

'You're so suspicious. I'm glad Mags is with a decent bloke, particularly after what Paul did, not that she's aware. Hayden was so worried about her before she met Damien.'

Lily pushes her bowl of chips aside. 'You won't think Damien's so wonderful after you hear what I've found out about him. Take a look at this.'

83

RED

Sarah and Lily's choice of café shows Red has something in common with them. The past has a hold on her too. There are places where Red can hear ghosts calling, smell the essences of childhood, and feel goosebumps of indelible memories rippling on her skin. Whenever she's in Great Parston, it's like entering a time tunnel.

Red raises the menu higher. She resists asking for a replacement not covered in stains. As she moves her elbow, her jumper sticks to the table. The cashmere is ruined. Red seethes but she must not draw attention to herself.

Unity is a greasy spoon and makes no apologies for it. Plastic chairs sweat from steam pouring out of the kitchen. Condensation runs into the window frames. Red assesses the other diners' food and is pleasantly surprised by the offerings. Meals are carefully presented and appealing. Red admires Unity for being what it is and sticking to its purpose.

'What can I get for you?' A young waitress blocks Red's view of Sarah and Lily's table.

'Tea, please.'

The girl reads out a long list. Red can't hear Sarah and Lily's conversation over the litany of herbal infusions.

'A basic cup of breakfast tea, for goodness' sake.' Red clutches the girl's forearm, too late to cage the raging beast.

The waitress' knuckles whiten as she trembles within Red's grasp. Red tries to rescue the situation, placing her hand on the girl's arm instead. The waitress jumps away and crashes into another table. Red's targets look over at the scene. Waiting for the performance to end, Red picks up a fork Red's purposefully knocked to the floor.

The waitress scuttles away. Red won't drink the tea. It will be topped with saliva or worse.

Crisis over, Red continues listening to Lily and Sarah. As Lily details Damien's damning past, Red cannot believe what she hears. She could never have prepared for this, and yet, it is perfect.

84

SARAH

On the way to see Damien, I wish I didn't know what Lily's disclosed. I've asked her to do the talking. Damning as it is, Lily's prepared to break the news. She can show her investigative prowess and how no one messes with Lily's friends.

I phoned Hayden and shared what Lily's unearthed. He tried to stay calm. Hayden's arranged cover at school so he can be at his mum's house too. I can't imagine how the Lawsons will ever recover from this.

Damien's face is ashen. His eyes shift around the room. No one offers him support. Damien holds Mags' hand. She emerges from the shock. Revolted by touching such a person, Mags shoves Damien away.

An expectant silence weighs down on us. The wait for the impending storm is unbearable.

'Why do you have these photographs of Tamsin?' Lily aims and fires at Damien.

Damien snatches the file from Lily. She's unprepared for the aggressiveness from a usually gentle man. Lily stumbles. Damien attempts to catch her.

Lily rights herself. 'Back off,' she says, holding out a hand against Damien.

'Why have you been snooping into my private life?' Damien asks.

'I can't believe you're trying to shift the blame onto me. I found these hidden at the bottom of your wardrobe. Sorry.' Lily glances at Mags. 'I shouldn't have been rifling through your bedroom but I had a hunch about Damien. I needed to see if I was right.'

Mags doesn't respond. Privacy is obviously the least of her concerns.

'Unfortunately, Damien is too good to be true,' Lily says. 'Whenever he looks at you, Mags, he either appears amazed or troubled. When Damien was telling us about Tamsin's body, he acted strangely. Damien wrung his hands at any mention of the park where Tamsin went missing. You'd be crap at poker, mate.'

'See? You can focus when you try, Lil,' I add.

'Not relevant right now,' Steve replies, glaring at Damien.

Damien stares at the floor.

'When did you take those photographs?' Hayden asks Damien. I'm surprised by how level Hayden's voice is considering the circumstances.

Damien's fingers tussle with each other.

'Stop fidgeting and answer the question!' Mags shouts.

'I took them the day Tamsin disappeared,' Damien replies.

Steve advances towards Damien, fists prepared for a fight.

85

DAMIEN

D amien grimaced as Paul clasped Tamsin's hand. That man didn't deserve his charmed life. It should have been Damien's. Mags was meant to be his. Tamsin could have been their daughter.

When Damien saw Mags in the pub, he was smitten. Call it fate, good luck or a curse, Damien hadn't intended to be there. After he'd worked on a complicated electrics job in Great Parston, a tired Damien decided to eat out. The Queen's Head suited his simple tastes.

Seeing Mags, Damien lost his appetite for steak and ale pie. He developed a hunger for her instead. The instant pull of attraction was unnerving. Damien was a loner. Unless he sorted out their electrics, women ignored him. His mum expressed confusion at how such a good-looking man didn't have a girl-friend. His workmates called him the "Secret Adonis", convinced he had a hidden harem.

Damien believed Mags was his soulmate. She was the first woman he didn't want to run away from. He found her confi-dence endearing but he couldn't approach her though. As soon as he spoke, she would have been disappointed. Being a solitary man killed his art of conversation. Damien needed to learn more about Mags before he approached. This time he had to get it right. Following Mags was wrong but Damien needed to be sure of the situation before he made a move.

Discovering Mags was married to Paul was a blow. Whenever a job came up near Great Parston, Damien took it. He wanted to be nearby even if he couldn't be with Mags. His colleagues joked about Damien having a bit on the side in the village. If she were his, Mags would have been everything, not an add-on.

Damien hadn't intended to be at the park. It was a difficult day, not helped by accepting Mags was unobtainable. The stalking had to stop because it was, he reasoned, exactly that. Damien despised the man he'd become. He resolved to let go of his infatuation with Mags. Then he saw Paul and Tamsin.

Father and daughter chatted as they walked to the park. Tamsin's happiness was infectious. Damien's anger slipped away. A scarf swamped Tamsin's body. She was a sweet girl with a habit of greeting everyone. Damien feared the over-friendliness made her susceptible to unsavoury individuals. The newspapers were full of it.

Paul stood at the ice cream van, ignoring his daughter while obviously doing something shady. The men spoke in whispers. Damien wondered why Mags wanted such a man. She deserved better. Mags deserved Damien.

The men at the van paid Damien no notice. If Paul thought Damien wasn't a threat, he'd made a huge mistake. Damien *was* a threat. He couldn't allow Paul to have everything. Paul was living Damien's dream life.

As Tamsin spun on the roundabout, Damien approached, ready to take what was rightfully his.

86

SARAH

Hayden's practically sitting on Steve after removing him from attacking Damien. From underneath Hayden's arm, Steve blasts threats. Although Mags doesn't speak, her eyes never leave Damien. He can't look at her.

'You killed my sister!' Steve breaks free and strikes Damien. Steve's signet ring catches Damien's cheek, making it bleed.

'Move out the way,' I say to Steve, blocking him from Damien.

'Let me see,' I say to Damien. I check the damage. 'It's fine. Only a scratch.'

'Thank you,' Damien says.

I face the others. 'Look, everyone, we haven't heard the full story yet. No one can accuse Damien of killing Tamsin when we don't have all the facts.'

Damien offers me a smile I can't reward. He might still be Tamsin's killer.

'He stalked Mags, Paul, and Tamsin,' Lily says. 'It's creepy enough.'

'Cheers, Lily, you're really helping,' I reply.

'I want to hear everything.' Mags' statement cuts through the conversation. 'Damien owes us an explanation and it better be the truth.'

Damien sinks into the chair. He takes a breath and resumes his story.

87

DAMIEN

28TH JUNE 2002

D amien only intended to make a stand. Taking snaps of Tamsin playing alone and Paul ignoring her were to reveal Paul's neglect. The camera had been an afterthought. Damien carried it in his pocket as part of the job. The rising problem of doctored electric meters led to his bosses demanding Damien gathered photographic evidence.

As he sat on the bench, capturing Tamsin spinning in circles, Damien wondered if he'd lost his morals. Hypocrisy twisted in his gut. He convinced himself it was a noble deed for Mags' sake. He'd send her the photos as proof Paul wasn't a doting father. Damien hoped Mags would dump Paul for mistreating her child. Mags wouldn't accept Tamsin being used while he engaged in dodgy acts. Paul's life wouldn't be worth living when she saw the photos.

When the camera clicked, Paul looked in Damien's direction. The air left Damien's lungs. He willed his body to disappear. The men connected in mutual fear. Both were behaving badly. Paul turned back to business. Damien relaxed.

He considered if the photographs would suffice. What did they show apart from a girl playing while her dad bought ice creams? Mags would be angrier with the photographer than Paul. She'd think *Damien* was in the wrong. He needed another tactic. Making Paul experience the pain of losing something he valued was a better option. Damien couldn't have Mags. It was Paul's fault. Chancers like him always won. Nice men finish last.

Damien devised a ruse to ask Tamsin to help find an escaped dog. The generous child wouldn't refuse. Damien had seen her coo over the family pet. The plan was for Tamsin and Damien to search for the "dog" in the woods, beside the park. Suddenly, Damien would recall the dog's habit of returning home when off the lead. It was a flimsy excuse, although believable to a child. Tamsin would be gone long enough to panic Paul, if he tore himself away from his selfish needs.

Satisfied he could make it work, Damien stood. Tamsin was in his sights.

88

DAMIEN

28TH JUNE 2002

Tamsin yelled a greeting to someone approaching the park. Damien stopped. Would Paul see a stranger advancing on his daughter? Damien concentrated on loosening the terror seizing his body. When Tamsin frowned at the pained-looking man, Damien came undone.

He couldn't do it.

The girl was innocent. It wasn't Tamsin's fault she had an unreliable father. Damien should have been a protector, not using Tamsin as a pawn in a badly executed game. Self-loathing made Damien question what he'd become; obsessive and a potential child abductor. Life before Mags was mundane and routine. Ever since Damien first saw her, he'd behaved like a man possessed. It had to stop.

He fought tears of shame. The park became busier and Damien's common sense dictated he couldn't ignite people's interest. He took a last glimpse at Tamsin. The child was saved from being misused by another self-interested man. Damien could and would be better than Paul.

Tamsin's screeches of happiness were Damien's punishment.

He wondered if he'd be able to look in the mirror again. A body slammed into him, disturbing his guilty reverie. Damien offered an apology for his inattentiveness. He ignored the abuse he received in return. Nothing anyone said could be worse than what Damien already knew about himself.

89

SARAH

'Why did you develop the photographs, let alone keep them?' I ask Damien.

'You won't believe me,' he mumbles.

'Speak up!' Mags yells. 'You've got this far. Finish the story. Why do you have photos of my daughter?'

'When I heard Tamsin was missing, I considered giving the photos to the police as evidence. Maybe the person who abducted her was in one of them. I couldn't do it. I didn't want to explain why I'd taken them.'

'That's because it's dodgy,' Steve says. 'Normal people don't hang around parks, watching and taking pictures of kids. They certainly don't consider going with them into the woods, searching for a fake dog. You're sick.'

Blotches appear on Damien's neck. 'I may be many things but I'm not a paedophile.'

Mags touches Damien's shoulder. 'Why did you keep the photos?'

After Mags removes her hand, Damien talks to the place where it lay. 'I forgot about them. I had lots of photos from over the years. When I moved in here, I shoved them in boxes. Recently, I had a sort out and found the shots of Tamsin and Paul. I panicked and hid them until I figured out what to do. I considered passing them onto the police, anonymously.'

'Like the coward you are,' Hayden says.

'You've got that right,' Damien replies. 'I *am* a coward but I *will* give these photos to the police and explain their background.'

'You expect us to believe you didn't kill Tamsin?' Steve stands. Hayden forms a barrier.

'I believe him.' Everyone looks at Mags as she makes the bold declaration.

'How can you trust what Damien says?' Hayden asks. 'Before you met him, he stalked you.'

'He confessed, finally.' Mags' dagger eyes pierce into Damien. 'I'm not happy about him keeping tabs on us. We'll discuss it later. Damien didn't abduct Tamsin, let alone kill her. Despite everything we've heard, I know Damien. He's a screwed-up man.'

Damien frowns, appearing unsure whether he should view Mags' speech as a show of solidarity or an insult.

'How did you two get together,' Lily asks, 'seeing as Damien was your stalker? I've not asked before.'

'You have,' Mags replies. 'As usual, you've forgotten.'

'May I tell her?' Damien asks Mags.

'Go ahead.'

'I did a wiring job on this house,' Damien says. 'I begged not to do it. My boss became suspicious, thinking I'd slept with someone's wife and was avoiding the husband. I was the only electrician available.'

'Unlucky for you, Mum,' Hayden adds.

Damien continues despite his discernible hurt; Hayden is like a son to him. 'Knowing Tamsin was missing, I couldn't look

Mags in the eye. I wanted to complete the job and get out of there. I tried my best.'

'I fell in love with him on the spot.' Mags' expression softens. 'Damien was so gentle and kind, although nervous. I soon brought him out of his shell. We chatted for ages, long after Damien completed the work. He even fixed my kitchen cupboards. They were falling off the hinges. I'd asked Steve many times.'

Steve straightens. 'I was going to do it. Damien only did it because of guilt.'

'Yes, initially I did,' Damien replies. 'But after a while it felt like Mags and I were starting again. In a few hours I learned more about her than I did watching from a distance. I tried to stay away as I couldn't be around Mags without feeling remorse. I loved her too much to hurt her.'

'Truth be told, I pursued Damien,' Mags says. 'I thought he was playing hard to get. I figured I was too stupid for such a clever man. He astounded me with facts.'

The couple are finding their rhythm, remembering how they fell in love.

'Mags, you're the most savvy and loving woman I've ever met,' Damien says. 'You were, and still are, everything to me.' It's obvious Damien means every word.

Mags approaches her husband. I swear there's a collective intake of breath. She pulls him up from the chair. I wait for a tender moment. The slap of Mags' hand against Damien's already-wounded cheek echoes.

'That's for lying, being a crazy stalker, and using my child to deal with your issues.' Mags flicks her hand, undoubtedly trying to summon feeling into it.

Damien opens his mouth to respond.

'Don't say a word.' Mags kisses the damaged cheek. 'That's

for being the man I love, the one who's underneath this. You've been through so much. More than they know.'

Damien smiles.

'Take the grin off your face,' Mags says. 'You've still got some explaining to do. The rest of you, off you trot. My husband needs to hear a few truths.'

We aim for the front door. Steve stands at the bottom of the stairs. 'I'm not being sent to my room like a kid,' he says. 'I have rights too.'

'Grow up,' I say. 'Stop being so self-absorbed and concentrate on the fact your sister's killer is still out there.'

'Find the bastard,' Steve replies.

'We will,' Lily says. 'Make no mistake about it.'

90

LILY

When your hair is greasy and you're wearing a grubby tracksuit, you're guaranteed to bump into an attractive man. Lily curses Sod's Law for her literally bumping into DI Chris Watts.

'Don't judge,' Lily warns as she scoops Dairy Milk bars from the floor. 'It's been a difficult time and I have a teenage daughter. All a woman needs to survive is a plentiful supply of chocolate.'

'I'm sure you need more than that.'

Lily doesn't respond to the innuendo. She's sworn off men. Damn Chris for having dreamy brown eyes. Who the hell says *dreamy*? Lily worries she's regressing to her younger, more awkward, self.

The local convenience shop isn't conducive to romance. Harsh strip lighting gives customers a zombie appearance. A stench of something past its sell-by date makes Lily's stomach turn. Imogen insists they support small businesses. Lily only goes there when she's feeling too lazy to drive into town. After paying for her goods, Lily can't wait to leave.

She looks behind at Chris following her. 'Policemen shouldn't pester women.'

'What if I ask you to join me for coffee next door to discuss something? Would it make this meeting more legitimate?'

'Perhaps... if there's cake too.'

Chris extends an arm, inviting Lily to lead the way to the tea room.

Lily concentrates on sipping her coffee rather than taking the usual slurps. 'I'm not an idiot. It's obvious you followed me into the shop.'

'Rumbled.' Chris holds up his hands.

'Why are you here?' Lily asks. Chris may be attractive but no one is allowed to keep tabs on her, especially the police.

'I'm checking you're not investigating Tamsin's death.'

'Of course not.' *Not at this actual moment*, Lily thinks. 'Scout's honour, I've kept my word.'

Lily begins the game of staring Chris out. She can win this. Chris flashes a cunning smile and Lily loses. The floral table-cloth becomes fascinating.

'Is she having a stroke over there?' Chris indicates the matronly woman at the counter, having an issue holding onto her eyeballs.

'Don't mind her. She's the village gossip. Everything all right, Barbara?' Lily gives the woman an exaggerated wave.

Barbara drops behind the counter. Lily grins at the thought of Barbara's wide girth squashed against the back wall.

Chris' phone rings. He moves over to the doorway to take the call. Lily checks her reflection in the window. A house of horrors would have healthier-looking faces. She resolves to use foundation again and not allow her cheating husband to bother her so much.

Chris returns and places a business card on the table. 'I have to go. Sorry to cut it short. Maybe I could make it up to you with dinner sometime?'

'I might be persuaded.'

'My number's on the card. I've got yours.'

'How? Oh yes.' Lily admires Chris' cunning in using police resources to secure a date. Perhaps he can teach her how to be an accomplished investigator.

Free to eat without resembling an underfed pig, Lily dives into a slab of carrot cake. She has a date with a policeman. Lily never considered being back in the dating pool. She hopes Chris doesn't think she agreed to it to extract information from him. Lily likes him. Is she a cheat, like Gareth? They're still married. He'll be livid if he finds out Lily's interested in someone else.

Lily will put herself first and enjoy the finer things in life, including Chris. She doesn't regret lying when she made her promise. Scout's honour means nothing. Lily wasn't in the Scouts.

Barbara hovers nearby, half-heartedly flicking a dishcloth across tables.

'I've still got it, Barbara,' Lily says, and continues having her cake and eating it.

'You'll pee yourself laughing when you hear what Barbara did, Mum.' Lily throws carrier bags down by the shoe rack and distracted, leaves her key in the lock.

Nothing has changed.

After seeing Chris, Lily went into town to splash out on a new outfit. It took longer than she'd expected. Lily left her wallet in the public toilets. Luckily, it was still by the sinks when she returned.

Nothing has changed.

'Barbara nearly had a fit when I popped in there with...'

Imogen and Myles' troubled expressions interrupt Lily's flow.

'Well, hello there, toy boy.' Lily can't resist teasing Myles.

Imogen looks behind Lily. 'Is Freya with you?'

'Not unless she's in my back pocket. She must be home by now.'

'Freya's not here.' Imogen's pitch rises.

Lily laughs, trying to reduce her mum's nervousness. 'I expect Freya's dawdling back from the bus stop, nattering to her mates.'

'She isn't.' Myles gives Imogen's mobile to Lily.

Lily reads the text, sent from Freya's phone.

When children like Tamsin and Freya go missing, it ends badly. Tell Lily she needs to be smarter than talking to the police. There are consequences when you cross me.

Attached to the message is a picture of Freya, waving to the camera. She looks happier than Lily's seen her in ages. How can an abducted person smile? What's the abductor doing to her child? Considering the sadistic possibilities and knowing how Tamsin died, makes it hard to breathe. As she tries phoning Freya's mobile, Lily's hands quiver. An automated voice announces the phone is switched off. Lily wishes she could disconnect from this nightmare too.

'We've tried her phone so many times,' Imogen says, clutching her mobile after Lily hands it back.

'Why didn't you call me?' Lily yells. 'My child could be in serious trouble!'

'We did,' Myles replies. 'It kept ringing.'

'What's this got to do with you?' Lily soon regrets her rudeness. 'Sorry.' She remembers how she was immersed in shopping. A check of her phone confirms it's set to flight mode. 'Damn it. Have I put Freya's life at risk with this investigation? I'll never forgive myself if anything's happened to her. What if she's...?' Lily can't finish the sentence. She pauses, swallows unspent tears, and tries to be rational. 'Let's approach this logically. Freya looks okay in the photo. It must mean she's safe and doesn't feel threatened. Right?'

No one replies.

'Right, Mum?' Lily pleads. 'Freya's going to be okay, isn't she?'

Imogen draws Lily close. 'Of course she is, darling.'

Lily loves her mum for trying but Imogen's voice betrays her. Fear binds them together in the horror of Freya's possible fate.

'I've been out looking wherever we could think of.' Myles brushes a hand through his hair. 'The police will be here soon.'

'Sorry for snapping at you,' Lily says. 'It's just... I...'

Myles touches Lily's shoulder. 'I understand. Let's focus on Freya.'

Lily has to make a difficult phone call. Gareth picks up after two rings.

'Hey, lovely Lily. You've finally called. I'm so pleased because I–'

'This isn't a reconciliation.' Lily practically spits out her reply. 'Get over yourself. Is Freya there?'

'You know she's not.' Gareth's gentleness switches to irritation. 'Freya lives with you, remember? You took her away from me.'

'I don't have time for this!' Lily shouts. 'Our daughter's missing. Have you told Freya to come and see you? At this moment, I don't care if you did. Even if you sent Mum a threatening text message. We'll deal with it later. Believe me, we will. Is Freya safe?'

'You seriously think I'd do something so nasty?'

Lily doesn't answer, remembering Gareth doesn't know she's investigating Tamsin's death. Gareth didn't send the text.

'Freya's not here,' Gareth repeats. 'What's this about a threatening text? I'd never do that.'

'I know,' Lily says, desperate to hear the opposite from her husband. 'Gareth, I don't know what to do. Someone's taken our daughter.'

'Who?'

Lily won't share all the information at this point. Why should Gareth be tortured too with Lily's suspicion Tamsin's killer has their child? Why would the text message mention Tamsin in the same context otherwise?

'I'm not sure who's abducted Freya. It's why I phoned you.'

'We have to find her,' Gareth says. 'I'm on my way.'

'No, don't, I...' Lily realises he's hung up. Facing Gareth is the least of her problems.

Lily thought nothing had changed. Life was getting better. She was wrong.

Freya's life might be over.

92

LILY

Lily continues calling everyone Freya and Lily know. Even the head teacher, one of Lily's friends, who wrangled getting Freya back into her old school quickly, couldn't help. Each person shares how little they know of the girl nowadays. It's another jab to Lily's heart, discovering Freya was struggling to fit back in. Freya's former friends were embarrassed at how they hadn't spoken to Freya since she returned. Lily forgot how fickle teenagers are. Concern for her lonely daughter as a prime target for weirdos, creeps into Lily's brain. She's watched enough *Criminal Minds* not to consider the worst possible outcomes.

At the sound of the bell, Imogen rushes to the front door. Chris enters the lounge. Searching for an anchor among the waves of fear, Lily hugs him.

'Someone's got my girl, Chris.'

Chris sweeps a hair away from sticking to Lily's mouth. Lily notes Imogen's questioning look. There will be a discussion later.

'I heard as I was driving to the station,' Chris says. 'The team will get here soon. Try to keep a level head, as much as you can. Have you contacted people Freya could be with?'

'I've called kids, the school, even parents from our toddler group when Freya was little. No one's seen her since school finished.'

A panic attack comes from nowhere. Chris guides Lily with breathing. She's never felt such despair. Her daughter is out there, possibly dead. Lily's lungs forget how to function. A balloon forms inside her, threatening to burst. The walls perform a circular dance.

Chris and Lily inhale and exhale together. As her breathing becomes even, Lily begs her faculties to return. Freya doesn't need her mum falling to pieces.

'Have you started searching for Freya?' Chris asks.

'Yes.' Myles steps forward and shakes Chris' hand. 'I'm Myles, Imogen's, er...' Myles glances at Imogen.

'Partner,' Imogen adds.

Lily notes Myles' expression change from surprise to happiness. His smile soon disappears. He's a decent man who knows it's not appropriate, given the current situation.

Imogen offers her hand to Chris. 'I'm Imogen, Lily's mother. You've obviously met my daughter.'

'I'd like to say I'm pleased to meet you,' Chris replies, 'but certainly not under these circumstances. How about we make a drink, Myles? It won't fix everything but a sugary cuppa will help with the shock.'

Lily doesn't reply, understanding the men want to discuss strategies away from hysterical women. Usually Lily would be offended. Even Imogen is too distraught to protest.

Lily lays her head on Imogen's shoulder and lets the tears flow. 'The person who killed Tamsin has got my baby,' Lily says.

'It might not be them.'

'You're wiser than that, Mum. They're warning me off and who knows what they'll do to Freya?'

. . .

Chris and Myles return, followed by a man and woman in uniform.

'I let these two in,' Chris says. 'They'll help you. I'm sorry, I've got to go.' He touches Lily's shoulder. 'We will find your daughter.'

Lily dare not speak her thoughts. Will they find Freya alive or dead?

93

RED

L ily needs to learn the differing values of give and take. Hypocrites claim it's better to give than to receive but Red knows otherwise. You must grab hold of what you want. No one will give it to you.

If Lily would give more to Red by behaving, she could receive so much from Red. Lily must learn to take what Red is giving. Red's mother called her attraction to new projects obsessiveness. The idiotic woman couldn't see it was love.

Giving attention to someone else angers Red. She had to take something to redress the balance.

94

RED

R ed's gran would be proud of how her favourite girl has
passed on an important lesson.

The music stopped. Red couldn't believe her luck as the parcel
landed in her lap. She began tearing off the paper.

'Stop.' Gran seized Red's prize.

The gathering of children and their parents silenced. Merri-
ment ended.

Red's mother tore herself away from flirting with someone's
father. 'What are you doing?' she asked her mother.

Gran ignored her and moved to the centre of the circle,
pushing her glasses up her nose. Red waited for the inevitable
speech.

'Children must learn to take as well as give.' Gran's booming
voice carried across the room. 'Your parents tell you it's the
opposite but there's a better way. My granddaughter is a
cautionary tale.'

Red shuffled on her backside, away from Gran's accusatory finger.

Red's mother staggered over to Gran. 'Mum, this isn't the time. Everyone's looking. Don't show us up.'

It was hard to tell if Red's mother fell or Gran pushed her. A girl began to cry after the woman landed on her. Red didn't care. She'd resolved not to like the girl that day. It regularly changed with that particular girl. She either had Red's complete devotion or utter hatred. Red's dislike of the other children was permanent. She hadn't invited them. Her mother used Red's party as a social opportunity. There was more alcohol than soft drinks.

As Red's mother soothed the crying girl, Red wished death upon the child for receiving what should have been hers. It was Red's right she should be first.

Gran placed the parcel into the hands of the upset girl. 'Have this. You're taking it because of the injuries received from my drunken daughter.'

The sobbing girl became mute. Her eyes widened as she regarded the gift. Red wished the girl would die and stop making Red's life miserable.

'Here.' Gran pointed to a space on the floor beside her.

Red scrambled to Gran, aware of being prompt when summoned. As if showing her off, Gran extended Red's arms out to the sides.

'This, children,' Gran said, 'is a child who didn't take. She refused to receive instruction. I told her the ways of sin and still she wouldn't listen. Instead, she pursued devilish pursuits from others leading her astray. I know who those boys are.'

Two boys sitting together visibly trembled. Red enjoyed their fear. Despite Red's public humiliation, Gran did an excellent job.

The vicar, who Gran always invited to gatherings, approached the sermonising woman. 'They are children,' he said. 'You cannot condemn them. Let's talk about this outside.'

'I will not be escorted out of my home,' Gran replied, her glare fixed on the vicar.

The vicar's trembling fingers riffled through his pocket Bible, which he always carried. 'Jesus said, "it is more blessed to give than to receive",' the vicar read.

Gran snatched the book and held it against her. 'I think you'll find, Jesus doesn't say that in any of the Gospels. The Apostle, Paul, was a law unto himself. I know what is true.' Gran tapped her hand against her heart.

The vicar approached Gran, reaching for his Bible.

'Get away from me!' Gran shouted. 'I've had enough of your loose theology. In my day, the Church was far more disciplined.'

'Yeah, and look at the damage it's done,' Red's mother remarked. 'You and the girl standing beside you are pure evil.' Alcohol often made Red's mother's mouth careless.

Red wriggled her fingers into Gran's tight fist. The usual scent of bleach was stronger than ever.

'We were only playing in the garden,' Red said, looking up at a pillar of piety.

Gran cast aside Red's hand. 'You call gambling *playing*?'

'Betting on a snail race isn't naughty,' one of Red's accomplices dared to add.

'Gambling is wrong.' Gran crouched towards Red. 'It's receiving ill-gotten gains.' Gran stood to address her captive audience. 'This party is over. The birthday girl doesn't deserve it. Everyone leave.'

The previously crying girl clasped the parcel as she left. Once again, she had what Red wanted.

~

Red wants something else now; to teach Lily the same lesson Gran bestowed.

Lily has lost her daughter. She gift-wrapped her for Red. Freya is another layer in Red's parcel of revenge.

95

LILY

Night had dropped over the sky. Lily tries not to visualise a frightened Freya. Whenever Lily shuts her eyes, she soon opens them. The darkness is unbearable. Her daughter may be trapped in it.

Lily is running on adrenaline. Tiredness will not claim her until they find Freya. She wants to be out searching, alongside the police, but they say being at home is best. Waiting isn't Lily's strength but she accepts she must be there when Freya returns. *If* she returns. Lily shakes her head, filtering out the disturbing thoughts. Gareth shoots her another pitiful look.

Her husband has only been here a few hours and already Lily can't stand the sight of him. It's not because of the affair. Gareth's face reflects Lily's grief. They should have conducted the separation with more dignity. Freya was torn between selfish parents, making her an easy target. She was probably grateful for the abductor's attention.

'Don't blame yourself,' Gareth says. 'You didn't make this happen.'

Lily stomps across the rug, annoyed by Gareth's ability to read her thoughts. 'This happened on my watch.'

Imogen laughs.

'How the hell can you laugh at a time like this?' Lily shouts.

'Don't raise your voice at me,' Imogen replies. 'Keep it together. Freya will need you when, and I mean *when* she gets home. You're not her bodyguard. She's capable of making her own decisions. Freya will be okay.'

'Much as I admire your optimism, Freya's not street-smart,' Gareth says. He recoils at Lily's glare. 'It's true. Freya grew up in a Buckinghamshire village where the biggest crime is to covet your neighbour's sheep and the like. Moving to London was a culture shock. Freya had to talk herself into walking to school alone. We held off and pretended we weren't concerned. Remember how shocked she was about knife crime?'

'You have a point,' Lily says. 'Freya thought living in London would be glamorous. She soon discovered the reality was different.'

'Freya's more courageous than you give her credit for,' Imogen adds. 'Whenever she phoned me, Freya said she was determined to integrate into city life and learn more about criminals' motives. Freya believed being close to it put her in a better position to be a PC. She's toughening up. Also, there's something you've forgotten.'

'What?' Gareth asks.

'Freya was abducted in Buckinghamshire, not London. She knows this area well.'

Lily's phone sounds. It's a text from Sarah. Lily had asked her to stop phoning in case Freya tried to call. When Sarah and Hayden offered to help search, Lily declined. She was ashamed to admit the situation felt more real if she involved them. Now Lily wishes her friends were here.

When Lily's mobile sounds again she decides to ask Sarah to come over. Lily needs her best friend. The message swims in front of Lily's eyes.

Your daughter is at Thornhill Park and Ride car park. You've been taught a valuable lesson about not crossing me. Hurry. I might change my mind and take Freya again.

96

SARAH

'Anna, by any chance?' I ask as Hayden ends the call.

Anna's phone calls have increased. Is she staking a claim or needy? Neither is a welcome prospect.

'Sorry,' Hayden replies, looking for his wallet and keys. 'Anna wanted to chat while she was waiting for the bus.'

'We need to wait to hear from Lily, anyway, so it's not a problem.'

I try not to sound annoyed with Anna's constant presence, even when she's not around. Besides, I'm more concerned about Freya. Since Lily sent a message stating Freya's at the park and ride, I can't focus on anything else.

It appears Tamsin's killer has upped the stakes. They probably thought taking Freya and leaving a callous text would deter us from investigating. Now they've made this even more personal. I won't stop until I find them.

Is Freya alive? It's the only answer I want. I check my phone again, despite knowing there have been no further messages or calls. Lily must almost be there. Please be alive, Freya.

'How are you holding up?' I ask Hayden, noting his deep frown.

He jangles keys in his hand. 'Wishing we knew about Freya.'

I take the bunch of keys from him. Either that or I'll batter Hayden for getting on my nerves.

'My question was more about your dad,' I say. 'You've had a lot to process.'

Hayden fiddles with the clasp on his wallet instead. 'I feel so let down. Dad was my hero. I never thought badly of him for killing himself. Suicide isn't selfish, it's desperately sad. Dad lying about his debt and considering drug dealing makes me so angry.'

I guide Hayden to sit. Continual pacing will wear him out. We've got a long night ahead of us.

'Try to remember Paul as the man who taught you how to fish, throw a rugby ball, and passed on a love of literature,' I say.

Hayden rubs his thumb between his eyebrows. A headache is forming. 'How do I tell Mum and Steve?'

Kissing Hayden's forehead, I say, 'I'll be there too. Let me get you some paracetamol.'

Hayden smiles. 'You know me so well.'

As I'm rifling through my medicine box, I remember something Hayden said earlier. 'How come Anna's catching a bus? Doesn't she drive?'

'Anna sometimes uses the park and ride. Getting a space at the hospital is a nightmare. Why she's getting a bus so late is beyond me. Perhaps Anna's found some friends and been out for the evening.'

'Which park and ride does Anna use?' Fear flutters in my throat, making it hard to speak.

'Bloody hell, it's Thornhill.' Hayden drops his wallet. 'Maybe Anna saw Freya or her abductor? I'll phone her.' Hayden waits for Anna to pick up his call.

Anna uses the same park and ride Freya is currently in, dead or alive. What if...? No. That's ridiculous. Anna's strange but surely Hayden would have concluded she's a potential killer first? He knows Anna better than me. No. Thornhill's a popular option. Many people use it as parking in Oxford is limited and expensive. Be sensible, Sarah. Reel in your overactive imagination. And yet...

'Anna's phone's turned off,' Hayden says. 'I'm sure if she's seen something she's already contacted the police.'

'Of course,' I say, trying to ignore a niggle. 'I can't sit here and wait. Let's drive over that way. I need to know Freya's safe.'

97

LILY

Throughout the journey, Lily barked orders at Gareth to drive faster. He was already above the speed limit but Lily needed to rescue Freya before the abductor snatched her again. If the last hope of seeing Freya disappeared, Lily wouldn't consider what she'd do. A child shouldn't die before their parents.

The second Gareth parks, Lily dashes out, leaving the door open. Gareth is close behind her. Desperate parents' cries sound across the car park.

Behind them, Imogen and Myles move at a more measured pace. When Myles phoned the police on the way, his calm authority and maturity surprised Lily. The attraction he held for Imogen became more obvious. With their flashlights, Myles and Imogen search the corners of the car park, highlighting the redundancy of Lily and Gareth's phone torches.

A muffled sound travels on the wind. 'What was that?' Lily asks. 'Stop talking, everyone, so I can hear.'

Whimpering; the sound of the wounded. Imogen trains her light towards the source.

'There!' Lily shrieks, darting along the line of the torch's beam.

A body is slumped against a tree. Lily's nightmare threatens to become reality. No signs of life. Freya's eyes are closed.

'Is she breathing?' Gareth's question sounds more like a plea.

'I don't know. Please, breathe!' Lily recalls Freya's birth. Upon entering the world, the infant was silent. Lily counted as a distraction from distressing thoughts. When Lily reached twelve, Freya's wails began. Once again, Lily counts, willing Freya to fight.

Imogen gently nudges her granddaughter. 'Freya, it's Nan. Wake up, my love.'

Freya groans. Twelve is still Lily's magic number. As she reaches for Freya, Myles pulls Lily away.

'What the hell are you doing?' Lily yells. 'She's my daughter!'

Taking Lily's shove with good grace, Myles doesn't flinch. 'I think she's been drugged,' he whispers.

Lily phones for an ambulance, finding the words hard to form; to speak them is to acknowledge what's happening. She wishes she could comfort Gareth who's weeping by a tree. Emotional exhaustion leeches Lily's energy. Dampness seeps into her jeans from the concrete, chilling her knees. Being next to Freya is all that matters.

'What's that noise?' Gareth asks as he joins Lily on the ground.

'Her teeth are chattering.' Lily places her coat over Freya. 'Bloody hell, her clothes are soaked. Where's the ambulance?'

'They'll be here soon,' Myles replies. 'Here, take my coat.'

Lily shakes her hand by way of a refusal. 'Don't worry about me. As long as Freya's okay, I will be too. Thanks though.' Lily resolves to be kinder to Myles.

Lily cups Freya's face in her hands, hiding despair at her

child's drowsy eyes. 'Freya, it's Mum. We're all here. Dad too.' Gareth and Lily cocoon their daughter.

'How did you get here, sweetheart?' Gareth asks.

'Don't barrage her with questions,' Imogen says. 'She's not up to it.'

'I'm fine,' Freya slurs. 'Bit sleepy.'

'Who brought you here, Freya?' The sooner Lily knows what happened, the sooner she'll find who did this. Someone's been watching Freya and Lily, probably the same person who killed Tamsin. It has to stop.

Freya blinks. 'I thought she was nice. She dumped me like I'm rubbish.'

Her child's wobbling voice threatens to break Lily's fragile heart.

'Who was she?' Lily asks. Aren't abductors usually men or does Lily need to research kidnappers more? A woman took her daughter and might have killed Tamsin. Lily swallows the bile threatening to make an exit.

When Freya doesn't answer the question, Lily decides to tackle other issues. 'Are you hurt?' She performs a preliminary check. But what about the inner scars?

'Tired. Freezing. Whose coat is this?'

'Mine,' Lily says.

'You said to take a coat. Sorry.'

'No, I'm sorry we argued over something so silly. From now on, you can be mouthy every day.' Lily pretends not to notice Imogen's raised eyebrows.

Myles bends on a knee to talk to Freya. 'How long have you been here?'

'So sleepy.'

To quash the tears and frustration, Lily has to step away. Someone dumped her unconscious daughter. Anything could have happened and not only at the hands of the abductor. Did this woman have an accomplice? Lily looks over at Freya's school uniform, checking if everything is in place. It seems to be in order but Lily isn't sure.

Waiting in the ambulance feels like an out-of-body experience. This sort of thing happens to other people, not Lily.

A paramedic places a foil cover over Freya. 'This will warm you up.'

'Mum!'

Lily reaches for Freya's hand. 'Don't be scared, darling. I'm here. No one will ever hurt you again.'

The crushing of Freya's grip makes Lily wince.

'You don't understand.' Freya's tears flow. 'She tricked me. I thought Scarlett was your friend.'

98

RED

R ed left Freya under a tree and out of the light, despite the temptation to dump her somewhere more exposed. Few people used the buses in later hours and Red knew enough of the car park to leave Freya in a secluded spot. The shadowy borders were helpful. Red gave Lily Freya's location too. There was a temptation on Red's part to drag it out. Lily should think herself lucky. Despite her annoyance, Red decided to show some generosity. Considering Freya's testing of Red's patience, the girl is lucky to be alive.

Freya finally stopped talking long enough to get into Red's car. It was almost admirable how the teen wasn't a pushover. She asked many questions before Red convinced her she knew Lily.

'Scarlett is such a cool name,' Freya said as she threw her school bag in the back seat.

Red sucked in air, swallowing her annoyance at the possible marking of the upholstery. Instead, she concentrated on her little in-joke. Eventually, Lily and Freya would understand the name's significance.

'I didn't know Mum had worked with a photographer. She's never mentioned it.' Freya continued her idle chatter. 'Although Mum's had lots of jobs. Sometimes it's hard to keep up.'

Red knew she'd have to talk to diffuse the girl's suspicions. 'Lily was a wonderful assistant. My photography was all the better for it. When Lily left, I missed her deeply.' As Red spoke the words, the pain of other losses haunted her.

Freya pulled down the visor and pouted in the mirror. A glorious image of smashing the girl's face into the windscreen softened Red's hurt.

'Do you really think I could be a model?' Freya asked.

'I've already said, haven't I?' Red's tone was snappier than intended. Time had been wasted convincing Freya of her connection with Lily and how Lily agreed to "Scarlett" taking test shots of Freya in Oxford. 'Apologies for my grumpiness. I'm a little tired. When I saw your photograph at the house and said you should consider modelling, your mother was ecstatic. It was a pleasant end to my impromptu visit.'

'Was Sarah there?' Freya asked.

Red knew Freya was testing her claim of being Lily's old boss. 'Sarah's still at the surgery, of course. I'll get to meet her in due course.'

While Freya fiddled with her hair, Red enjoyed the girl's nervousness.

'Being a model long-term won't work for me,' Freya began. 'Getting into the police means lots of study.'

Red stifled a laugh at abducting a future police officer. 'As I've already said, you can be a teen model. Think of the money and how it will buy you fancy clothes and gadgets to impress your friends.'

'What friends?' Freya asked. 'Since I returned to my old

school, it's been hard. People I thought were friends have moved on.' Freya began to cry.

Grimacing at the closeness, Red risked giving Freya a hug.

'Poor girl. Models always have lots of friends. Everyone wants to know the rich and famous.'

Freya wiped her cheeks with her sleeve. 'Really? I'd love that. Thanks so much, Scarlett, for asking me.'

It was almost painful to witness Freya's gratitude. Almost.

'What are you doing?' Red asked as Freya typed on her phone.

'Texting Mum. Better double-check she's okay with me going to Oxford. I'm not usually allowed out on school nights.'

'What part of me being Lily's friend and having consulted with her do you not get?' Red didn't apologise for her abrasiveness. Lessons had to be learned.

As Freya moved away, Red stroked the back of the girl's neck, considering whether to kill or soothe. When Freya recoiled, Red's prudence returned.

'I'm so sorry.' Red affected upset. 'Things have been difficult for me recently. My mother died.' *If only.*

'I understand.' Freya leaned into the back of the car to put her phone in her bag. 'Of course I don't have to ask Mum again. This is going to be so much fun.'

It certainly will be, Red thought.

99

RED

R ed and Freya toured Oxford, seeking the most scenic backdrops. The river mesmerised Red.

'Watch how the rowers move their arms in unison.' An enthused Red tried to engage the obviously bored Freya. The girl's apathy stoked Red's malice. 'They could teach you a lot about being part of something; how to belong. Maybe you'd have more friends that way.'

'Okay,' Freya replied, looking down at her shoes.

Red's burgeoning hatred simmered. Being with the girl had become a chore and a reminder of Red's weakness. Red wasn't any better than Freya, craving acceptance. Red *must* be alone. It's the only way. Picking off the people who've hurt her led to living a solitary life. The dead don't make great company.

Freya's ignorance of Oxford's attractions grated on Red. The girl knew every shop's location but hadn't heard of the Ashmolean Museum, Bodleian Library or Sheldonian Theatre. People who lacked sophistication made Red nauseous.

Children have always been an enigma to Red. Their neediness repulses her. She fast-forwarded to adult independence. There was no choice considering Gran insisted on it, stating self-sufficiency made her less of a burden. Childhood frustrated Red. She refused to accept its limitations.

Throughout the afternoon, Red toyed with ending Freya's life. At least she wouldn't grow up to be a needy adult.

~

'I'd rather not do that.' Freya folded her arms. 'Draping myself around this column will look a bit silly, won't it? I don't want to come across as cheap. Can we do something else, please?'

Red laughed at Freya's defiance, offset with manners. 'You remind me of your mother. She's defiant too. Good for you, finally standing up for yourself.'

'Thanks.' Freya blushed. 'If it's okay with you, can we take a break? I'm just popping to the loo.'

'Of course.'

Thankful for the opportunity to be alone, and having watched Freya key in her passcode earlier, Red grabbed Freya's phone from her bag and sent a text to Imogen about Freya's abduction. Previously Red considered messaging Lily but decided second-hand knowledge was better. Lily deserved punishment. Flirting with the lead on Tamsin's case was unfor-givable. Lily claimed to be a maverick, above the law, when she's practically in bed with them.

To add to Lily's misery, Red switched off Freya's phone. It served Lily right for letting Red down.

Hurt Red, know torment.

100

RED

A ball of anger formed in Red's chest as she watched Lily and Chris cosying up in the café. Red had started caring about Lily and the woman abused it. It felt like a sister's betrayal.

Red didn't go in. The café was tiny and her actions were unpredictable when enraged. Instead, Red drove to Freya's school, rage pressing on the accelerator.

Red previously considered a warning for Lily to keep her child safe. There are villainous people out there. Originally, Red planned to take Freya away for a short while to shake things up. Lily nuzzling up with Chris changed everything. It was Lily's fault Freya got into Red's car and spent the rest of the day with a stranger. Lily should have warned her daughter of potential dangers instead of indulging Freya's whims.

When Freya asked Red to take a photo on Freya's phone, it offered a perfect opportunity to add a picture to the text Red sent to Imogen. A happy abducted child would cause confusion.

As time wore on, Red found the whole thing tedious. Her boredom threshold was never high. Red enjoyed having this in common with Lily.

Freya had to go.

244

Red carried a mini pharmacy for every occasion and used it to lace Freya's latte with a sedative. The silence in the car as the medication kicked in was bliss. Red checked Freya's consciousness by turning the music up. No movement. As the track changed to "Killer Queen", Red sang along.

Despite the apparent evil of drugging a child, Red did Freya a favour. She was alive. So what if it was an arctic damp night? Freya would survive. Red knew the park and ride well. She'd picked a good spot. It didn't matter the police could detect Red's number plate from surveillance. She had contacts who supplied cars not theirs to sell. The registrations never matched the vehicles and Red changed her cars regularly. Freya would describe her abductor as a short-haired brunette with blue eyes, thanks to Red's extensive collection of wigs, contact lenses, and clothes.

This investigation is between Red, Sarah, and Lily only. Hayden and Sarah will pay. Lily's life prospects are dwindling.

101

SARAH

Today's patient list included a man with suspected liver failure, a severely depressed woman, and a teenage serial killer in the making. I love my job but sometimes the demands are exhausting. Maybe meeting with Anna is a mistake.

I'm still coming to terms with Freya being abducted and drugged. She looked so young and helpless in the hospital bed. My doctor's head says Freya's physically fine and the drug's no longer in her system. The part of me that loves Freya wonders about the mental damage. Lily made several phone calls, rallying people to find who did this to her daughter. Lily has contacts for every situation. She knows many people, usually from the various jobs she's had. Everyone who meets Lily likes her.

What kind of sick person sedates someone, particularly a child? I'm still reeling from hearing it was a woman. Lily was frantic at the thought of Freya being assaulted. I had a chat with the registrar who confirmed it wasn't the case. I've never seen Lily so vulnerable and was glad to put her mind at rest.

We're trying to figure out who Scarlett is. It's obvious she's scaring us off and somehow knows Lily. Aware someone might be watching us, we're trying to be more vigilant. Every female patient I see must be questioning my scrutiny.

Does Scarlett know how Tamsin died? Did she kill her? Thinking of Freya, unconscious in the company of a child killer, is disturbing. What have I got myself into, investigating and possibly facing such a person?

Preparing myself, I switch my thoughts to Anna. I asked to meet at the practice so we're on my territory. She won't catch me off guard again. I'm more prepared, although I don't know more than Anna's already shared. Lily's been distracted after Freya's abduction and hasn't had a chance to check Anna out. Whenever I ask Hayden about Anna's background he's evasive. He says she wants to leave it behind. It's piqued my interest. What's Anna done? What's she capable of?

On cue, Anna enters without knocking. 'Hi, Sarah.'

She's wrapped up against the coldness outside. Assessing her in the patient's seat, I appreciate the set-up. Let her feel like this is an interrogation. I'm still annoyed she made Hayden keep her a secret from me.

Anna takes off her outdoor clothing. 'Now you've got me here, doc, do I have to talk about my childhood? Is head shrinking part of your repertoire?'

'I'm not a psychiatrist, just a plain old GP.'

'I was teasing, Sarah.' The friendly smile morphs into a rigid line. Anna's moods change in an instant. She's fascinating and infuriating.

'Did you have a good childhood?' I'm half joking, while hoping she'll answer.

'You couldn't resist. My childhood was fine. I grew up without a dad but many kids do. Mum tried to make up for it although she was somewhat unpredictable. Being a worn-out teen mum contributed to her moods. When my father died, the chance to reunite disappeared. I moved on.'

Anna's trying to be stoic. To an untrained eye and ear, she's doing a good job. I detect the slight wobble in her voice, fingers drumming on her knee, and how she scans the room. Like she did at my house, Anna's scoping out the place. I'm glad I tidied. Phoebe threatened to charge the crap on my desk rent, seeing as it had taken up residence.

'How's Freya?' Anna asks. 'It's terrible what happened. If only I'd been at the park and ride around that time, I might have been able to help her.'

'She's fine.'

For some reason I don't like this woman mentioning Freya. I want to protect her from bad people. Is Anna one of them? Women commit crimes too.

'I'm so glad Lily and you have Hayden to support you through the aftermath,' Anna says. 'He dotes on Freya.'

'I expect having Hayden around was a comfort to you too when you were younger,' I say. 'He was a decent kid most of the time.' My attempt at not asserting my first acquaintance with Hayden fails. My inner bitch is clawing her way out.

Anna's smile returns. 'He's a great guy, always has been. Being quiet kids, we bonded. Don't worry about the kiss. It changed our relationship and not for the better.'

'How? You're still friends.'

When Anna looks at me, I wish she hadn't. Goosebumps erupt on my forearms.

'We were apart for a long time,' she says. 'Life and other people got in the way.'

'Do you mean his ex-wife?'

Hayden doesn't often talk about Verity. Whenever he does, a vein bulges in his temple.

'Did you hear how Verity insisted on a country manor wedding with all the bells and whistles?' Anna asks. 'Steve was so wasted he threw up on the dance floor and fell on the DJ's equipment.'

'I heard.'

It's never spoken about in the Lawson household. Arguments still start between Steve and Hayden if it arises.

'I'm glad Hayden's with you,' Anna says. 'Verity was a monster. Hayden deserves someone nice. What you're doing with this Tamsin investigation is amazing. Are there any leads yet?'

Anna was asking questions last time too. I decide not to answer but use it to my advantage. 'Did you know Tamsin well?'

'Yes.' Anna straightens. 'She was a lovely girl. I joined the search party when Tamsin went missing.' Anna's tone is far too chirpy for someone discussing a kidnapped child. 'Tamsin being murdered is unbelievable. The person who did it deserves to rot in hell.' Anna's fingers pinch the cushion she's holding. 'What will you do if you find Tamsin's killer? Will you take revenge on her behalf?'

In a refusal to rise to Anna's bait, I keep my face neutral. 'I'd let the police do their job, as it should be.'

Anna inspects her nails. 'I thought you'd put up a good fight against Tamsin's murderer. It could be quite a match. I'd like to see that.'

102

SARAH

To break Anna's intense stare, I sit on my desk. I'm aware I'm taking the high ground, asserting superiority. My cat taught me all she knows.

'I'm sure there will be justice for Tamsin soon,' I say, 'without anyone else getting hurt. Can I get you a drink? I should have asked sooner. Excuse my terrible manners.'

'Do you have gin?' Anna asks.

'We don't keep alcohol on the premises. Imagine how unproductive I'd be if I was wasted.' I force a chuckle despite Anna's expression. She's wound so tight I consider shouting *Boo!* in her ear to see how high she'll jump.

'Worried about getting addicted? I've heard it can be genetic.' Anna's mouth forms into a sly smile.

'What do you mean?' I reply, trying not to sound defensive and failing. 'Do you want something to drink or not?'

'No thanks.'

I'm torn between punching Anna and phoning Hayden to give him an ear bashing for telling her about my parents. I ball my hands into fists instead. Think first, act later, and smash her gob in another time.

'It's great to see Hayden in love. You must be doing something right.' Anna needs to tell her face to match her words. Lines deepen in her forehead.

'He's a good man. I'm very lucky.' And he's mine, bitch.

'I was done with love years ago,' Anna says. 'It only brings anguish and pain. I was engaged once. He let himself be led astray.'

I note the odd phrasing. It takes two to have an affair.

'After he left, I vowed to be alone. It's safer. This is getting deep. Moving on.'

'How was work?' I ask. People often like talking about their jobs and I want to learn more about Anna.

'Same old.' Anna wrinkles her nose. 'Being a ward clerk isn't as interesting as working as a GP, I'm sure. A&E will do for now.'

'I did a stint, training in A&E. It opened my eyes to hospital life. I bet you've seen some sights.'

'More than you could possibly know.' Anna stares out the window. 'Actually, I wanted to be a teacher. Hayden and I bonded over our ambitions to teach English. I'm clever enough.'

'I don't doubt it,' I say, aware Anna needs approval. She's begging for it.

'Due to unforeseen circumstances, I couldn't finish teacher training. After, I became a teaching assistant and then a learning support manager. Wow, what is it about you, Sarah, making me want to spill my life story?'

'You don't have to share anything. I'm not grilling you.'

'Of course. We're both in charge, right?'

'How come you're no longer working in education?' I need to keep Anna talking.

'It's too tedious to mention.' Anna waves her hand away. 'Let's say love got in the way again. You look tired, Sarah. Are you working too hard?'

'I'm fine.' I cross my arms. 'Nothing staying on here this evening won't fix.'

Before Anna puts on her bobble hat, I search for the roots Lily mentioned. Anna's hair is glossy brunette. She's either had her hair coloured or Lily's newfound powers of observation need work. I'd put money on the former.

'Got to go.' Anna aims for the door. 'Things to do. No rest for the wicked.' She leaves without looking back.

Who is this strange woman?

RED

B itch! Who does Sarah think she is with her interrogation? She's no match for Red though.

Mission accomplished. Anna has surpassed Red's expectations. Sarah has her fighting claws out and is even more confused about Hayden's friend. It will give Sarah something to simmer over while Red puts the next stage into action.

Sarah thought she had the advantage in inviting Anna to the practice. She's played right into Red's hands. Red lets others think they're in charge. They become careless. Defences crumble. Red swoops in.

Seemingly fortuitous events are actually opportunities. Anna reunites with Hayden and then Tamsin's body is found. The past creeps back in and Red manipulates it. Anna and Hayden's resurrected friendship brings Red closer to him and Sarah.

It's getting interesting. Sarah's cattiness will be punished. Preparing for vindication, Red flexes her fingers.

SARAH

Who the hell does Anna think she is? She reminds me of the spiteful kids at school. Mags tried to help me integrate in the short time I was at the school in Oxford. I couldn't tell her how a gang formed, determined to make me feel inferior for being a foster kid and the daughter of addicts. No matter how much you try to hide your background, someone finds out and uses it against you.

I was lucky to have Lily. She was my defender and often in detention because of it. I joined her. The teachers taking detention stopped asking why I was there too. I was never in trouble at school. I had to show solidarity with my best friend. Lily and I enjoyed those sessions; whispering at the back and catching up on gossip.

When I tell Lily about how Anna behaved earlier, Lily will do time for me again. Lily's a grown-up now and it won't be a simple detention. I'll tone it down as I could do without Lily being incarcerated.

The coffee machine is taking forever. I lean against the wall and consider the admin I must catch up on. I need to be more organised. These extra hours won't help when I'm trying to investigate.

I can hear the hoover nearby. I'm hiding in the kitchen so the cleaner won't see me. She has a habit of asking me to diagnose her ailments, her husband's, and those of distant relatives.

A red light flashes on the machine. The coffee pod explodes.

'Shit!' Scalding coffee splashes on me. I switch off the machine and place my burned hand under the tap.

The room's light goes out.

Fantastic. The bulb has blown. This isn't my day. I trail my hands along the wall to navigate my way out.

A body slams against me.

An arm seizes my neck.

The hold tightens.

I struggle to breathe.

Fingers press into my trachea.

I kick at the person holding me.

'Die.'

The whisper is a command. My body is ready to obey.

105

LILY

Lily takes charge. 'Get in the ambulance!'

'She's right,' the paramedic says. 'I'd feel much better if you went to hospital. You should be okay but it's best to make sure. You know the drill, doc.'

'Okay, okay,' Sarah says. 'For you, Lil.' Sarah steps into the ambulance.

Lily shoulders drop in response to Sarah's compliance. Freya's abduction and drugging has shaken Lily. It's made Lily want to hold her loved ones closer. Despite this, Freya's staying with Gareth as a temporary measure to keep her safe. Lily can't lose her best friend too.

~

'Which cubicle? Where is she?'

'In here,' Lily says, her head appearing around the curtain to reply to a frantic Hayden.

Hayden rushes past Lily to hug Sarah.

'Not so tight,' Sarah says, her voice a rasp.

Hayden clenches and unclenches his hands. 'I'll kill whoever did this. Look at the state of your neck.'

Lily doesn't want to look again. The bruising already rushing to the surface of Sarah's skin makes Lily feel queasy. For a while, she'll insist Sarah wears polo necks.

'Those scummy junkies,' Hayden says. 'This is the second time it's happened at your surgery. I thought Phoebe was stepping up security?'

'We can't be certain it was an addict.' Sarah sips water from a plastic cup.

'I'm so sorry,' Hayden replies. 'I didn't mean to–'

'Don't worry about it,' Sarah says, recovering from coughing. 'Addicts are desperate. If anyone understands that, it's me. Nothing was stolen from the surgery though.'

Lily raises her hand.

'You're not at school, Lil.' Hayden chuckles. 'You can speak without asking permission.'

'I'm working on not butting in when others are talking,' Lily replies.

'Good for you, Lil. I was–'

'I'm wondering if it was Tamsin's killer.' Lily slaps a hand over her mouth, recognising her interrupting habit has returned. 'Stuff it. I've started so I'll finish. Your attacker didn't have time to scope out the place. I think they were looking specifically for you.'

Sarah pales. 'I hoped it wasn't the case.'

'Me too,' Lily adds, 'but the stupid cleaner left the door open just before you were attacked. I spoke to her. At least she had the sense to call for an ambulance. Her husband was helping out. He saw someone running down the stairs but couldn't keep up with them. Dicky ticker. There could have been two of you in here tonight if he'd attempted it.'

Hayden grasps the back of a chair, swinging it backwards and forwards.

Lily expects an outburst in five, four, three–

'I told you investigating is dangerous!' The vein in Hayden's forehead threatens to burst. He looks to Sarah. 'From now on, I need to know you're safe. Regular clocking in. No negotiation. Whoever did it isn't getting away with this; killing my sister and hurting you.'

'And abducting my daughter,' Lily adds. 'I'll kick their arse for that.'

'I'm worried,' Sarah says. 'This is getting dangerous. When my attacker whispered in my ear, it sounded like a woman. It's probably the same woman who took Freya and killed Tamsin.'

Lily's defences lower. Sarah's worried face reminds Lily of the thirteen-year-old girl she protected.

'If you want out, I understand.' Lily sits on the side of the bed and holds Sarah's hand. 'I'd rather die than let anything happen to you.'

'The way this person is carrying on, we're probably going to die if we don't get to them first,' Hayden says. 'It's your call, Sarah. I can take over.'

Sarah sits up, wincing as she does. 'I'm not leaving you two alone to investigate. I'll feel safer with you both by my side. We're the three musketeers, right? We see this through to the end.'

No one speaks. Lily knows they're all wondering if it will be *their* end.

RED

Red watches Sarah and Hayden, sitting on a bench by the pond. The perfect couple are having a perfect day. How disgustingly nice for them. Red prepared to leave until they began talking about the attack on Sarah, along with Lily's renewed determination.

Red has continued following Lily. She's aware Freya is staying with her dad and where Gareth lives. It's ridiculous Lily took the unnecessary step as Freya's served her purpose. Red has no intention of being near the girl a second longer. Her mother is far more interesting.

Unfortunate little Sarah had an unsettling liaison with Anna, and then Sarah was strangled. The three musketeers, as they're calling themselves, have realised it was a direct attack. Red doesn't want a random person taking credit for her efforts, not that it required her usual meticulous planning. She always knows how to get her hands on Sarah.

RED

R ed waited across the road from the surgery. The drizzle threatening to seep into her clothes wasn't a deterrent. Sarah's clipped comments and negative assessment of Anna had to be repaid. Later, Sarah will be more appreciative of Anna's visit. Not everyone gets prior warning.

Red calmed her breathing. The hitching in her throat would do her no good. Violence was better executed by steady hands and a controlled mind.

A car made Red startle. Who would turn up at a GPs' surgery in the evening? The man getting out of the Rover could have been a problem. Instead, he opened a literal door of opportunity.

The woman Red understood to be the cleaner opened the main door. She greeted the frail man with a kiss, beckoning him in. They propped the door open, preparing for a task requiring easy access. Red slipped inside the surgery.

She was already aware of the building's layout. The GPs' rooms were on the ground floor. Everything else was upstairs.

Red peeked through the rectangle of glass within Sarah's door. The desk held a mountain of paper and junk. Sarah soon made a mess of her office. Did she think Anna wasn't aware how slovenly Sarah is? Sarah didn't need to clean up on Anna's account.

Hearing conversation, Red hid behind the reception desk. She peered around, watching the cleaner go outside. The woman returned with a variety of containers. Her husband had brought more supplies.

How much polish did one building require? From what Red had seen, the cleaner hardly used it. A sheen of grime covered computer monitors. Mugs' ring marks on the desks were indelible. Red was glad she wasn't a patient in this surgery.

The man puffed out exertion as he carried a box. Filling the cleaning cupboard took time Red didn't have patience for. She considered disposing of the couple to get to Sarah. They were saved by the woman going into an office to clean, reluctant husband in tow.

Red crept upstairs. Despite her solidness, she'd mastered the art of treading without making a sound. With a mother like Red's, she had to.

Light spilled from the open doorway of the kitchen. Red heard the coffee machine whirring, along with Sarah's expletive. It was showtime.

A flick of a light switch began Sarah's terror.

Red exhaled on the back of Sarah's neck, enjoying the woman's shivers.

As Red pressed her fingers in deep, Sarah's pulse slowed. Life faded in Red's hands. The excitement was exquisite.

When Sarah's flailing limbs gave up the fight, Red recalled a similar death; her first and best.

Red's reverie was broken by the cleaner's voice. Sarah's body dropped to the floor.

The cleaner's husband's attempt to catch Red was embarrassing. He barely shouted, let alone gave chase. His wife tended to Sarah. They wouldn't be able to identify Red. Disguise did its magic again.

Imogen sweeps a finger along the surfaces in her lounge. 'Has someone replaced my daughter with a domestic goddess? There's not a speck of dust and the carpet is visible.'

'Ha-bloody-ha. You're such a comedian.' Lily doesn't look up from her laptop. 'Maybe if you cleaned more often, I wouldn't have to do it.'

'You've done a good job, darling.' I know Imogen can tell when Lily needs a boost.

'I thought of starting a cleaning business once,' Lily replies.

Imogen and I give each other our "Lily look"; the one reserved in response to Lily's schemes.

'How are you doing, Sarah?' Imogen asks, sweeping me into an embrace, within her roomy kimono. She's a dramatic woman who should have been on the stage. Out of curiosity, I attended one of Imogen's lectures. Her performance entranced the students. No wonder one of them became her partner.

'I'm okay. A bit sore and I sound like a forty-a-day smoker. Apart from that, I'm good.'

Lily's phone rings. She glimpses at the screen and kills the call. It's the third time in a row.

'Don't mind us if you want to answer it,' I say.

'I don't.' Lily snaps her laptop lid shut.

'Is it the lovely Chris?' I try to coax the old Lily back to life.

'Yes. He wants a date. I've separated from Gareth and need space. Freya isn't here and I miss her every minute. I'm done with men. Does that answer your question?'

Afraid to speak, I nod. Lily marches out.

Imogen leans in towards me. The sweetness of marijuana is her perfume. Imogen is partial to a daily joint, for medical reasons, of course. Lily makes Imogen smoke outside. I appreciate Lily is anti-drugs on my behalf.

'She's not been herself,' Imogen says. 'Whenever I offer to help with anything, she snaps. It's not like my Lily.'

I agree. Lily is fiery but she's never disrespectful to those she loves. Since Freya's abduction and my attack, Lily's been defensive. I can tell she's worried about something else happening but is too proud to say it. Lily won't confess investigating is a treacherous business.

'I expect Freya being with Gareth is getting on top of Lil,' Imogen says. 'It's hard not having your daughter nearby. I didn't tell Lily how much I missed her when they lived in London. I've never held her back. When Lily returned, although it was under terrible circumstances, I'll confess I was relieved. I understand how she's hurting at Freya not being here.'

The conversation ends as Lily returns. She takes a seat and opens her laptop.

'Let's check how we're doing so far.' Lily is strictly business. 'We've eliminated Paul because he was busy being the worst dad ever, trying to score drugs instead of looking after his daughter. Steve was with his secret lover. I hope they don't cheat on each other.'

Imogen and I make eye contact, as if to warn the other to watch our words.

'Mags was at a friend's house. Hayden was at college.' Lily notices I'm poised to reply. 'Not that anyone considers Hayden as a suspect. We have to eliminate people. Damien was a stalking idiot but we agree he wouldn't have taken Tamsin. Guess what I found out?'

'Don't you hate it when someone expects you to guess something without giving any context?' Imogen asks me.

'So annoying,' I reply.

'All right, sarky pants,' Lily says. 'I've been looking into Paul's background. We've eliminated him as Tamsin's killer but I think he's a major part of this. Paul took Tamsin to the park where she disappeared. Turns out I was right to be suspicious. Paul had a daughter.'

'Yes, darling, that would be Tamsin.' Imogen adopts her condescending intonation, reserved for idiots and students.

'No, *darling*.' Lily imitates Imogen's voice. 'Paul had another daughter.'

'No way.' My mouth could catch flies. 'He kept that quiet, particularly from Mags.'

Lily sneers. 'You can't be shocked about Paul being shady after finding out about his gambling and attempt at drug dealing. I trawled through some birth records. Paul had a child before he married Mags. The mother, Ruth Hawkins, was eighteen.'

Imogen rubs her hands together. 'This is interesting stuff.'

Lily continues. 'Paul and Ruth had a daughter called Naomi. She disappeared off the face of the planet in 2006. Anything linked to Naomi ends there. There isn't a death certificate though.' Back in investigator territory, Lily becomes more animated.

'Curiouser and curiouser,' I say.

Lily finally smiles. I hoped the *Alice in Wonderland* reference would please her. It was a favourite when we were younger and baffled.

'It is weird,' Lily says.

'Hayden will be devastated when I tell him,' I say.

'About that.' Lily draws up her knees, hugging them. 'We're not telling Hayden about this yet.'

'Right, *we* aren't, are *we*? Why aren't *we* telling Hayden?'

'The Lawsons are dealing with enough as it is. Hayden's still processing about his dad's dodgy habits. I think it's best not to say anything. Ruth said she wouldn't speak to us if I mentioned her to Hayden.'

'Why Hayden in particular? Don't you think it's odd?' Ruth Hawkins is already making me defensive.

'Absolutely but I'm playing this her way to begin with. It's the only way I could get her to agree to a meeting. I asked about Naomi but Ruth got upset. I didn't want to shut her down. When I mentioned we're investigating Tamsin's death, Ruth couldn't agree fast enough to a chat.'

'How come? Why does she care about Tamsin? Surely Ruth wasn't happy Paul had another child he acknowledged and raised.'

'This is where it gets interesting.' Lily bounces in the chair. 'Ruth lived in Great Parston, on Oak Road, a few doors up from the Lawsons. She knew the whole family, including Tamsin.'

110

RED

L ily and Sarah are like sisters. The knot in Red's throat twists whenever she considers it.

Despite her unconventional families, many people love Sarah. She's even had more than one set of parents. Red would have settled for a decent mother or father.

Those in troubled families say your friends can be family. Utter rubbish. Blood is significant. The life-giving fluid binds you, like it or not. What runs through your veins connects you with your family forever. Because you share the same blood, you can choose to make it shed; theirs not yours.

No one's pain is off limits to Red, not even young girls'.

111

RED

～

'Your cat's up the tree in the park,' Red said. 'I'll help you get it.'

The girl followed, delighted at the prospect of finding her pet. The cat had been missing for days. Red watched the girl put up posters on every road in the village, while Hayden helped her look. It was the only reason Red invested in the fruitless search.

Red knew where the cat was. She stood on its grave, next to Mags' puppy, Joy.

Along with Hayden, Red had walked the streets of Great Parston, knocking on doors and asking about the cat. She needed Hayden to see the kindness she mustered. Chasing a boy who didn't want her was pathetic. Red was a young woman and male attention wasn't lacking. She wanted something pure though, something real: Hayden Lawson.

The girl stood under the oak, chewing her nails, despite Red's efforts to make the youngster break the habit. Red considered if there was space for a body next to the dog and cat. The girl had everything. If she was gone, Red might have it all instead.

'I don't see her.' The girl shielded her eyes from the sun to scan the branches.

Red shoved the girl behind the tree. 'Stupid child, you should know better than to trust me. You've had long enough to figure it out.'

Enjoying the violence, Red shoved the girl to the ground. The little upstart had manipulated Hayden's attentions and affections for too long.

The girl scrabbled to stand. She cried as twigs gouged her hands.

Red leaned over, blocking the sunlight. 'Leave Hayden alone, this is your first and last warning.'

The girl gasped. 'I just want to be his friend.'

'Which is exactly why you must stay away. It's dangerous. Do as you're told for once!'

A penknife skirted the girl's neck.

Blood stained the girl's shirt collar.

Red watched its beauty bloom.

112

SARAH

I open the door. No one's there. The doorbell definitely rang. Someone's playing games. I stand on the front step, looking to the left and then right.

'Surprise!'

A hand seizes me, pulling me outside.

'You scared me.'

'I thought I'd be more spontaneous in my old age,' my mum, Denise, says, rifling through carrier bags.

Whenever Mum visits she brings groceries, worrying I don't have enough time to eat and shop. I've told Mum to stop but she's selectively deaf. Her hearing aid is top-notch. I researched and bought it for her.

'You're so sneaky.' I waggle a finger. 'You didn't mention visiting when we chatted the other day.'

'It's only a short visit. I've got to get back to Thame soon. A man's coming to check the boiler.' Mum wraps me in one of her soothing hugs. I feel like I can breathe easier when she's around.

'I know you, Mother. You're checking up on me. I'm fine. The bruises are healing and there's no permanent damage.'

Mum scowls. 'Not physically, love. How about in here?' She taps my head. 'You've had so much to contend with. I don't want anything tipping you over the edge.'

Hayden joins us in the lounge and is rewarded with a Mum cuddle too.

'I've seen Mags,' Mum says to Hayden. 'I wanted to pay my respects.'

'Thanks, Denise,' Hayden replies. 'I'm sure Mum appreciated it.'

'It's regrettable we didn't keep in touch,' Mum says. 'I'll always be thankful to Mags and Paul for looking after my Sarah though. I can't tell you how happy I am you two have made a go of it.'

I sigh. 'Stop being so slushy, Mum.'

'She can be as slushy as she likes,' Hayden says. 'Denise is a top mum, apart from my own, of course.'

'No parent should lose their child.' Mum stares at the wall. I expect she's reflecting on the struggles she endured with my dad, Zeke, to conceive and then adopt.

'You're looking well,' Hayden says. He's astute at reading body language and knows Mum needs a distraction.

It's true though. Mum does look better. Since Dad died three years ago, Mum has struggled. He was the other half of her. Without Dad, she's been lost. Mum's expression of desolation made me want to cry.

'I'm doing okay,' Mum says. 'Zeke wouldn't want me to mope around, so I'm trying for him. How's the investigation going?' Mum asks me, then turns to Hayden. 'Sorry, Hayden, my condolences to you. Tamsin was a lovely girl. Do you mind us talking about it?'

'It's fine. I'm glad Sarah and Lily are investigating. I'm

helping where I can too. Tamsin deserves the best.' Hayden kisses my cheek.

'My daughter's lucky to have you,' Mum says. Her happiness is infectious. It's great to see Hayden brighten a little.

'I'm the lucky one,' Hayden replies.

I smile. 'Someone had to have you. It might as well be me.'

Hayden tickles me until I scream for mercy. 'Now I've annoyed you, I'll stick the kettle on,' he says.

After Hayden leaves, Mum joins me on the sofa. I fill her in on the progress Lily and I have made so far. Sharing the details makes me wonder if we're getting anywhere. There are too many false leads and not enough evidence. Tamsin's killer is always ahead of us.

Mum clears her throat.

'Spit it out,' I say.

'I'm concerned about you investigating. Please stay safe.'

'I will,' I reply, aware I can't offer a guarantee.

'You'd do well to consider how secrets are often hidden within the family. What goes on behind closed doors can be where wrongdoers are created. That's where you'll find this hideous person. Functional loving families are wonderful. Look at us. We've made this family work, despite your beginnings. No one understands better than you that when the rot sets in, rotten apples appear in the family orchard. The blight can taint the good apples.'

Mum's referring to Kayleigh and James. She becomes emotional whenever we discuss them. Mum can't even say their names. She's the gentlest person I know. The anger she expresses is surprising but not unjustified.

'Have you told Hayden yet?' she asks.

'What about?'

'What happened in the squat.'

I check the open door for signs of Hayden returning. 'No. I'll lose him.' I rub my hands along my arms.

'Hayden won't leave you. Give him a chance.'

'Let's not talk about it.' I can't control the quivering in my voice. 'I'm still a good apple, aren't I?'

'The best.' Mum hugs me. 'You're my world.'

I need to change the subject. 'You could be on the right track, about the family thing. I believe Tamsin's death is rooted in the family and someone had an issue with the Lawsons. It feels personal, not calculated. A suitcase as a burial place suggests something opportune, like the killer grabbed it as the best option. They would've had some front to kill a child and leave her there while they went suitcase shopping.'

Mum shivers. 'It's too horrible to contemplate. I can't imagine what the Lawsons are going through.'

Hayden enters with our drinks. 'Sorry it took so long. Anna called.'

'It's fine,' I say. Anna won't spoil my time with the people I love most in the world.

Mum sips her tea and grimaces. 'No sugar.'

'I forgot.' Hayden slaps his head. 'Here, I'll sort it.' He reaches for Mum's cup.

'Don't worry,' she says. 'We'll get some biscuits on a plate while we're at it. I picked up some lovely cookies.'

How many people does it take to add sugar to a brew? I ponder how rubbish they are at keeping secrets. They're probably discussing my birthday present.

My thoughts are disturbed by a smash. I run to the kitchen.

Mum shakes glass off her cardigan while Hayden stands in apparent shock.

'What the hell happened?' I ask, surveying the debris on the floor.

Mum reaches for a brick that's landed on the rug.

'Don't touch it!' I shout. 'There might be fingerprints.'

I slip on rubber gloves lying by the sink and turn the brick over. A note is attached, held in place by a hairband, covered with snagged red hair.

Enjoy your family time. Such a shame Tamsin can't.

113

RED

Red sat in her car, listening to the radio. The pacifying tunes from Classic FM brought a welcome calm. Peace was hard won. Red's job demanded so much. People always wanted something from her. Following Lily, Sarah, Hayden, and the Lawsons was tiring too. Red wished she could clone herself. The thought of world domination by a group of redheads made her laugh.

As a woman approached Sarah's cottage, Red's smile slipped. She recognised the visitor as Sarah's mother. Denise paid regular visits. Of course, Red knows her name.

When Sarah's at work, Red sometimes looks through the windows of Sarah's home. Photos cover every available side in the lounge. Denise and a man Red guesses was Sarah's adoptive father, take pride of place. Red deplores the desperate ploy to appear popular. Her house doesn't have photographs on display. Sentimentality is for losers. The only reason Red would have a photo of her mother up on the wall would be for target practice.

Sarah's smiling face as she spotted Denise stirred Red's annoyance. Red wanted a decent mother, father, sibling, *anyone* to care about her. Why did Sarah have everything?

The radio station's relaxing music changed to "Carmina Burana". A rising crescendo elevated Red's serenity to fury. Thinking of her own mother always enraged Red. Denise's display of maternal love highlighted Red's lack.

Red would shatter the family, taunting her in Sarah's house.

114

RED

Red slammed the car door and paced the street, muttering oaths against Denise, Sarah, and Hayden. Their offensive domesticity had to end. A brick fallen from a crumbling wall of a nearby house offered a solution.

She returned to her car, ripping off a sheet of paper from a notepad in her glovebox. It didn't matter that the handwriting could identify her. Red wouldn't be caught. Evidence is no use if it can't be matched to the culprit.

Red secured the note against the brick with her hairband. The stray hairs clinging to the band weren't a problem. Attaching a part of herself to the weapon was perfect.

As the brick hurtled towards Sarah's kitchen window, Red congratulated herself. She hadn't aimed for bodies but if they got hurt it was their problem. Red ran, hoping the house's occupants were distracted by the attack, rather than seeking the offender.

As Red drove away, she reasoned her actions were wise. Now Denise would worry even more about her pathetic daughter's safety. Also, Sarah and Hayden were reminded of Tamsin's death.

Playing happy families doesn't alter the fact a child died.

115

SARAH

I turn to Lily, ready to comment on how nervous I am about being with Mags. Lily isn't here. She's visiting Freya in London. I'm so used to having Lily around it's strange when she's not.

She offered to come with me today, after hearing about the brick hurled through my window. Lily can't apologise enough for getting me involved. I could tell she wanted to keep me safe by giving me a chance to back out. We have to see this through. When someone tries to hurt my mum, I come out fighting.

I attempted to put Mum at ease about the brick incident but I could tell she wasn't convinced. I reported it to the police, not disclosing the details of our investigation. They think the message was aimed at Hayden because of the reference to his sister. I'm not so sure. If Tamsin's killer's aware Lily and I are investigating, what does this mean for us? More incidents? Death?

I'm wary of being alone with Mags. We haven't discussed our argument at length yet. I'd rather move on but Mags likes to talk things out. Being here without my wingman, Hayden, and wing-woman, Lily, doesn't help.

Mags places an overladen tray on the table. She's put a lot of graft into what is supposed to be a cuppa and a catch-up. A porcelain teapot stands on a doily, flanked by matching teacups. I recognise the best tea set, inherited from her grandmother. Mags regards the spread before us. The array of cakes and biscuits could feed an army.

'You didn't have to go to all this effort on my account,' I say.

Mags' cheeks flush. My attempt at putting her at ease has failed.

'I've gone overboard, haven't I? I promise some of this is sugar-free.' Mags twists her hands around each other. 'Damien says I shouldn't worry about being with you. I'm trying too hard. Sorry.'

'No need to apologise. I'm touched you did this for me.'

'I want to get it right. Not talking to you was horrible. I've got a lot of making up to do.'

'You love Hayden, which makes you protective.'

'I love you too, you silly girl.'

'Less of the girl.'

Mags smiles. 'There's my confident Sarah. I wondered where you'd gone. I missed you.'

I understand she's missed the girl who depended on her. Does she care about the woman she became? 'We all have to grow up, Mags,' I say.

'I was heartbroken when you went to live with the Jessops.' Mags blushes again. 'Ignore me. I'm being silly.' Her tongue pokes out the corner of her mouth as she pours the tea. Her concentration habit is endearing.

'Go on. Tell me what you mean.'

'I reacted badly when you and Hayden told me you were together because I viewed you as my daughter. I got more attached to you than any other child I'd fostered. You fit in. I can't explain it but I felt an instant connection with you.'

'I'm not sure what to say. I was close to you but I thought you treated all your foster kids the same.'

'I'd like to think they all felt equally cared for. You were special though.'

'Not so much.' My pathetic giggle indicates my inability to receive praise.

'I'm so embarrassed at how I reacted about you getting together with Hayden. It's a great thing. You might be my daughter again, of a fashion, if you two get married.'

'Sneaky.'

We drink our tea, lost in our individual thoughts. The grandfather clock ticks. I used to sit underneath it at the house in Oxford. Time passed when I didn't want to lose a second in my new home. Every tick signified my security being taken away.

'Did you give up fostering after Tamsin disappeared?' I ask Mags.

She shakes herself from a seemingly intense memory. 'I gave it up after you left. I couldn't have a child wrenched from me again. Turns out I had no choice when someone took Tamsin and...'

Mags can't speak about what happened to her daughter. It makes me feel sick whenever I think about it. Hayden's having nightmares. The past few nights he's woken up, lashing out, after dreaming he was trapped in a small space. Tamsin's killer has damaged us all.

I lean across to touch Mags' knee. She places a hand over mine.

'Have you got your diabetes under control?' I ask. Putting on my GP head helps to deal with the tsunami of emotions.

'I have. Damien's feeding me up. I've told him not to. I could do with losing weight.'

'Lack of eating was making you ill.'

'I know, I know.' Mags hates being told what to do. Woe

betide the person who tries. I'm brave enough to take her on with medical matters.

'Thanks for helping the other day, when I had a funny turn,' Mags says.

I concentrate on the sound of the clock, waiting for what's coming. I will the ticks to speed up and get us through the next part unscathed.

'Damien says you panicked and couldn't inject me.' Mags comes straight out with it. 'Did the needle freak you out?'

'Not at all.' I make my voice carefree, despite knowing it won't pass Mags' bullshit detector. 'I'm a doctor, remember. Needles are part of my life.'

'Was it because of your parents?'

'No. I often see addicts in my surgery. It's not an issue.' Care-free is becoming manic. I'm talking so fast my brain can't keep up with my mouth. 'I reacted badly because of how much I love you. Not professional but there it is.'

'Love you too, Sarah.'

I should be pleased with the declaration I've been waiting to hear. All I feel is guilt at lying to Mags.

She gives me a sideways glance. 'Can I ask another question?'

'It seems to be the afternoon for it.'

'Why won't you move in with Hayden?'

'It's complicated.'

'Isn't that a Facebook status? In all seriousness, confront your hang-ups or you'll lose him. Hayden's patient but you can't expect him to wait forever.'

Mags means well and she's right. I *do* need to sort out my trust issues. I'm convinced Anna is waiting for an opening to be with Hayden. With me out of the way, she'll make it happen.

116

RED

Red waited for her chance to be with Hayden until she had to accept it wasn't to be. He's stolen years from her. She cannot claim them back but Red can be satisfied with taking the future Hayden would have had.

The list of failures and losses began before she met Hayden. Generations before them created a catalogue of tragedies and deaths. Red is delighted to add to the collection.

117

SARAH

Mags' stern advice to sort out my relationship with Hayden makes me regress to my younger self. I realise I'm sitting straight, deferring to the adult, and fearing what they'll say. No more of this. I'm not that girl. Mags is not an unforgiving parent.

'It was lovely to see Denise,' Mags says. 'I was touched she came here to pay her respects. Denise is a decent woman. I'm glad you have her.'

'I wouldn't be without Mum. It was hard settling in at first but Mum and Dad were so patient and kind. Receiving your letters helped me make the transition. Then they stopped. Why?'

Mags hangs her head low. 'Paul said I had to let you go and I should concentrate on our children. I cried for weeks after you left. Paul thought I wouldn't move on and you'd never integrate with the Jessops if I stayed in touch. I regret it though.'

'I understand Paul meant well. Thank you for explaining. I'll confess it felt like another abandonment.'

'Oh, sweetheart. I never abandoned you. You were always with me.' She holds her hand against her heart. 'Right here. It's where I keep my special girls.' Mags focuses on a photo of Tamsin. 'Damien reckons if I say to myself, "I'll get through the next five minutes" then I'll cope with Tamsin's death. Sometimes it works. I try to stay busy for five minutes and the despair passes. I'm living life minutes at a time.'

'Your husband should be a therapist.'

'Damien's a clever man. I'd be lost without him, even after hearing what he did before Tamsin disappeared.' Mags coughs. 'We're working through it. I'm still annoyed but trying to understand. Damien was lonely. He wanted a partner and that was me. It's flattering but freaky too. When we properly met, it was a fresh start. The obsessive nonsense was over. I fell in love with him. Damien didn't force me. Steve said I should get a divorce but he doesn't know what Damien's been through. He's a good person.'

'I'm glad. You deserve it.' I consider my next words. 'Can I ask what's in Damien's past to convince you he wasn't interested in Tamsin? Sorry if this sounds harsh but many mums would be wary of a man who'd taken photos of their child.'

After checking the hallway, Mags shuts the door. 'Damien and Steve are out but I don't want to take chances. Seeing as we're sharing confidences, I'll tell you. Not a word is to be shared with anyone else, understand?'

'Can I tell Hayden? I'm fed up of Lil instructing who I can and can't speak to about developments.' I realise my error and hope Mags won't ask for an update. She needs to hear about Paul's past but I'm not the one to do it. Mags and I are in a better place and I hate heaping bad news on her.

'Hayden will be kind about it, so go ahead. It sickens me to say it. When Damien was a child, his uncle sexually assaulted him. It continued for years. The uncle threatened to kill Damien if he told. Damien found the courage to speak to a teacher. He looked to another adult for hope and was let down. The teacher called Damien a liar and accused him of attention seeking. Damien was always the quiet sort. How could anyone accuse him of such a disgusting thing?'

'I can't imagine what Damien must have gone through. Did his parents find out?'

'No. The teacher said he'd let him off for his "naughtiness" and wouldn't tell Damien's parents. Damien was even more alone and confused. If I'd seen that teacher I wouldn't have been responsible for my actions.' Mags scrunches the paper doily from the tray.

'You knew Damien couldn't hurt another child because of what happened to him.'

'Yes. I'm aware the papers report on some abused kids becoming abusers. Damien isn't one of them. He can't even kill wasps. He won't be comfortable with you knowing but I need you to believe in him. He used to self-harm. There are deep scars in his thighs where he shredded them with scissors. He hated himself so much. Whenever I see the marks, I try not to cry. When Steve accused Damien of being a paedophile I was devastated.' Mags throws the balled-up doily into the fireplace.

'What happened to the uncle?'

'He died a while back. Damien needed to go to the funeral to check he was really gone. Damien had to accept he was free. I went too. Between us, I spat on the grave after everyone left for the wake. Damien's an idiot for following me and thinking of getting Tamsin involved but you have to know his past to understand. His motives are good, if not muddled. From the moment I met him, Damien's been my rock.'

'I'm glad you have him. We're all here for you, me included.'

'I'm so grateful to you and Lily for investigating. You must keep safe though. I won't think any less of you if you back out after what you've been through already.'

'No chance.'

'Thank you. I'm lucky to have such supportive people around me. As ever, Hayden is a diamond. Even Steve's calmer. I explained what Damien means to me. Steve's trying to be more civil to him. Since someone outed him, Steve's changed. I wish he'd told me himself but at least it's out in the open. As long as my sons are happy, so am I. I'm meeting Reuben next week. We're having a family dinner. You're invited.'

'Thank you,' I reply, hoping Reuben's prepared for Mags' scrutiny.

I consider parenting and how I've got to broach a difficult subject. I plump for Mags' no-nonsense method of diving right in. 'Did you know Paul had another child?'

Mags spits out a mouthful of tea. She wipes at the stain already forming on her skirt. 'Are you joking?'

I have to finish the bombshell. 'Paul had a daughter. She was born in 1985. Her name's Naomi.'

118

SARAH

When Mags sways, I'm ready to catch her. Fainters are my forte.

Mags slaps her cheeks to rouse herself. 'You're not joking, are you? Paul had another daughter.'

'Yes, he did.'

'Why did he lie to me? We were young when we met. I didn't think he'd already have kids, so I didn't ask. As you know, I was pregnant with Hayden when Paul and I married. He was a bit strange about the pregnancy. I put it down to first-time parent nerves. As Hayden grew, Paul often talked to my tummy. It was so lovely. I expect Hayden was a reminder of the child Paul already had. How devious can you get? My taste in men is appalling.'

I nibble a biscuit as Mags spends the next few seconds calling Paul a string of names.

Finally, Mags settles. 'I wouldn't've minded Paul having a child. It would have been a shock but I willingly took in other people's children. Maybe it's why Paul was reluctant about fostering.'

'He seemed detached. I put it down to him feeling awkward around me.'

'Paul was like that with all the foster children. He was never mean and always friendly but I could tell his heart wasn't in it. He fostered because of my need to fill the house with children. Any child of his would've been welcome in our family. Why didn't he say anything?'

'Maybe it's because he was embarrassed.'

'Do you have any info on the mother?'

'Lily's been in contact with her. Ruth's talking to us tomorrow. She knows your family. She lived in Great Parston.'

Mags stands. 'Do you mean Ruth Hawkins?' Mags glares at me, demanding answers.

I lean back. 'Yes.'

'What the hell?' Mags shouts. 'Ruth lived on this road. We had evenings in the pub together. I can't believe she drank wine with me when she had Paul's child living with her a few doors down. I shouldn't be surprised. Ruth has form. I wonder if Paul knew about Naomi. Was everyone lying to me?' Mags' head collapses into her hands.

'I'm so sorry. Lily and I aren't sure if Paul and Naomi were aware of their connection. Ruth will hopefully shed some light on it.'

Mags' face emerges. 'To think I let Naomi babysit Tamsin. They were related! Can you not tell Hayden yet? I'll announce it when we meet for dinner. At least give me some control over this crappy situation.'

'Okay but please make sure you do it soon. I don't want to keep things from him. It's caused enough problems.'

'I understand.' Mags stares into the distance. 'Secrets are painful when they're revealed.'

I'll have to jot down who knows what so I don't slip up. When this investigation is over, I'm never lying to Hayden again.

Not even about stealing his biscuits when he goes out. I can't stand the guilt.

In response to a key turning in the door, we compose ourselves. Hayden enters the room. Gus yaps and bounces alongside him. The shadow of a beard sprouts across Hayden's chin. Dark circles under his eyes make me wonder what's troubling him. Hayden usually sleeps like the proverbial log. The nightmares are doing him in.

'How are my favourite ladies?' Hayden plants a kiss on Mags' cheek and one on my lips.

'Great,' I say.

'Fine,' Mags adds.

'Any tea left in the pot?'

'I'll make a fresh one,' I say, 'while you have a chat with your mum about *the thing*.'

'What *thing*?' Mags asks.

'In a sec, Mum.'

Hayden and I give each other a look, knowing he will tell Mags about Paul's gambling and the failed attempt at drug dealing. I hate heaping these revelations on Mags but keeping it from her will damage the trust between us.

You're a hypocrite, Sarah. You're lying to Hayden because Mags asked you to. Is omission a lie or kindness? Lily's asked me not to tell Hayden about Ruth Hawkins either. There's the second lie, both about Ruth. I haven't met the woman yet and I'm already pissed off with her.

'Before you go into the kitchen,' Hayden says to me. 'Anna's invited us for dinner at hers, tomorrow night.'

'I'm meeting up with Lily.'

'You see her all the time. She won't mind if you postpone. Just this once, please? Anna wants to get to know you more. She's only available tomorrow and she's really looking forward to it. I'll explain to Lily.'

'Okay. Good luck with Lil. She's not herself at the moment.'

'I hope she's okay. Lily annoys the hell out of me sometimes but I don't like seeing her hurt.'

'We'll look after her. She's with Freya today, which should give her a boost. Lily's got the investigation to focus on too.'

I try not to sulk at missing out on talking to Ruth. Lily can handle it alone but I want to hear Ruth's story first-hand. For Hayden's sake, I'll make an effort with Anna. I'm also intrigued by the changeable woman.

'I'll tell Anna we're on for dinner.' Hayden grabs his phone and writes a text. 'It means so much to her. Anna says she's got it all planned.'

119

RED

Red sneaks a glimpse over the hedge and wishes she hadn't. Through the voile curtains Hayden and Sarah are kissing in Mags' lounge.

The Lawsons are drawing closer. They've forgiven Damien – Red heard him grovelling to Mags in the garden – and they're letting Sarah in.

Watching Hayden kissing another woman resurrects memories of hoping he'd place those lips on her. Missed opportunities were Hayden's downfall. Red wishes she could travel back to when the possibilities seemed endless. A confused night, where Hayden's inhibitions disappeared, ruined everything.

Now it's his turn to suffer.

R ejection is the foundation of Red's life. Her earliest memory of being cast out was when she was three. It sticks in her mind as a betrayal of her love, viewed as a hateful act.

The baby's cries sounded an alarm in young Red's head. She had to make it stop. The wails threatened to shatter Red's heart. Someone needed to soothe the child.

Red passed the form, snoring on the settee. She lifted the woman's arm and gave it a tug.

'Get lost.' The woman pushed Red and turned away from her. She always did. Once again, Red was alone.

Red followed the beacon of distress. The cries increased. Red had to make it better.

A smattering of stars shone on the ceiling, guarding the child underneath. Above the cot, a mobile of the solar system tinkled, celebrating the baby's importance in the universe. Red made the comparison with her own sparse box room. Peeling woodchip wallpaper yellowed, and damp ate the window ledges. Her few toys were shoved under her bed. Red wanted to lie under constellations too. She wished people and the planets gravitated towards her. Maybe then her dreams would have been more peaceful.

She peered into the cot. 'I make it better.'

The baby's surprised O of a mouth widened around the screams. A stench reached Red's nose.

'Naughty baby.' Red feared for the child. Lack of control was a punishable offence.

Red lugged the footstool from the bathroom, hoping the scraping wouldn't disturb the woman downstairs. Balancing tiny feet within the prison bars of the cot challenged Red. She curled her toes for anchors and leaned in. The hold on the infant was clumsier than intended. Red didn't realise babies were heavy. Until then, she'd never held the child. As Red's socks slipped off, the anchors gave way. In a fitful embrace, the children toppled to the floor. The baby's sobs became cries of terror.

The woman ran into the room. 'Get away, demon child! You're hurting the baby!'

Red untangled herself from the wriggling infant.

The woman seized the baby. 'Look what you've done, you spiteful girl!'

'Baby cry. Help.' Red's limited vocabulary was gibberish to someone who'd already reached a guilty verdict.

Red couldn't deny life without the baby would have been better. Maybe Red wanted something at a tender age she wasn't able to define: death.

121

SARAH

For the umpteenth time, I check my hair. No matter what I do, frizziness tries to win. I laugh when people admire my curls. It's a mission trying to tame them. It's important to look and feel good tonight. I'm not in competition with Anna but she elicits the awkwardness within me. She's the kind of woman who has men rushing to help. Not that she needs it. Anna's tougher than she looks.

There's a tension between us. Is it as simple as competing for Hayden's affections? Anna should have realised she's already lost. She's taking all my assessment skills to figure her out. I'm determined to crack Anna's code. Tonight could be the night.

I realise putting on lipstick and wearing a new top doesn't make me superior. It's protection. Women can be brutal to each other sometimes. Lily and I don't invest in such crap but we're always alert. I have the comebacks, Lily has the bolshiness. The two often see us through when we go to the ladies' toilets where the bitches congregate.

Despite her limited finances, Kayleigh slathered on make-up, usually cosmetics she'd shoplifted. I remember her putting on her face, using the sliver of a mirror left after addicts had

295

smashed it to snort off. Kayleigh was an attractive woman until heroin took a hold. She slapped on extra foundation, trying to hide sunken eyes, acne, and protruding cheekbones. Instead it highlighted the ravages under an orange veneer.

One of my fondest memories is of Kayleigh putting make-up on me. It was before she discovered the needle, and a joint or a snort were her limit. James had broken into an enormous house obviously belonging to wealthy people. The feeling of opulence as I trailed my hands over silk furnishings and thick carpets was novel compared to our usual surroundings. The indulgence continued when Kayleigh found an abandoned bag of expensive cosmetics. Our eyes almost exploded from their sockets at such treasure. We spent an afternoon painting our faces and giggling. I wish every memory was so precious. James stole those memories from me with what he made me do.

As I apply eyeshadow, I stick up two fingers, pretending my reflection is my birth father. I'm not keeping his secrets from Hayden any longer.

'Wow, Sarah. You look amazing.' Hayden sneaks an arm around my waist and nuzzles into my neck. I still shiver at his touch.

'You scrub up well yourself, Mr Lawson.'

'Don't call me that. It feels like I'm in the classroom.'

Hayden spins me in a circle and we kiss. I wipe lipstick from his mouth.

'I flipping love you, Sarah.'

'Where's this coming from?'

'Stop fretting.' Hayden pulls me inwards. 'Not everything has a motive. I'll never leave you. Only death could separate us.'

Hayden's declaration stirs something inside me, like a warning. 'You're not going anywhere.'

Hayden checks his watch. 'We *are* going to Anna's. I can't

figure out why I'm so nervous. It's only dinner, although I've never been to Anna's house.'

'Don't you think it's strange?'

Hayden sits on the bed. 'She's reclusive. I guess Anna's home is her sanctuary. She comes to my flat, so it's not a problem. Hey, maybe Anna's hiding a dastardly secret. Perhaps she runs a brothel or is a secret crime lord.'

I can't join Hayden in the laughter. Going to Anna's house is making me wary. Why?

I sit next to Hayden. 'I need to tell you something I've been too afraid to share.'

'Okay,' Hayden replies. His forehead vein begins to protrude.

'Don't worry,' I say. 'We're fine. I love you. Please remember that after I tell you this. You may not want to be with me after I do.'

122

SARAH

S arah's body melted into the floorboards. She tried to lift her arm to look at her watch. Sarah had to get up before Kayleigh and James returned. Her limbs felt like they were glued to the floor. She lay heavy, fighting to keep her eyes open.

His face loomed over her, licking his lips. His legs straddled across her. 'I'll take you to heaven, sweet girl.'

Sarah's mind gave up the fight. She drifted into a dangerous sleep.

～

'Get off her, you animal!'

Sarah's eyelids struggled to prise apart. The sound of Kayleigh's screaming hurt her ears. Why wouldn't her mum be quiet and let Sarah sleep?

Sarah ached. Ripples began in her tummy, rising to her throat.

'You filthy little whore!'

Sarah awoke. The man was covered in vomit, Sarah's vomit. He released his grip on Kayleigh's throat.

James shoved the man away, instructing him to never show his face in the squat again. Sarah was glad. Heroin wasn't for her anyway.

~

'My poor baby.' Kayleigh held Sarah in her lap, despite her daughter being a teenager. 'I'm so, so sorry.'

Sarah didn't reply. For days, Kayleigh had repeated her apologies. The displays of affection came too late. It didn't alter the fact her parents had left her alone with a bunch of vagrants.

Sarah was too ashamed to confess she'd asked the man for a hit. She wanted to see what it was like; to experience what her parents loved more than her. Knowing how sick it made her added to Sarah feelings of inadequacy. Kayleigh and James chose *that* over her.

'Stop fussing over her,' James said as he prepared his next fix. 'Sarah's fine. No harm done.'

'Are you kidding me?' Kayleigh yelled. 'He would have done something if we hadn't got here in time.'

'Chill out.' James grew testier. He always was when he needed to shoot up. 'He didn't attack Sarah.'

Kayleigh tried to cover Sarah's ears. Her daughter pushed Kayleigh away. It was too late for protection.

'I dread to think what would've happened,' Kayleigh said, looking at her daughter. 'Stop shooting up in front of Sarah. Why do you think she tried it? My daughter won't become an addict.'

James slammed his fist against the floor. 'Sarah's seen needles before. She's a dab hand with them too.'

When Kayleigh stood, Sarah scurried to a corner. Her parents' rows often became violent.

As Kayleigh advanced towards James, Sarah looked for cover. James had revealed their secret.

'Have you been showing Sarah how to take skag?' Kayleigh's voice reached screeching level.

James laughed. 'We had a practical lesson. Sarah's an expert at finding my juicy veins, aren't you, kid?'

Sarah retreated further into the darkness, trying to hide her shame. Her father hadn't given her a choice. Threats to abandon her unless she injected him made Sarah comply. James was so lazy he forced his daughter to administer his drugs. Whenever she did it, Sarah felt another piece of her dignity crumble away.

Kayleigh raised her fists and ran at James. Knowing previous consequences, Sarah darted from the house. She couldn't take anymore. Someone was going to get hurt.

123

SARAH

Throughout my telling of the worst day of my life, Hayden has been silent. It was hard to speak when he didn't respond. With each sordid detail, it felt like Hayden was slipping further away from me. I get up to undress.

'What are you doing?' Hayden asks.

'There's no point in wearing this if we're not going to Anna's.' I have to force the words out against the pain in my chest. 'Sorry I lied to you. I'm no better than my parents. If you're leaving me, I don't blame you.'

Hayden stops my fumbling fingers taking off my bracelet. 'I'm not leaving you.' He turns me to face him. I can't make eye contact. 'Please look at me,' he says.

I do and then I realise. He's the one I want to spend the rest of my life with. Hayden wipes away tears running down his face as he leads me back to sitting on the bed.

'I'm furious,' he says. 'Not with you, never with you. How could a man do such a thing to his daughter? I heard your birth parents were messed up but never expected this. Mum shared some of your background before you came to live with us. Does she know about this?'

'No!' I grab Hayden's hand. 'Please don't tell Mags.'

'It's not my story to tell. If and when you're ready, we'll do it together. Mum will react like I am now. She'll want to tear James' heart out of his throat.'

I can feel my body decreasing in size. I'm the girl in the squat again, cowering in a corner, trying to be invisible. Will the shame ever end?

124

SARAH

'I need you to be brave,' Kayleigh said.

'Aren't I always?' Sarah replied, weary of mustering up courage. Sometimes she just wanted to be a teenager, not the pseudo adult.

'James is out but he'll be back soon. We have to do this as quickly as possible.' Rifling through her pockets, Kayleigh produced a leaflet from a Jehovah's Witness. She sneered at the headline. 'God isn't going to save me now, is He? Have you got a pen?'

Kayleigh knew Sarah would because of the girl's love of writing. It was Sarah's escape. When she couldn't sleep, she lit a precious candle she'd found in a drawer. As Sarah wrote her stories, she escaped to other worlds where junkies didn't groan for a fix, perverts didn't eye her for loathsome possibilities, she always had food in her belly, and a clean body.

'You write what I say,' Kayleigh instructed Sarah, handing over the pen.

Sarah knew Kayleigh struggled with writing. They had learned to read and write at the same time. The primary school readers Sarah brought home, when she was younger, provided a double education for mother and daughter.

Kayleigh's parents gave up on her before she hit her teens. As she drifted into the wrong crowd, Kayleigh played truant from school. Her parents didn't care their daughter was semi-literate. When the handsome, seemingly clever, and older James came along, Kayleigh was easy pickings.

As Sarah wrote the words ending her relationship with her parents, she cried. The tears didn't stop as she walked to the police station and handed over the note.

Please look after my Sarah. She's too good for me. Mums have to do what they can for their kids, even if it hurts. I love you, Sarah.

125

SARAH

I can't stop talking. Hayden's silence is worrying me. I have to fill in the gaps. Trying to decipher his reaction, I scan his face.

'For some reason, it seems right telling you tonight,' I say. 'I can't get rid of this strange feeling of dread.'

'It's probably more relief that you've finally told me.' Hayden holds me against him. 'I can't believe what James did. Coercing your child to inject you with drugs is unforgivable. Making light of a man trying to attack your daughter is even worse.'

Years of suppressed anguish tear away from inside me. As I rock backwards and forwards, wailing, Hayden moves with me.

'We'll work through this together,' he whispers in my ear. 'I love you and we'll be okay. You'll be okay.'

'When Kayleigh sent me to the police station, the day she let me go, she said she was trying to make up for being a terrible mother.'

'It sounds like she tried her best.'

I think about Kayleigh and how she veered between apathetic and nurturing. Mothers don't have it easy. They try to love their children the way they see fit. They don't always get it right.

I catch my reflection in the mirror. Kayleigh looks back. I offer a nod of thanks, hoping wherever she is, Kayleigh will feel it.

126

RED

Red doesn't need a mirror as proof she's looking hot. Prettiness is overrated. Attractive girls blur into one. Red is unique.

Her determination frightens others. Such intensity is wasted on them, whereas Red gets high on it. It makes her even more focused.

With a flick of her hair, Red remembers how her crowning glory was mocked in the playground. Insults of *carrot top* and *copper nob* never bothered her. Red's superiority highlighted their mundanity. She was a threat.

It's a relief to discard her work clothes and wear something stunning. Red hopes tonight's proceedings won't be messy. The outfit was expensive. She doesn't want it ruined. Blood is a chore to wash out.

They've already wrecked her life. They'll never sully anything precious to Red again.

R ed isn't a stranger to saying goodbye to those she loves. Killing Hayden will be nothing compared to the pain of Gran's death.

~

'She's gone.' The nurse removed his fingers from Gran's neck.

Red grabbed his arm. 'She hasn't. Use the stethoscope again.'

The nurse stepped away, offering the pitying expression reserved for the bereaved. 'She's died. I'm sorry for your loss.'

As she watched him leave the room, Red resisted forcing the nurse to get it right this time. She was alone.

The rest of the family were having a break. Red had watched them leave. They'd banned her from being with the only person who understood. Because of them, Red spent the night sleeping in corners of the hospital, hiding like a criminal. It wasn't fair but she won in the end. Red was the last person Gran saw before she died.

Needing a connection, Red draped herself over her gran's body. The closeness was a strange solace. Gran wouldn't tolerate sentimentality, particularly from a grown woman. Although Gran withheld affection, she had shaped Red's life. She taught Red to toughen up, guard her heart, and not allow anyone to steal it. The moment she saw Hayden, Red let her gran down.

Red looked one last time at the only person who'd known her. For courage, Red repeated Gran's last directive. 'Whatever you do, however you do it, always do it for love.'

Red placed a crimson kiss on her gran's cold lips, sealing their deadly deal.

LILY

Lily's grateful Ruth lives on one of Bicester's main roads. Wherever she goes, Lily looks for exits. A secluded avenue would have been challenging.

'Freya is safe and you are too,' Lily reminds herself. Talking to herself is a habit formed from when Freya was a baby and lacked the art of conversation.

Lily checks the arsenal of self-made weapons in her handbag: perfume to spray in an attacker's eyes, keys to stab, and a whistle to deafen.

Thankfully, Ruth lives alone. Ruth's responses showed she found it odd how often Lily asked, but Lily won't take chances after what happened to Sarah. Planning this meeting was Lily's way of showing she can be organised. Her usual spontaneous approach isn't appropriate for an investigation.

The textured glass front door hinders Lily's assessment of the form approaching her. Ruth is short and hopefully not imposing. To release the tension, Lily exhales. Whenever Lily bunches up her shoulders, Sarah jokes how Lily is tall enough. Thinking of Sarah gives Lily courage.

As she follows Ruth into the dining room, Lily notes the

emptiness of the house. There's nothing on the walls, not even a photo. Cabinets and dressers are bare. The carpet is worn where rugs would have preserved them. Despite the radiators pumping out heat, Lily shivers. A hospital waiting room is more welcoming.

'Have you recently moved in? It's almost empty in here!' Lily shouts through to the kitchen where Ruth is preparing drinks.

'I've been here ages,' Ruth says as she gives Lily a full wine glass. As a rule, Lily doesn't often drink. She's excitable enough without alcohol and her body is a temple she worships at the gym. Today, Lily might need Dutch courage. She will only have a little, knowing she has to drive home and keep focused. The bitterness of the wine soon changes her mind.

Ruth looks around. 'I suppose it is sparse. I don't notice until someone visits and I see it through their eyes. Are you always so brutally honest?'

'Sorry. My friends and family keep telling me to think before I speak. We can't all afford the decorative stuff some people go mad for.'

The grimace on Ruth's face is confusing. Was it Lily's comment or the acidic plonk that's caused the reaction?

'I've got money, thank you very much,' Ruth says. 'I had a great job, practically running my boss' business until I retired. Mementoes aren't my thing. There are too many memories vying for attention in my head already.'

As the chill in Lily's bones increases, she pulls her jacket tighter. Is she ill or are the thought demons playing with her? She focuses on Ruth, wondering if she's seen her before. There's something familiar about the woman. When Lily's mind wanders, the thought slips away.

'Where do we start?' Ruth is practical. Lily will use this. Idle chit-chat won't work.

'Do you mind if I record our conversation?' Lily asks, grabbing a notebook and readying her phone.

Ruth's pencilled eyebrows rise. 'Yes, I do mind. This is between us. I'm only doing this for Tamsin's sake. No one must know you've been here. It's important.'

'No problem.' An intrigued Lily places her mobile and notebook aside. She doesn't add how annoyed she is that she'll forget some details if they're not recorded.

'Promise.' Ruth reaches for Lily's arm. Despite herself, Lily pushes Ruth away.

'So sorry.' Lily frowns at her betraying hands. 'I didn't mean to react. I'm not usually like this. Please, forgive me.'

'Someone's hurt you, haven't they?'

Is Ruth being sympathetic or enjoying Lily's pain?

'Not at all,' Lily replies. 'I'm a lean mean fighting machine who forgets her own strength.'

Their mutual laughter is hollow and forced.

Lily assesses Ruth. Muscular arms show she takes care of herself. Is it for self-improvement or defence? A set of weights and a medicine ball are in a corner of the room. Although Lily would love to offer Ruth advice on better equipment, she has a feeling Ruth wouldn't be receptive.

Chatting in the dining room is a strange interview choice. Most people lead visitors to the comfort of their lounges. Then Lily figures it out. Ruth is at the head of the table, with Lily seated at her side. This is professional. No cosy sofa where Ruth could slip up or lose her composure.

The earlier flighty thought lands back in Lily's head. 'You remind me of someone. It's bugging me I can't place who it is.'

'Have you heard of Rita Hayworth?'

'Oh yes, that must be it. My gran loved those films. She had a colour picture book of the old movie stars. Looking at Rita's photo amazed me after only seeing her in black and whites. You and Rita could be twins with your flame-red hair.'

129

SARAH

'Red suits you,' I say, as Anna takes our coats.

Anna scowls and then swishes her hair, shampoo advert style. 'I changed back to my natural colour. I've been dyeing it for years but decided I should stick to my roots.'

'Very funny,' Hayden says.

'What is?' Anna clutches Hayden's jacket.

'Roots? Hair? Forget it.' Hayden shrugs.

'Oh, I get it.'

Anna's sudden shrill laugh makes me startle. She's always on edge and it's catching. When Anna tugs her hair, I wince on her behalf.

'You look tired,' Anna says, assessing me.

No matter how much repair work I've done to my face, the puffiness around my eyes remains. Hayden offered to cancel tonight. I need to carry on with life. Already my body feels lighter. I hope my mind will eventually follow.

'Long hours at the surgery,' I reply to Anna.

'How's Lily?' Anna asks.

'She's fine.' I don't mask my confusion. Lily and Anna didn't hit it off when they met. I guess we're doing pleasantries.

'It's an awful business, her daughter being abducted.'

'Indeed,' I reply, not wanting this woman to talk about Freya.

'I hear you've been in the wars too.' Anna inspects my neck.

'If you call being attacked "being in the wars", then yes, I have.'

'Anyway, ladies.' Hayden plays peacemaker. 'Shall we get more comfortable? Lead the way, Anna.'

Anna's spartan lounge houses only essential furniture. The clinical white walls are so bright I have to blink. A cactus is on the windowsill; the only personal touch. The spikiness reflects its owner. Anna favours the minimalist look I hate. Being as disorganised as I am isn't conducive to minimalism. Sentimental items make a house a home. This house is soulless.

'How long has she lived here?' I whisper to Hayden, as Anna checks dinner.

'Years. You wouldn't think so looking around though.' Hayden scans the lounge and adjoining dining room. 'Perhaps Anna's decorating.'

'I'm not a fan of tat and tacky family photos,' Anna says, entering the room with a tray of nibbles. 'Hayden, you under-stand why I don't want to be reminded of certain people. Nostalgia is overrated.'

Hayden nods. Curiosity is killing me. I hate it when others know things I don't.

Anna places plates of food on the floor. 'I've never seen the point of having a coffee table.' Her shaking hands betray her composure. Canapés fall on the laminate.

'I'm such an idiot.' Anna rubs her neck. 'Why can't I do anything right? If only I could get it right.' The distress in her voice becomes angrier.

I fear for Hayden as he places an encouraging hand on her shoulder. Anna looks set to kill.

Oblivious to her rage, Hayden scoops up a cracker and eats it. 'Ten-second rule applies. Delicious.'

Anna laughs.

Unaware I was holding my breath, I exhale.

Hayden helps Anna pick up the rest of the food. Her focus on him is hard to define: love, pity or both.

'I need to carry on with dinner.' Anna skitters away.

'What on earth is wrong with her?' I ask Hayden.

'Haven't a clue. Anna's worrying me. Recently, she's become erratic. She needs more help than I can give. Can you suggest counselling?'

'I expect we'll both be in counselling soon. I've decided to do it again.'

'That's a great idea and brave too.'

'We'll see how brave I am once I'm in therapy. I'll mention counselling to Anna if it comes up in conversation but I won't force anything on her. Counselling is the client's decision. To be honest, I don't understand what Anna needs. She hasn't opened up to me, and you're being cagey about her past.'

I don't mean to sound bitter but I'm tired of Anna's games and people's secrets.

'If Anna doesn't share tonight, I'll tell you her story later,' Hayden whispers. 'It's time you knew. I was wrong in keeping it to myself. This whole thing is twisted and beyond my capabilities. Believe me, I thought I was doing the right thing. Before, when Anna needed a friend, I wasn't there for her. Anna's family background explains her strange behaviour. It's right you should know about them. After all, you've shared your secrets with me.'

'Thanks for trusting me. We'll try to get Anna the help she needs. Oh, I forgot to give her the wine.' I grab the bottle and enter the kitchen.

'Sorry to disturb you. Were you on the phone?' I ask Anna.

She drops a ladle into the casserole. It splashes over her

apron front but luckily not on her stunning dress. It must have cost a fortune and is extravagant for a dinner party.

'No. I'm busy cooking.' Anna wipes away sauce covering the stove.

'I thought I heard voices. Don't tell my practice partner, Phoebe, she loves head-shrinking her staff.'

Anna doesn't laugh.

Freezing night air creeps in. 'Shall I close the door?' I ask.

'Please do. I opened it to cool the kitchen.' She leafs through a recipe book. Sticky notes bookmark favourite dishes.

I hold the bottle, turning the label towards Anna for her approval. She takes the wine from me with a shaky hand. 'Is red okay?' I ask.

The bottle slips through Anna's fingers, shattering on the granite tiles. Anna is a nervous wreck covered in claret.

130

RED

Anna must rein in the terrified helpless woman act. She's losing control. The end is close. It's integral Anna remembers how to play her part. She's given an accomplished performance so far.

Sarah and Hayden's behaviour in Anna's house compromised Red's strategy. She considered shredding their smug faces with a kitchen knife. Instead, she took some air and talked herself out of it. It is not yet time.

As the lovebirds mock their hostess, Red decides they'll pay for that too. Let them have fun while they're able. Their laughter will soon become silence.

Sarah and Hayden's ignorance shows how little they care for Anna. The doctor, Sarah, is quick to diagnose people as what she wants them to be. Nobody is ever only one thing.

Without Anna, Red barely functions. She tried and suffered for it.

Anna is Red. Red is Anna.

No one will come between them again.

131

LILY

Lily pinged an elastic band on her wrist throughout Ruth's recital of the redheaded celebrities she's been likened to. Tedious as it's been, Lily has learned Ruth is chattier when her ego is stroked. The alertness trick from Sarah works, even if Lily's wrist is smarting from the twangs.

'So, Ginger Spice.' Lily winks at Ruth. 'I expect your good looks caught Paul Lawson's eye.'

Ruth's mouth tightens into a thin line. 'I suppose we've got to talk about him. You don't get to judge, right?'

'No judgement from me,' Lily says. 'I've seen and heard everything, and no doubt done most of it myself.'

'I met Paul at Langston Brothers, a biscuit factory in Aylesbury we were both working at. I was picking and packing full-time. Mum wasn't happy about it, saying I had responsibilities at home but I needed my freedom. At the end of a shift, Paul's girlfriend appeared. Paul and I were fooling around in the car park. This girl came along, shouting at me for stealing her boyfriend. I could have died of shame. You could hear my work mates' gasps.'

'I bet Paul didn't apologise to you or his girlfriend.'

'You got that right,' Ruth replies, clutching her knees. 'The cocky beggar made a joke out of it. Anyway, we split up and Paul lost his job because he was slacking off. He didn't care about either. I should've known it was a bit of fun for him. I had a habit of picking wrong 'uns and making the family live with the consequences. It's why I've stayed single for years.'

Lily can relate. She's made a similar vow to steer clear of relationships although Chris is rather foxy.

Ruth continues. 'Then the proverbial hit the fan. I was pregnant. The timing couldn't have been worse. Before you ask, she's definitely Paul's.' Ruth gives Lily a hard look. 'I didn't bother telling Paul at the time. He wouldn't have been interested. I had his child and kept her a secret. I shouldn't have. Naomi was distraught when she found out her father's identity.'

132

LILY

Ruth drains her wine and pours another. So Ruth doesn't notice Lily's glass is still full, she moves it away.

Before she speaks, Ruth takes a swig. 'Naomi was devastated when she found out Paul was her dad. My mum waded in, saying I should've done a better job of hiding it. She was ashamed of me for letting the family down again. When Mum heard I was pregnant, she called me all the names under the sun. Great behaviour for a devout Christian, don't you think?'

Lily shakes her head in sympathy.

Ruth continues. 'I tried to make amends, letting Mum name my daughter after a woman from the Bible. Mum said a godly name atoned for having a child out of wedlock. Apparently, I had a habit of repeating mistakes. A child of God would be a reminder and a warning of my sinful tendencies. Mum said calling me Ruth was a mistake and I'd betrayed my biblical namesake. I was a single mother, living with my parents. It was a miserable existence. My dad tried but was under the thumb. I vowed Mum wouldn't take my child. She'd never steal from me again.'

'What did she take?' Lily asks.

'It doesn't matter. My mouth runs away from me sometimes. Pay me no attention. Mum often called me Jezebel and pointed at my daughter as a mistake.'

'That's not acceptable,' Lily says, feeling even more thankful for Imogen. 'You shouldn't have been treated like that, by your own mother.'

'Don't pity me,' Ruth says. 'Mums can be hard taskmasters. I didn't always do a good job and wasn't the best mother. Being young, I wasn't prepared to have my wings clipped. Naomi is everything to me. It made others jealous to see our bond. They couldn't understand why I gave so much of myself to my child. Making up for my errors and getting it right with Naomi was important. I vowed never to be parted from her. That was ruined too.' Ruth clutches the pendant around her neck. It disturbs Lily for a reason she can't define.

'Is Naomi still alive?'

'Of course.' Ruth's eyes narrow. 'Why wouldn't she be? What do you know?'

'Nothing.' Lily affects nonchalance. They'll talk about Naomi all night if Lily doesn't lead the conversation. 'Did Naomi know Tamsin? You lived on the same road, right?'

'We did. Naomi doted on Tamsin. I worried she used her to get closer to Hayden. I confronted Naomi about it. Her reaction was terrifying. Naomi looked like she wanted to strangle me.'

133

RED

When Red's family moved to Oak Road, her life began. The Lawsons gave her a purpose, and later, reasons to destroy them.

Intent on leaving Great Parston, Red's mother took some persuading to stay. Red enjoyed her discomfort. As usual, Gran proved to be a useful conspirator, demanding the family stayed close. When the property on Oak Road became available, Red knew it was meant to be. A strategically placed home was the least Red's mother owed her.

While the others carried boxes into the new house, Red sat on the front wall. She watched Hayden, walking with his shoulders stooped. In the time she'd known him, Red understood he was shyer than he allowed others to believe. Books were Hayden's refuge.

Red learned all she could and wheedled into Hayden's life and his family. When Mags and Paul went out, and Hayden was studying, Red looked after Tamsin. Whenever Mags wanted a confidante, Red sympathised.

Red had all the Lawsons in her clutches, except one. She

couldn't reach Hayden. He said they were friends. It wasn't enough. Red had to have all of him; his whole life in her hands.

134

LILY

The jigsaw pieces of Tamsin's death are slotting together. Ruth is unleashing clues pinging around Lily's mind. She tries to concentrate on the revelations, cursing Ruth for insisting Lily didn't record their conversation.

'I didn't want to live near Paul but my daughter demanded it,' Ruth says. 'She said it was the least I owed her after telling so many lies.'

Lily covers her glass as Ruth offers the wine bottle.

'Kids can be hard work sometimes,' Lily says, while wishing Freya was with her.

'Don't I know it,' Ruth mumbles. 'After Naomi found out Paul was her father, things escalated. We had to live near him. There was no other way. It was bad enough when Paul moved into the village, worrying he'd find out about Naomi. Then he did.'

'What happened?'

'When I heard his family were living in Great Parston, I almost had a breakdown. Mum accused me of conspiring with Paul. She thought we were having an affair. As if.' Ruth opens a drawer and takes out a pack of cigarettes and an ashtray. 'Do you mind if I smoke? I kept these as a reminder I'm stronger than the habit. Turns out I'm not. This talk of the past is doing me in. Do you want one?'

Lily hears Sarah's warning voice, telling her not to. 'No thanks. Go ahead, as long as you won't regret it.'

With the first drag, Ruth closes her eyes. 'There are many things I regret. This is low on the list. Anyhow, I spotted Paul soon after they moved in. I hid in the local shop, thinking I'd avoided him. Imagine my horror seeing him waiting outside. Paul said he knew I lived nearby and had seen me with a girl. Then he asked if she was his daughter because she looked the right age. I couldn't lie. Paul still had the charming grin. I confessed she was his and told him to stay away from her. When I said we wanted nothing from him, his relief was obvious. We agreed to keep the secret to ourselves. Paul didn't want Mags finding out. I didn't tell him that my family, including Naomi, already knew. I made the wrong decision and should've told the truth.'

'How did Naomi behave around Tamsin, knowing she was her half-sister?'

'She loved Tamsin. To my knowledge, Naomi never approached Paul about being her dad. We carried on as normal. None of the Lawsons knew the truth about Naomi. She loved Tamsin like a sister. It was difficult to witness. Naomi was almost, what's the word? Yes, she was possessive. My mum was annoyed when Naomi started babysitting Tamsin. She didn't want any of us in what she called "a den of depravity", because of Paul.'

Lily stops biting her nail. 'I'm sorry to ask, was Naomi ever angry with Tamsin or Paul? Would she have taken out her hurt at Paul's rejection on Tamsin?'

'I won't have any accusations against my Naomi.' Ash drops from Ruth's cigarette as she stands and points to the door. 'If you're going in that direction, get out.'

'Apologies.' Lily backs away from Ruth's scrutinising stare. 'I didn't mean to offend.'

When Ruth takes her seat, she taps her knee. 'Naomi was a wonderful girl. Awful things happened to her. She couldn't help how they affected her decisions. If I'd been a better mother, Naomi wouldn't have latched onto Hayden. She made a dangerous choice trying to be part of the Lawsons. There were consequences. Paul told me to make Naomi back off. I tried but nothing deterred her from being with Hayden and Tamsin. Naomi wanted siblings who could love her without conditions. I waited for it to come crashing down. That's what love, used the wrong way, does.'

135

RED

Red watches Hayden and Sarah, fingers entwined, waiting for their meal. Little do they know, there's more than food being dished up tonight.

Red focuses on Hayden. It takes supreme resilience not to kill him right now. Hayden doesn't appreciate how often Red has given him back his life.

136

RED

Hayden has never been out of Red's sights. After he left for college and then stayed in Leeds for university, Mags never stopped talking about him. The information Red gleaned was worth enduring cheap coffee and Mags' incessant chatter.

On an emotionally weak day, Red travelled to Leeds. She waited outside Hayden's halls of residence. Red learned from Mags that Hayden had moved out of his uncle's house to have more independence. Hayden's absence confused her and Red needed to make sense of her feelings. Did she still want him?

After their confrontation, before he left for college, she should have continued hating him. Taunting her with the evidence of her following him should have been a deterrent. Red was often flaky around Hayden. It was his fault; sending her confused messages. One moment he was a friend, the next, more of an enemy.

The Indian summer beat down upon Red. Her clothes glued to her skin and her temples pounded as she waited. Hayden's eventual appearance eradicated Red's discomfort. He chatted with another young man. No threat there. A woman would have met with an unfortunate accident.

Hayden's awkward stoop had disappeared. His strides were purposeful and he'd stepped into a new, more confident, skin. Studying to be a teacher had transformed him. Red refused to be happy for him. Hayden didn't deserve it.

Red was still invisible, even when standing across the road. She vowed Hayden would never forget her.

137

RED

Red had her satisfaction when Hayden came home to search for Tamsin. She was gone and Hayden was back; how it should have been. His distress at his missing sister pleased Red. Tamsin was no longer an obstacle.

Years later, when Anna bumped into Hayden, he applauded the magic of fate. Red would give him that. It *had* been unexpected. Everything else that happened after, Red won't allow anyone but herself to take credit for.

Hayden's reunion with Sarah was the catalyst. Until then, Red had been a watcher. Red couldn't confess how unguarded dreams elevated her to Hayden's significant other. The beginning of his relationship with Sarah destroyed Red's fantasy. It's only fair Red destroys them.

138

LILY

Ruth has taken up smoking again with a vengeance. The ashtray is half full and she shows no signs of stopping.

'You must see the weirdness of Naomi getting close to Hayden and Tamsin, considering she's Paul's secret daughter.' Lily's tried subtlety but Ruth isn't getting it. It needs a direct approach, despite the fear Ruth invokes in Lily.

'Naomi went through so much.' Ruth's fierceness re-emerges. 'She loved those kids because they were related. Don't you dare taint something pure by making it more than it is. There's nothing Naomi wouldn't have done for the Lawsons. I told her to rein it in. She should have been revising for exams rather than babysitting Tamsin. Mags had a habit of taking advantage, aware Naomi wouldn't refuse.

'Despite my connection to Paul, Mags and I were friends. Paul hated seeing me with her. There were a few occasions when I was so drunk I wondered if I'd blabbed that Naomi was Paul's daughter.'

'Mags knows about Naomi,' Lily says.

Smoke rises as Ruth puffs out a sigh. 'It's okay. If it helps with your investigation, then it's worth it. I'm not bothered. Mags is no match for me.'

'It must have been difficult, living near Paul, seeing as he was so attached to Tamsin.'

'Ain't that the truth? I felt like murdering Paul sometimes. Even after all those years, I carried a torch for him. It's why I became friends with Mags. I liked her but she was hard work. Being around Mags meant getting nearer to Paul. He often took me aside and told me to go home. I'm cringing at how grateful I was when he noticed me. When Paul died, I didn't grieve. I realised it was over. I had a fresh start and Naomi didn't have to fight for her father's recognition any longer. Paul's constant rejections cut both of us deep.'

Lily realises Naomi is the key to unlocking the investigation. Taking a more friendly interest in Ruth's daughter is the best approach.

'Do you have any photos of Naomi?' Lily asks. 'I'd love to see what she looks like.'

Finally, Ruth smiles. Lily wondered if she was capable. Mothers love bragging about their offspring; the decent ones at least. Ruth opens the same drawer that held the cigarettes; a place where she hides her secrets. She holds a frame in front of her. An initial scowl makes way for a wide grin. Lily takes the offered photograph.

'This was taken not long before Tamsin disappeared,' Ruth begins. 'Mum insisted on a family photo at a church dinner. None of us wanted to go but Mum always got her own way.' Ruth points at the photograph. 'There's Mum, looking mardy and, as usual, in her Sunday best. She wore the same A-line skirt and plain blouse every day. She bought duplicates. After she died, I binned the lot.

'That's Dad, standing next to Mum. He's smiling, despite being forced to wear a suffocating starched collar. Mum pitched a fit when Dad dared to wear jeans. She made him return them to the shop. Dad even did his gardening in decent clothes in case someone saw him. He'd return from the allotments, trousers filthy and torn. Mum mended them and put them in a boil wash. I miss Dad so much. He tried to be a good father.'

Lily wonders why two completely different people get married. Then she remembers her own parents.

'There's me.' Ruth taps the glass covering the photo. 'Mum was furious with me for wearing that. I did it on purpose.' She chuckles at her triumph.

The woman with big hair and cleavage spilling out of her blouse makes Lily smile. Younger Ruth seems more carefree than the version sitting here.

'Naomi's the one with her arm around me,' Ruth says. 'My lovely girl.'

As she tries to interpret the scene, Lily grips the frame. When she first glanced at the photo, Lily thought she recognised the person but wasn't certain. People change, faces not so much. Lily would know the girl anywhere and is aware of where she is right now. Yet, something doesn't make sense. 'This may be a stupid question, seeing as she's your child, but is your daughter definitely called Naomi?'

Ruth grasps the pendant around her neck. 'It's not a stupid question. Naomi changed her name by deed poll.'

'Weren't you upset?' Lily asks, recognising how Imogen would be gutted. Her mum named Lily after her best friend.

'Of course I was upset.' The brittle tone bites back. 'What mother wants their child to change their name? No good ever comes of it. When Naomi said she had a new name, I was devastated.'

'What's she called now?' Although Lily knows the answer, she needs to hear it.

'I don't know.' Ruth lays the frame on the table. 'She

wouldn't tell me. When Naomi cut off contact, she said she needed another identity so no one could find her. I had to trust the name was appropriate.'

Once again, Lily regards the family of redheads in the photograph. Dread coils in her stomach. Lily recognises the girl. Lily's also met her as a woman.

SARAH

'Is Anna always clumsy?' I ask Hayden. 'She's dropped the wine and splashed casserole everywhere.'

'I thought I heard something. Anna used to be so together. We joked about how annoyingly organised we were. Now she's nervier than ever. She wasn't always like this, although she was sometimes edgy around Mum.'

'Mags would frighten the SAS when she's having a bad day.'

'True. At least I could go to Anna's house.'

'What was Anna's mum like?' I ask.

'Unpredictable. Anna said she had major mood changes. I never saw it though. It wasn't a chore going around there, seeing as Anna lived a few doors down.'

'You've never mentioned Anna lived on your road.' My skin prickles. Has Anna opened the back door again?

'I thought I had,' Hayden garbles through a mouthful of crackers. 'I met Anna at school. Although she was older than me, we got along. When she said she lived in Great Parston I was surprised. I hadn't seen her around but, to be fair, I stayed in my room a lot, being a mopey teenager. Then Anna's family moved to our road. I remarked on the coincidence of a house becoming available when her mum wanted to move. It puzzled me how Anna said it wasn't a coincidence.'

'I don't believe in coincidences either,' I say.

'Anna said us living near to each other was part of a plan, bigger than we could imagine.' Hayden laughs. 'I teased her for believing in fate. She said strong forces plot everything. Anna's a stickler for having an agenda. When she's got an idea in her head, she won't budge. It's why Anna lives alone and doesn't have any friends, other than me.'

'What has Anna been through?'

Hayden looks towards the kitchen. 'I can't get into it here. Let's say Anna must always be aware of what's happening and see her ideas through to the end. It's a family trait. Her lot are stubborn and scary. Some of Anna's ideas are way out there though, like changing her name.'

'You what?' The chill isn't coming from an open door.

'She chose the name, Anna Hart, a while back,' Hayden says. 'When we met up again, she insisted I never use her birth name again. Don't tell her I told you. She hates being reminded.'

'Why did she change it?'

Hayden glances at the kitchen again. 'Keep your voice down. Anna had a difficult time with her family. Changing her name by deed poll meant they were less likely to find her. She hasn't shared everything with me. I'm slowly chipping away.'

'What was Anna's old name?'

'Naomi Hawkins. She said *Anna* was to remember her gran, which was odd as she wasn't called that. The surname is a reminder of love. Hart is spot on.'

Naomi Hawkins enters the room.

RED

S arah knows Anna's secret. It doesn't matter. Naomi and Red are ready to emerge from the shadows.

Anna can be known by the name her gran gave her and the one Red prefers. *Naomi* was appropriate. The biblical Naomi was faithful to the women in her family, despite her own misery.

This Naomi deferred to her religious gran by choosing the name, *Anna*. In the Bible, Anna had foresight. This Anna tried to prepare for the future. Others got in the way and blinded her to the truth.

Red watches Hayden, cutlery poised, ready to eat. To draw out the conclusion, Naomi took her time making the meal.

Cautious Sarah can't hide her anxiety. Her hawk's stare tracks Naomi's movements. Sarah thinks she has everything figured out. When Red shares her story, it will blow Sarah's mind and shatter her heart.

LILY

Lily couldn't leave Ruth's house quickly enough. As soon as the photo appeared, she recognised Anna. Lily should have trusted her instincts. Her muddled mind had struggled to process Anna's deviousness.

Ruth remembered the picture was taken in 2002, at the local church's hundredth anniversary. Naomi, as Lily now knows her, was seventeen. Her hair was longer and its natural red. Naomi's face is Anna's.

Lily didn't tell Ruth she's seen her daughter. Although Ruth would be overjoyed, Lily believes she made the right decision. It's obvious Ruth is hiding something. The woman had Lily seizing her handbag and recalling the weaponry it held throughout their conversation.

Sarah and Hayden are having dinner with Naomi. They're in potential danger. Lily didn't trust Naomi, as Anna. She was always guarded. In a matter of minutes, Naomi swung from over-friendliness to irritability. What does this mean for Lily's friends?

Lily can't yet prove Naomi killed Tamsin but the evidence is veering towards her. Naomi lived on Tamsin's road and was overly protective of the girl. Against that, Paul lavished affection on Tamsin while shunning his other daughter. A younger child took Naomi's place. People had lost their temper and mind for less. Did Naomi murder Tamsin to punish Paul and eradicate the other daughter? What does this mean for Hayden, one of Paul's remaining children? Steve could be at risk too.

Lily is on the way to Naomi's home, grateful she had her suspicions about Anna. Expecting she'd need it, Lily had previously found Anna's address in Haddenham. Hayden *does* have an address book. Lily sneaked a look at it when she visited him. She knew not to ask. If she had, Hayden would have been defensive about his troubled old friend.

On the side of the investigation, Lily was looking into Anna. She did it for Sarah although Lily doesn't know much more than Anna disclosed. Time conspired against Lily. If Lily had more information, Hayden and Sarah wouldn't be at Naomi's house. It's true Lily needs more training in investigation but time is running out. Her friends' lives are at stake.

Lily almost admires Naomi's cunning. She "died" in 2006. All traces of her disappeared that year. Imogen helped Lily to research birth and death records. Before she spoke to Ruth, Lily rehearsed how to offer condolences. Sarah would have been better placed to do it. When Ruth talked about her very-much-alive daughter, Naomi became more of an enigma.

As Anna, Naomi had various jobs, leaving each one within a short space of time. Lily could relate, although for Naomi it was a strategy. If you stay in a place too long, people get close and start asking questions. Lily's certain Naomi is an accomplished liar but everyone slips up. Starting a new job and living in a different area meant she could be whoever she wanted. Naomi's acting skills are superb.

Following hunches has worked for Lily. She knew Ruth was important to the investigation. When Ruth produced the family photograph, she helped Lily unlock a mystery. It not only revealed Naomi's new identity but told a more damning secret too. Naomi has more sides to her than Lily and Sarah realised.

142

SARAH

After placing serving bowls on the table, Naomi takes a seat. She hugs herself, staring at the casserole dish as if something will burst out.

I try to process what I've learned and the frightening feeling accompanying it. Naomi lived on the same road as Hayden. Later, she changed her name and came back into Hayden's life. She knew Tamsin, loved her like a sister, she claims, and joined the search when she went missing. Killers often get a kick out of returning to the scene of their crime and witnessing the family's misery.

Naomi couldn't have been closer if she tried. She's always been in the perfect position to orchestrate events. Despite his rejection, she still saw Paul around. Did she enjoy reminding him of her existence? Was babysitting Tamsin a ploy to torture Paul, seeing his children together? Did Naomi bond with Hayden to annoy Paul and her mum? I'm angry on Hayden's behalf. He assesses the food before him, oblivious to the fact his half-sister is seated at the same table. I couldn't eat even if I was starving. When Hayden offers roast potatoes, I give them back.

'No thanks. I'm dieting.'

Hayden looks at me as if I've sprouted an extra head. 'You've never dieted in your life and don't need to.'

'When we get older, the fat doesn't shift so fast,' I say, wishing telepathy worked.

The rational part of my mind wants to flee but my investigative brain demands I find evidence. This may be my only opportunity to discover if Naomi killed Tamsin. There it is. I believe Naomi might have done it. She's too evasive and unhinged for me not to consider her as a murderer. The killer is probably female, after all, and Naomi's connections with Hayden and his family are strong.

'Can I use the bathroom?' I ask Naomi.

Her eyes dart to the kitchen. 'I'll show you where it is.'

Hayden eases Naomi back to her seat. 'Enjoy your food. You deserve to after making this effort. It's upstairs, first on the right, Sarah.' Hayden used it earlier when Naomi and I were in the kitchen.

I leave Hayden with Naomi, hoping she won't hurt him. She's had many opportunities before tonight. I hope the love she has for Hayden is built on compassion. Maybe it will keep him safe.

I bypass the bathroom and head for a door on the left. As I suspected, it's Naomi's bedroom. I'm surprised to see trinkets and photographs on the window ledge. The rest of the house is almost empty. This is Naomi's sanctuary and I'm invading it.

The photos are all shots of Naomi at various gatherings. In one, her arms are locked around Hayden's waist. From the group in the background, it's a teenage party. The revellers are all smiling, apart from a girl on the right. There's always a party pooper.

In front of the others, Naomi gazes up at Hayden like a starstruck fan. Hayden leans away from her anaconda hold. They say the camera never lies and it didn't on this occasion. Naomi was obsessed with Hayden. She probably still is.

I'm hoping Naomi hides her secrets where many of us do; under the bed. I lift the edge of the comforter, opening the stage curtain to reveal the scene. Boxes and bags squash against the bed frame. This might take time. Time I don't have.

My flailing hands strike a metal box. It's the only one of its kind and is a good enough place to start. It's not well hidden but doesn't need to be. No one comes here. Why has Naomi invited Hayden and me to her home tonight? He's never been in this house. Why is Hayden allowed in when I'm here too? Our presence on this particular night isn't a fluke. We're here because Naomi wants us to be.

I push away the rising panic to concentrate on the box's contents. Exam certificates with Naomi's name on them are useless. Trinkets and jewellery rattle. A ruby pendant catches my eye. It looks expensive. I check the time. I must go downstairs soon. Naomi will be suspicious.

I hit gold; a bundle of newspaper clippings. They report on Tamsin's disappearance, including the discovery of her body. I could attribute this to Naomi being a family member but it's more sinister. Paul and Tamsin's names are underscored. Doodled broken hearts frame photos of Tamsin. A picture of Paul and Mags has knives added to their chests.

I put the articles back in the box. My finger catches on something sharp. I take out the offending item. My heart beats in my throat. I'm holding a badge. It's Tamsin's.

I remember Hayden pinning it to her scarf. It's a *Doctor Who* one, of course. When Hayden gave it to her, Tamsin said she'd never remove it. As far as I know she didn't. Hayden asked the police about the missing badge. Tamsin was fastidious with her badges. This token was too precious to lose. The killer sent me one of the others as a warning. They kept another as a souvenir, in this box, under Naomi's bed.

Hayden and I must leave. I was foolish to think Naomi

wouldn't hurt him. Naomi killed Tamsin. She's obsessed with the Lawsons.

I rise from the floor. My head throbs. Darkness.

143

LILY

As she drives, Lily waits for Chris to pick up his phone. It keeps going to voicemail. She has to do this properly and get the police involved. Now she must confess she's out of her depth.

Lily's tried phoning Sarah but her mobile is turned off. There's no point in calling Hayden. He wouldn't conceal his anger in front of Naomi when Lily shares what she's learned. Accepting she needs backup, Lily knows Chris is her best bet. Lily won't underestimate Naomi, based on her being female. Women can be calculated killers and kidnappers too. If Naomi is intent on lashing out, Lily's not offering herself as a victim.

Does Naomi want to hurt Hayden or Sarah? She's had plenty of chances to kill Hayden. There's a reason why she hasn't so far. Lily saw it whenever Naomi mentioned Hayden's name: love. Love makes people lose their minds. Sarah's a barrier to obsessive Naomi having all of Hayden's brotherly attention. Is Sarah the target? Naomi's dinner party isn't an innocent affair. A fan of trusting her instincts, Lily keeps trying Chris' number.

'You took your time,' Lily says as Chris answers.

'Nice to talk to you too. I wondered if you were avoiding me. You keep ignoring my calls. Shall we arrange our date?'

'Stuff the date!' Lily shouts. 'Why do blokes only think about getting their leg over?'

'Woah there. I'm not like that, Lily. I'm upset you'd believe it of me.'

Lily smacks her palm on the dashboard. 'It's not about me and you. We've got to get to Anna's, I mean Naomi's house. I think she killed Tamsin.'

'Is she called Anna or Naomi?'

'She's both. She changed her name from Naomi Hawkins to Anna Hart.'

'Who *is* this woman?'

Lily explains Naomi's links with Paul and the Lawsons. She's glad Chris doesn't comment on how Lily's continued the investigation.

When Lily mentions the photograph and the evidence, convincing Lily her friends are at risk, Chris ends the call, saying he needs to get there. His concern does nothing to alleviate Lily's.

Sarah and Hayden are in danger.

144

SARAH

D amp air tickles my throat. My head rumbles. I try to dislodge the sound, then realise it's a tumble dryer.

I can't see. I attempt to move my hands to check if I'm blindfolded. They're tied behind me. When I wiggle my nose, there's nothing covering my eyes. I'm in darkness.

My movements are slow. Someone's given me a sedative. The thought of a drug coursing my veins makes me nauseous. I don't want poison in my body again.

I scoot along the floor, feeling for my mobile in my back pocket. It's gone. Rope tied around my chest and waist tethers me to a beam. Shards of wood scratch my fingertips. I must have been out of it for a while. I don't remember a thing. Being handled by a killer when unconscious is terrifying.

I call out for Hayden. No reply. My breathing becomes ragged. Memories of being shut in a wardrobe loom. James' face appears before slamming the door. A key turns in the padlock. I can almost smell the odour of wetting myself, left in a prison for hours.

I concentrate on the present. James is no longer my enemy.

Naomi is. I stare into the gloom, distinguishing the outline of boxes and shelves. This must be a basement.

Despite its monotony, I miss the company of the dryer's sound. I don't want to be here alone. I don't want to be with a murderer. Desperation makes me struggle against the restraints. Rope gnaws at my wrists. I recall stories of prisoners who cut off their hands in similar situations. Aware I'd bleed out, I'd rather keep mine. If I think, I can escape. My woolly brain can't catch up with my determination. As I lean against the post, a lump on the back of my head smarts. Naomi will pay for this. When I get out of here, I will see that she's punished.

Frantic clapping sounds near my face.

'Who's there?' I hate the sound of my fear. Naomi can't break me.

A breathy laugh tickles my ear. The clapping gains momentum.

'You're not scaring me, Naomi.'

Silence. Where is she? Is Naomi standing next to me? I wait. Footsteps move away.

The light flicks on. My eyes adjust. Tears obscure my vision. I blink to focus. My sight clears.

I wish it hadn't.

Hayden's head slumps on his right shoulder. Please, not him.

Is Hayden dead?

145

SARAH

Desperate for a response, I shout out Hayden's name. I won't accept he's dead. Hayden doesn't move from where he's tied to a filing cabinet. It's difficult to see if he's breathing underneath the ropes. Frustration at not being able to check his vital signs makes me struggle against the restraints.

What will I do if Hayden's gone? Without him, I might as well die too. There's no choice. This is how it ends. I'll be dead soon.

No. For Hayden's sake, I'll keep going. I must make it out of here alive. If I give in, Naomi will get away with another killing. I don't understand why she kills those she loves. Why murder her half-brother? Maybe believing Hayden will reject her when he knows the truth was Naomi's tipping point. I'm an obstacle to Hayden too, for someone who clearly wants all of him. The desperate measures Naomi has taken prove it. Hayden's death isn't the end. Naomi wants me to die too.

This must be her basement. I should have checked it out earlier. Usually, I consider all angles. In my line of work, my mind needs to be sharp. Emotions got in the way. My annoyance with Naomi's secretiveness made me careless.

The beam I'm tethered to is in the middle of the room, making me a centrepiece and a sitting target. Pushing against my ties and the pervading grogginess is tiring. Naomi's blow to my head did the trick. At least it wasn't strangulation this time. I've wondered if it was her who did it. Now I know.

I search for escape routes. No windows but there are stairs. Their closeness taunts me; so near and yet impossible to reach.

Naomi's barren house is reversed in the basement. Ornaments, pictures, vases, and figurines cover shelving units. More photos of Hayden stand behind his body, creating a grotesque shrine. I won't mourn. I'm not giving up.

I've never seen so much stuff in one place. Naomi must have cleared everything out before Hayden and I arrived. She hid the clues. Personal possessions show so much about a person, particularly obsessives. Holiday souvenirs sit alongside folders, labelled as English schemes of work. I recall Naomi's thwarted teacher training. Next to me, photo albums are categorised by date. Video tapes and cassettes reveal Naomi's hoarding tendencies. Every item bears homage to the past.

I dare to look at Hayden, hoping he's breathing. It's hard to tell from a distance but I can't see the rise and fall of his chest. I suppress the animal cry building inside me.

'Why did you kill him, Naomi?' I shout, sensing her presence. 'If you wanted a brother, you've put an end to it. I wouldn't have minded you having a relationship with him.'

An embittered laugh travels from behind the partition. She steps out. I recognise the scarlet shoes I admired earlier.

'Sarah, you'd rather die than relinquish Hayden. Good. It can be arranged.' She moves towards me, swishing her red hair.

146

RED

The girl, Red, tried to settle as she tucked herself in with a story. She had learned to read at a young age.

Waiting for her mother or Gran to bond with her at bedtime was futile. Gran only appeared when there was a lesson to give. Red's mother wasn't present unless she was reprimanding her daughter.

Red admired the princess in the picture book. As Red looked at the image of the prince placing a glass slipper on Cinderella's foot, Red regarded her own feet. Nothing dainty fitted her giant feet. Like an ugly sister, the prince would reject her too.

Red would never be the heroine. It wasn't an issue. Even minor characters can rewrite history to become the main attraction.

147

SARAH

'How does it feel knowing your beloved Hayden is dead?' the redhead asks.

The confirmation is a punch to my core.

'Where's Naomi?' I ask a question instead of satisfying her with an answer.

The woman leans in. 'All in good time.'

I take in her appearance. She's tall and well built. Deep red hair is the main attraction, fanning across her shoulders. It seems more threatening than beautiful. Her solid frame strains against the tailored lines of her suit. Small eyes, set back in a large face, are devoid of kindness. They resemble lumps of coal; dark and dull but ready to burn. I expect she attracts masochists, desperate to prove they're not scared. She probably terrifies them. Her glare transports me to a locked wardrobe and a twisted father.

The woman edges closer, drawing out each step. She plays the villain with practised ease.

'How do you know me?' I ask, trying to turn away from her. Her nose almost touches mine. My head swims. Is she aware Kayleigh wore the same scent? Is this a game?

My captor snakes a finger under my chin, pushing it up. I look into her eyes, resolved in staying defiant. She won't see my unease. I wish I'd given her what she wanted and kept her near me. She cannot be next to Hayden.

'I make it my business to know everyone in Hayden's life.' She strokes his face. 'Including you, Sarah Atkinson. Sorry. My bad. That's Kayleigh and James' surname. I mean Sarah Lawson. Oh, wait, they didn't want you either so some other suckers took you in. Sorry, Sarah Jessop. Right?'

I focus on the floor, refusing to rise to her bait.

'I've heard you hate being reminded of your addict parents. You get testy when people talk about them. I can use that.'

I continue staring.

'Ignore me all you want, Sarah Atkinson. I know you have addicts' blood running through those veins. I shot you up with an added little extra. Was it a thrill realising a drug is coursing through your body, just like old times?'

'I will kill you!' The rope crushes against me.

The woman raises an exaggerated eyebrow. 'There it is; junkie rage. I wondered how long it would take. You're a disappointment. I thought you'd last longer and we'd have some fun.'

'Who are you?' I ask.

The woman takes a bow. 'I'm Red.'

'Who the hell is called Red?' I realise my mistake as she advances.

The cool steel edge of a knife catches my throat.

148

SARAH

A scream comes from across the room. Someone rushes from behind the partition. They apprehend Red, who's holding the knife to my neck. My potential rescuer is pushed away. She lands on the floor.

'I told you to stay back!' Red shouts. 'You must stick to the plan.'

'I'm not standing by any longer. You said you're sorting things out so we could move on. I didn't agree to killing them.'

'You always were naïve,' Red says. 'Did you seriously think I'd tell you everything?'

Naomi looks at me. I won't disguise my hatred for her plotting with this Red woman.

'Please.' Naomi tugs Red's arm. 'Don't hurt Sarah. You've done enough.' Naomi sobs as she looks over at Hayden.

Red applies pressure. Blood trickles down my neck.

When she withdraws the knife, Red flashes it in front of me. My blood stains the edge. Red watches Naomi. The stranger's face veers between disdain and adoration. Conflicting exaggerated expressions remind me of someone else.

Then I see it. Then I know.

149

SARAH

Red drags over an empty crate to sit next to me while Naomi lingers by the stairs. The coward is searching for a way out. She's lured Hayden and me here but can't face the consequences of her actions. If I'm going to die tonight, the duplicitous bitch will watch it happen. I hope our deaths give her nightmares for the rest of her miserable life. Naomi's led us to the madwoman in the basement.

'So, you *do* have a sister, Naomi,' I say. Both women cannot mask their feelings. 'Another of your many lies. How does it feel, Red, knowing your sister doesn't acknowledge your existence?' I shouldn't rile this woman but Naomi's deceit has unleashed my anger.

Red shrugs. 'She only did what I told her. Naomi's proud of her big sister, aren't you?'

We regard Naomi, who couldn't look more ashamed. Red clenches her jaw. Like her sister, her face is a canvas of emotions.

Naomi spots me looking at Hayden. 'I begged him not to tell anyone I have a sister. Hayden understood why I'd rather forget about her although he hated keeping it from you. He didn't know Esther was back though.'

'Good old faithful Hayden,' Red says. 'My sister knows fully well no one calls me Esther. Pleased to meet you.' Red holds out her hand to me. 'I forgot. You can't shake my hand, being tied up.' The cruel laugh matches her husky voice. There's nothing delicate about Red.

I assess the sisters. Both have red hair, although Red's is darker than Naomi's strawberry hue. Given how Naomi cowers, it's obvious she's the more passive sibling. Red dwarfs Naomi. I won't allow the difference in size to make me pity Naomi. She lured Hayden and me here.

Red prods Hayden's head. I mentally beg him to respond. Please be alive.

Nothing.

'Leave him alone.' Naomi rushes to Hayden. She's lucky I can't move.

'Back off.' Red points the knife at Naomi.

Naomi steps away. 'Esther, would you really hurt me?'

'It's Red, not Esther. Don't you ever listen? I'm here because of you. This is your chance to be avenged.' Esther waves the knife at Hayden and me. 'It all comes to an end tonight.'

150

NAOMI

After I posted the birthday card to Mum, I wondered if I'd made a mistake. Until then I was safe and living under a new identity. Loneliness travels with me wherever I go. Sometimes it's so strong, I feel like I'm suffocating.

Although Esther was my sister, I never wanted to see her again. She twists love into hate and violence. The jealousy she harboured towards, and for, me, ruined any relationship we could've had. For some strange reason, Esther either tries to gain retribution on my behalf or she ruins my life. I've never asked her for anything, certainly not to hurt anyone.

I understand Esther is hurting too. Mum wasn't always the best mother, particularly with Esther. Whenever Esther asked about her dad, Mum told her to go away. The pain it caused is unforgivable. Maybe Esther would have been happier if she'd known her dad.

Esther grew up calling Ruth, *Mother* because Mum demanded it. I was allowed to call her *Mum*. It's one of Mum's biggest mistakes regarding Esther. The constant comparisons Mum made between Esther and me has probably led us here.

While I realise I should have done more to show Esther she wasn't lacking, I couldn't approach her. Esther terrified me.

Where Esther was labelled a *handful* and *spiteful*, I only knew Mum's love. Her adoration for Paul Lawson made me the favoured child. I never felt comfortable with it. When Esther discovered the identity of my father, Mum was devastated. Paul was *her* secret.

Many times I asked Mum to give Esther the treats I got. Of course, Esther will tell you different. I did the best a child could do to make it fair. Our mum is a hard woman to reckon with sometimes.

Although Mum's complicated, I missed her. The longer we were apart, the more I suffered. I'd managed to avoid Esther by moving home several times and I got complacent. It was madness to write my address in a card I sent to Mum. I swore Mum to secrecy and thought we'd be okay. We never mentioned Esther in our phone calls and emails, foolishly believing it meant she didn't exist.

Often Mum's said how happy she is to be back in contact. She didn't tell anyone where I live. Mum will still do anything for me. It's a shame she's not so thankful for Esther, although it's understandable.

As soon as she was old enough to learn, Esther bullied us. We had to endure living near the Lawsons because of Esther's manipulation. She threatened to kill herself if we didn't move. Esther never considered my agony of living near the father who didn't want me. On reflection, she probably planned it.

I know Esther sometimes wishes I hadn't been born. Without me, she may have known love. Mum might have invested all her attention and care in one child. It's obvious Esther struggles between loving and hating me. The story of how she banged my head on the cot when I was a baby is infamous in my family. Esther claimed she was trying to soothe not hurt me. With Esther, I never knew what to believe.

When she returned from her trip to Oxford to find Paul, Esther wrecked my world. Until then, my father was anything I wanted him to be: an author, an actor or a pop star. Portraying their relationship as a brief encounter, Mum said he was a handsome stranger. Her eyes practically lit up whenever she spoke of it.

As soon as Esther overheard Mum arguing with Gran about Paul, Esther had ammunition. Shattering my illusions with the truth invigorated her. Because Esther's dad had abandoned her, she wouldn't allow me to have a fantasy. As far as Esther was concerned, I had everything already.

Mum's lies, a waster dad, and my sister's cruelty crushed me. Those who hadn't met Esther would have viewed her intervention as kind. A caring sister doesn't state your father loves his other daughter more. A loving sibling wouldn't ridicule you for being unwanted. A sister who already knew rejection should have shown empathy.

Esther said I didn't need a dad because she was all I needed. I'd never felt more afraid or alone. Life with Esther was a prison sentence. Hayden's friendship was my refuge. I needed the caring sibling relationships with Hayden and Tamsin, even if they believed I was only a friend. I no longer had the only option of a bitter sister.

Esther could have been a better person if it wasn't for Gran. She tried to keep Esther in line, viewing her as a project in turning a bad child good. Gran's attention came from discipline and rule. It's no surprise Esther grew up believing controlling people is how to love.

When Gran died, Esther fell apart. It was a turbulent year. Tamsin went missing too.

151

SARAH

Naomi pauses telling me about her life with Esther.

Red gives a round of applause. 'The prize for stealing the limelight goes to...'

'Sarah needs to hear it all!' Naomi shouts. 'I'm fed up with the neglected Red routine. You claim to love and need me, but you've terrorised and tortured me. I've done everything you demanded: meeting with Sarah and Lily, spending time with Hayden, and reporting everything back to you. I hated every minute but I did it because you forced me. You win, Esther. I'm scared.'

The knife in Red's hand lowers. She takes a moment before responding. 'You selfish madam. I've always been second best. Everyone loves Naomi. Sweet Naomi. Beautiful Naomi. I loved you and did your bidding.'

Naomi sits on the bottom step, laughing until she struggles to breathe. 'You don't know what love is. Everything you touch, you ruin. You pushed us away with your spite. Even Gran had enough of you by the end.'

'Don't bring Gran into it.' Red drags Naomi up to stand. 'She never let me down, unlike you.' Red strokes her cheek, as if seeking comfort. No one else will provide it.

Naomi struggles within Red's grasp. 'Gran was evil too. She gave you attention because she saw herself in you. How could you love someone who mistreated you? You never knew if she would hit or praise you. That's not love, Esther.'

'Shut up.' Red pushes Naomi away.

I'm still trying to loosen the ties around my hands. I need to keep them talking to stall for time. 'You're not much better, Naomi. You arranged for Hayden and me to be here so your sister can kill us.'

Naomi kneels towards me. 'I didn't expect her to do this. Please believe me. I had no choice. Esther threatened to kill us all if I refused, including Mum. Did you notice how jittery I was? Esther was hiding in the garden. It's why the back door was open. She had that thing in her hand.' Naomi points to the knife lodging in Red's pocket as Naomi goes to Hayden.

'Run to Hayden, as usual.' Red sneers. 'I suppose Naomi has been useful in seeing this to its fruition. I needed to prompt her but deep down she's enjoying this.'

'I wasn't the one obsessed with Hayden,' Naomi says. 'You've always envied our relationship.'

'Boys like Hayden seem nice,' Red replies. 'It's a ruse to get you in the sack. So funny he didn't know he kissed his own sister! I was a better choice but wasn't good enough for Mr Wonderful. You, my dear Sarah, are collateral. You took Hayden from Naomi and me.'

Red returns to sitting on the crate. 'I've followed you and lover boy for a while. It's been a blast getting so close I could touch you. You never suspected a thing. Some investigator you are. Remember all those dead crows and the signature I left in their blood?'

'It was you.'

'Remember the woman who spilled a drink over you in the pub?' Red continues.

'Do we have to keep doing this?' I affect a bored tone despite my fear. 'You again?'

'How about when the BMW knocked into you?' Red grins, obviously enjoying sharing the list of what she's done to me.

'Hmm, let me think. Could it possibly have been you?'

'Sarcastic, aren't you? Recall those fingers wrapped around your neck?' Red's eyes flash with fire. 'I enjoyed that.'

'I've already worked out it was you but thanks anyway.' Red won't break me. I'll keep up the fight until my last breath.

She extends her arms. 'Ta da! I've been with you every step of the way. Did you feel like you were being watched when you were at Mags' house, the pond, the park or your twee little home?'

'Why are you so focused on this investigation? What have you done?' I ask. 'You might as well say, seeing as I won't make it out of here alive.'

'Clever woman. I've been guiding Naomi ever since I found her again at the hospital. A porter cut his hand open. I'm a sous chef.'

'Congratulations.'

'I'm the one holding the knife, remember.' Red brings it up to the light. 'You should see me gut and fillet a fish, although I lost my job recently. Stalking takes up a lot of time.'

'Shame,' I reply.

'Keep it coming, Sarah, if bitchiness makes you feel better.' Red laughs. 'As I was saying, I took the porter to A&E. There was my sister, doing her ward clerk thing. You covered your tracks well until then, Naomi. Then, up she pops. I left the porter there. The reunion had to happen on my terms.'

Naomi shifts around on the step. 'She broke in here and left objects which could only be from her.'

I startle as Red thumps the crate.

'Be quiet. This is *my* story. Naomi had reunited with Hayden. Then I got her involved with you too. Naomi's visit to your house was my doing.'

'Of course it was,' I say.

'Be aware, I can do nasty things to you.' Red kicks my knee. 'Your hero, Hayden, is dosed up with night-night pills. I have my pharmaceutical sources.'

It explains Red's wild-eyed look. I'd worked out she's functioning on more than anger and misplaced revenge.

The tapping of Red's foot shows her anger is increasing. 'While you were snooping upstairs, Hayden had a taste of wine and was out for the count. You were supposed to drink it too but went off seeking buried treasure. I adapted by hitting you on the head. And here we are.' Red swishes a theatrical arm.

I check Hayden. Breathe, damn you, breathe.

'It wasn't easy lugging you two down here,' Red adds, 'but Naomi was most helpful.'

'She threatened me with the knife!' Naomi shouts.

'Such a liar. You want them dead as much as I do.'

'I don't, please believe me, Sarah.'

'Save it for someone who cares,' I reply, not knowing what to think. 'What did she leave on your kitchen side, by the way?'

'A family photo with Mum's and my faces crossed out and...' Naomi hesitates.

'Go on.' Red paces. 'This is the best bit.'

'A badge from Tamsin's scarf,' Naomi says.

152

SARAH

'You killed Tamsin.' I'm not asking Red for confirmation but the words must be spoken. The investigation is over.

'Well done. Call yourself an investigator? Couldn't solve it, could you? The clues were there. You needed to dig deeper instead of fixating on Naomi. Even being obvious with smashing a brick through your window didn't work. You've proved to be most disappointing.'

'Why didn't you tell someone what she did?' I ask Naomi. 'I thought you loved Tamsin.'

Naomi lifts her head. 'Tamsin was everything to me. I didn't know for certain Esther killed her. Esther told me recently to keep me in order. I wanted to back out of this stupid scheme. I packed a bag and was leaving to start over again.'

Red tuts. 'You should write a book, considering the stories you tell. The fact is, Naomi, I'll always find you.'

'I promise, Sarah,' Naomi begins, 'I haven't known for long about Esther killing Tamsin. If I had, I'd never have let it get this far. Esther tricked me. She's making me do what she wants, with threats. She forced me to return to my natural hair colour. I hate it. I don't want to be like her. Esther laid out this dress and shoes on my bed so we'd look similar. She said there would be consequences if I didn't wear them.' Naomi tugs at her hemline. 'I detest red in more ways than one.'

Red holds up a hand. 'Enough, Naomi. You keep forgetting, my name is Red.' Red turns to me. 'No one calls me Esther, apart from my family. They won't let me move on. I started calling myself Red a long time ago. It sums up so much more than my hair colour. Red is about fire, purpose, and passion.'

'Boring.' It slips out.

In response to Red's kick, waves of pain shoot up my leg.

'Why did you kill Tamsin?' I ask through a grimace.

'It's simple,' Red says. 'Love.'

153

RED

28TH JUNE 2002

D ays after her gran's funeral, Red's temper showed no signs of abating. An altercation with the chef at the Queen's Head spiralled out of control.

Red believed she was capable of more than waitressing and washing up. When Red claimed her culinary skills were superior, Chef called her a slut. The chef got a black eye and Red was sacked.

She had to dampen her rage before she returned to Granddad's. Red vowed to stay calm around him because no one else would have her. As she walked, Red kicked objects in her path, punishing her toes rather than people. A child's cry struck her heart. The sound of joy mocked Red's turmoil.

Paul chased Tamsin across the park. The girl shrieked at the inevitability of being caught. Red moved behind the oak tree to avoid idle chat. Not that she needed to. Paul never spoke to her in public.

When Red looked after Tamsin, Paul begged her to stop. Red enjoyed his annoyance. Threatening to tell Mags about his secret daughter and gambling addiction made Paul civil. As she grew closer to Mags, Red lorded over Paul. It wasn't enough. She blackmailed him into sleeping with her too.

No matter how hard she tried, Red couldn't have Hayden. Paul was a poor second but he sufficed. It was also guaranteed to make her mother angry when Red dropped not so subtle hints of Red's affair with Paul. Everything Red did was a game she played with her mother.

Paul begged Red to stop. Whenever they had sex, he shut his eyes. Paul's disgust taunted Red. He always came back though. A sexless marriage with Mags made him susceptible. For that, Red loathed him even more. She pondered why she'd never had a normal relationship. Why did Red have to manipulate to get what she wanted? She blamed it on her father, who disappeared when Ruth announced her pregnancy. They were both sixteen and neither was ready for a child. If Red's father had been decent and stuck around, maybe Red could have had normal parents, a normal family, and a normal life; not one of hurting others to get what she wanted.

Red's throat closed in response to Paul and Tamsin holding hands. It was what she'd craved. As a child, she attempted to hold Ruth's hand. Her mother pushed Red away, disciplining her for showing them up. Ruth always walked ahead, pretending not to be a mother. She said she wanted to be a teenager without responsibilities. When Naomi came along, a crowbar couldn't prise her off Ruth's hand. It confirmed Ruth's lie. She wanted a demure daughter not an antagonistic aberration.

Red tried to connect with Naomi. Sometimes she succeeded, like when Naomi's father was giving his love to a different child. It should have been Naomi's prize. Red would claim it for her sister.

154

RED

Tamsin spun on the roundabout, her head lolling from dizziness. Across the park, Red saw the man on the bench, staring at the child. The man expressed more than a natural interest. Red spotted the camera. She had to act. Rescuing Naomi's sister would deepen Red's bond with Naomi. Taking Paul's daughter away for a short while was a bonus.

The man made a quick departure. As a warning of her observance, Red barged into him. His apology for perceived clumsiness was met with profanities.

Red didn't expect to see the man again and learn his reasons for being in the park. It was Damien's fault she approached Tamsin. If Damien hadn't been there, Red might have left the child alone. The idea to worry Paul wouldn't have entered her mind. Maybe.

Paul was busy conducting a deal at the van. He tried to act the hard man with a heart. Where was his heart? Not with his daughter, left to play alone. Paul tended to his own needs. Selfish people had to learn the consequences of their self-interest.

Red advanced upon Tamsin. The girl's scarf flew behind her

as she spun. She shouted a greeting at the familiar face. Red stopped the roundabout and placed a finger on Tamsin's lips. It was guaranteed Tamsin would obey.

Red picked up Tamsin, surprised again by the lightness of the child. Tamsin wriggled, reaching back for the safety of the playground.

'We need to be very quiet,' Red whispered as she led Tamsin into the woods. 'See the ice cream man talking to Daddy?'

Tamsin nodded.

'The bad man's got a gun. He said if we don't leave the park he'll kill Daddy.'

155

RED

28TH JUNE 2002

'Why can't I go home?' Tamsin asked. 'I only live there.' She pointed to her house.

After shoving Tamsin through Ruth's front doorway, the child tripped. She looked at Red, knowing not to cry.

Red pulled Tamsin up. 'The bad ice cream man has a friend. He has a gun too and he's in your house, holding it to Mummy's head.'

As Tamsin's eyes widened, Red drank in the girl's terror. Dragging the child along the hallway, Red mentally thanked Ruth for not changing the locks. Once again, Red had been evicted and sent to live with her granddad. Assured Ruth would be at work, Red knew she would be safe. Red hoped Naomi was out with the friends she favoured over her sister.

Red seated Tamsin at the kitchen table. The girl's lips trembled. With her penchant for wearing weird clothes, Tamsin asked to be bullied. Odd children had to be harder, smarter, and stronger. Disappointment with Tamsin fired Red's animosity.

She blamed Hayden for Tamsin's deficits. He should have toughened her up. Caring Hayden doted on his little sister and ignored anyone else who laid a claim on him. Red imagined

Hayden's distress at thinking Tamsin was abducted. It made Red smile.

A check of every room confirmed Red was alone. She contemplated her next move as Tamsin sobbed into her milk. Red tuned it out as she remembered the shed. It was quieter and, most important, concealed. Putting Tamsin in there long enough to worry her family was perfect. Meek little Tamsin wouldn't say where she'd been. The gunmen would return if she did. It wasn't a foolproof strategy but Red was confident she could execute it.

Red imagined Paul diminished with the pain of losing a loved one. He'd previously cast Naomi out. Tamsin's absence would make him understand the torment. As a bonus, Hayden would be punished too. It was coming together.

Tamsin's crying pitched to a howl. Red slapped the child. A livid mark spread on Tamsin's cheek. The girl chanced a desperate cry for her mum. Red had to make it stop.

156

RED

28TH JUNE 2002

Red seized Tamsin's shoulders. 'Don't be such a baby. Do you want me to tell Hayden what a wimp you are? Stop shouting or I'll give you something to shout about.'

Tamsin slipped from Red's hold and off the chair. She'd never retaliated before. As Red held the girl in a perverse embrace, Tamsin kicked out. Red clamped a hand over the Tamsin's mouth to muffle the screams.

The kicking slowed.

Fighting ceased.

The six-year-old girl obeyed with silence.

Red lowered the child to stand.

Tamsin's corpse hit the kitchen floor.

157

SARAH

I can't erase Tamsin's face from my mind. It changes to a grotesque death mask, trapped in a narrow space. I must hold on to the happy girl I loved. Tamsin isn't a pile of bones. She's a glorious set of some of my best memories.

'Our granddad had a plot at the allotments, didn't he, Naomi?' Red looks to Naomi for confirmation and receives none. Naomi resembles the proverbial rabbit in the headlights. She appears as shocked as I am to hear what her sister did.

Red continues. 'It was a good place to dispose of evidence. A great idea, don't you think, Naomi?'

Obviously disgusted by her sister's depravity, Naomi turns away.

The devious Red grins. 'I hid in Granddad's shed until it got dark. It was so boring. I should have taken a book.'

'My heart bleeds for you,' I say.

Red ignores me again. 'I waited until no one was around.'

'What a hardship,' Naomi says.

'Watch it,' Red replies. 'I can cause trouble for you.'

Naomi focuses on Hayden.

'I dug up Granddad's plot. There wasn't much in it. Lazy old duffer only bothered when the council threatened him with fines. Digging a hole took ages. I pushed in the suitcase, covered it over, went home, had a shower, and got into bed.'

'I bet you slept like a baby,' I say.

'I did, thanks. Destroying Paul and the Lawson family was exciting. I watched them trying to find a child who wouldn't return. Sometimes I felt sorry for him.' Red points at Hayden. 'I couldn't say his sister was lying underneath the vegetables though. I thought we'd all moved on. Then the diggers came in for building the new flats and Tamsin's body was discovered. I had a wobble but soon recovered. Who would suspect me? You and Lily didn't.'

'We'd have got there eventually,' I reply.

'I'm bored with talking about Tamsin,' Red says. 'It's time to bring this to completion.'

158

SARAH

Despite my devastation, I won't reward Tamsin's killer with my tears. I have to keep Red talking while I figure out how to escape. Maybe Naomi will help. She's made it clear she doesn't want this to happen. We must join together against her sister.

'I don't understand how you can talk of what you did to Tamsin without any remorse or regret,' I say to Red. 'You never intended to let her go home. Killing Tamsin was a thrill. Admit it. You enjoyed it. You're evil.'

I wait for a beating. Red plays with her hair instead.

'I can categorically state I didn't take Tamsin intending to kill her,' Red says. 'Things worked out better than I thought. Let's say things happened that day to provide extra inspiration. The right people got hurt and continue to suffer.'

'You're not my sister. I refuse to call you it ever again,' Naomi says.

'Stop with the amateur dramatics. I killed Tamsin for you, you pampered princess. I expected Paul to be grateful for you, after the shock of his daughter going missing. With Tamsin dead, Paul had a reason to reunite with you. Paul deserved for his child to die. He had a replacement and he still rejected you.'

'You didn't do it for me. I didn't ask you to kill Tamsin.'

'It didn't do you any harm her being dead. You're gutless. Every major thing that happens in your life is because of others' actions. You're quick to reap the rewards though. I did it for you. When the life drained out of Tamsin's body, I connected with you. I held her tight because it felt like I was holding you. After all, she was your sister. Why can't you understand how much I love you?'

'That's not love. Your hate killed a child.' I'm determined to defend Tamsin until my last breath. 'You could've said it was an accident. It's not right but you would have got away with it. You'd have spared the family decades of confusion and upset. I guess you want their misery.'

'Are you so innocent?' Red asks. 'Why do you get to hide your secret? Is there a different standard for you? You're no better than me.'

'I don't know what you're talking about,' I reply.

Red pauses for a moment and then speaks. 'I was petrified of being found out. Looking at the body, I panicked. Remembering her size helped. Tamsin and I used to play a game of locking her in a cupboard, timing how long she'd last without crying. As suspected, she fitted into one of Mother's suitcases. It was a squeeze. Tamsin's arm snapped but it worked.'

I don't want to give Red the satisfaction but my disgust won't hide. Red nods, as if giving her approval.

She continues. 'I took some badges from Tamsin's scarf. I'm glad I did, so I could share them with you two. Trip down memory lane, right, Naomi? Nice deviation, Sarah, but you don't get away with it so easily. Here's something you'll enjoy.' Red pulls out a pouch from her inner jacket pocket. Steady hands place two syringes and vials on the crate. 'I'll let you administer this, seeing as you're so practised in shooting up.'

159

SARAH

'Off you go then,' Red says, holding out the drugs paraphernalia towards me. 'Show us how it's done.'

'How did you find out?' I ask.

'Our meeting at the surgery wasn't the first time I've been there,' Red replies. 'Why do you think I knew the layout so well when I attacked you? Phoebe needs to turn off her computer in the evening. Your file was on the screen, begging to be read. Worried about you, is she?'

Phoebe and I had an appraisal recently. That must be it. She'd tell me if she had concerns about me or my work. I won't allow Red to manipulate me.

'So, Phoebe carted you off to a shrink,' Red says, giving a self-satisfied grin.

'A counsellor actually. Not that it's any of your business.'

'Your counsellor's notes were thorough. They made for compelling reading. Did Phoebe not trust you to work with patients until you'd had your head sifted through?'

When Phoebe offered me a partnership in the practice, she asked if I would see a counsellor. Phoebe was aware of some of my issues, from when we trained together. She suggested counselling to make sure I'd cope, particularly with addicts. I was initially upset, believing she'd questioned my fitness to practise medicine. Then I realised Phoebe was looking out for me.

Red tries to force me to take the syringe.

I clench my fists so tight my nails dig into my palms. 'If you want to kill me, do the job yourself, you coward.'

'Okay. It's more fun this way.'

Naomi creeps forward. She reaches for Red. Red is always watching. She pushes her sister away. I wince as Naomi hits the ground.

'You don't need to do this,' Naomi says, rubbing her back. 'Leave. I'll cover for you. No one else has to die.'

'You keep forgetting I'm doing this for you,' Red replies. 'After these two are erased, we can move on. It's unfortunate you want to have a relationship with Hayden but you must let go. He'll never be ours. She saw to it.' Esther glares at me.

'Hayden doesn't want you and I expect he never did,' I say. 'Get over yourself, Esther, Red, whatever you are. Why would a decent man be interested in such a desperate and callous wench?'

Red winds her hand in a circle like cranking a handle. 'Keep the insults coming. Go out in a blaze of fury. The fact is you and Hayden must die. Then Naomi and I can be together.'

Naomi's laugh makes me shiver. 'I don't want you. Why can't you understand? You're unlovable. You smother people and suck the life out of them. I couldn't love you less if I tried.'

'It's not true.' Red's pitch increases to a screech. 'You *do* love me. I've given up so much for you.'

'I did love you, but you ruined it. You've wrecked so many lives. People do what you demand out of fear, not respect. You kill everything good.' Naomi makes a bold move, standing in front of Red. 'You're a disgrace. If Esther doesn't get her way, she throws her toys out of the pram. Stealing others' joy isn't making you happy. Stop taking my happiness. You ruined my degree by sending a plagiarised dissertation to the supervisor before I could send the real one. You knew I wouldn't tell.'

'Don't ignore me then.'

Naomi jabs Red's shoulder. 'You broke me when I found you in bed with my fiancé.'

Red backs away from the prodding. 'If he cheated so easily, he wasn't worth marrying.'

'You drugged him, Esther.'

'He would have done it eventually anyway.' Red grins. 'Shall I get the violins out to accompany your tales of woe? Best you don't play though. You were awful at it when you were younger.'

Before she continues, Naomi gives Red a wilting look. 'Then Esther found me at a school I was working in.'

'It didn't take the work of a sleuth, like our Sarah here. Your picture was in the paper. You slipped up there, Naomi.'

Naomi addresses me. 'The local newspaper promoted a school fundraiser. I knew Esther would find me as soon as I appeared in print.'

'She came out fighting though,' Red says. 'Naomi punched me when I turned up at her school.'

I want to cheer for Naomi as she pushes Red away. 'You goaded me and I was stupid enough to react. I lost my job because of you.'

'Be grateful I didn't press charges.'

The fight is leaving Naomi. She sits on the step as if spent. 'I thought changing my name meant I was safe. Hayden took me in and listened. He knew what a handful Esther was. Still, Hayden was horrified when he heard what she'd done and I gave him the watered-down version.'

'He wanted to get into your pants.' Red kicks Hayden. He doesn't respond. I will not fall apart.

'It isn't like that, Sarah. Hayden only loves you. Please believe me,' Naomi says.

'I believe you,' I reply. Naomi should have shopped Red to the police but she didn't have a choice. The evidence is right here of how dangerous Red is.

'Naomi's duped you too.' Red laughs. 'She's got a talent for it.'

Naomi brushes away a tear. 'Stop lying. Hayden is my family. He helped me start over. I was so pleased to have his friendship again. Now you've killed him.'

Red looks at Hayden. 'I expect so but it's best to make sure. Time to die.'

160

NAOMI

I relish Esther's frown as she watches me kiss Hayden's forehead. My sister doesn't move. Confusion has rendered her immobile.

The Red show must end. My part is over. Too much has been taken by both of us. It's now time to give.

As I look at Sarah, I wonder if I can atone for some of my mistakes. There are so many, some made more willingly than others. When Sarah smiles at the kiss, I accept her forgiveness. Sweeping Hayden's fringe away, I focus on my half-brother, for courage.

It is time.

This is love, not Esther's hateful parody. She's never known affection. All I have for her now is pity. We could have given love to each other. I'll teach Esther how to act in the name of love.

This is over.

Esther has taken too much. I did too. Coming back into Hayden's life wasn't my right, despite our family connection. Hayden had a promising future which Esther has killed. If I'd stayed away, he'd be alive.

Running away has taken its toll. There were many years of

trying to be a few steps ahead. Esther will always find me. Our performance is over.

A powerful force drives me across the room. My purposeful hands strike Esther. The syringe drops to the floor. Air slices. I fall. Screams penetrate my ears.

Wetness slicks my hands as I hold my side. Icy shock competes with a warm pool of blood.

A sister's arms cradle me but she won't let go of the knife. It's a token of our common blood. The aftermath of our lifelong battle drips from the blade.

It is over.

Esther's tears splash upon my face, mingling with my own. Realising I've done something right, I take a final look at Hayden. Goodbye, brother.

I must be good, one last time. A rejected broken-hearted sister looms over me. We will always have a connection.

'I love you, Red.'

161

RED

Red's primal howling reverberates around the basement. The stone floor glistens with blood.

Red holds her sister's body, whispering into Naomi's ear. 'Wake up, Sleeping Beauty. The ball is beginning, Cinderella.'

Naomi is still.

'You killed her!' Red screams at Sarah.

If Sarah hadn't played victim and riled Naomi, this wouldn't have happened.

Sarah stares at Red. 'You did it all yourself. *You* stabbed Naomi. *You* are a killer, *Esther*. Call yourself Red? Red is strong and vibrant. You're nothing but a cheap imitation.'

Red regards the knife. It will be fitting to murder Sarah with the same weapon that killed Naomi.

Defiant Sarah keeps her eyes open.

Good. Let her look into the face of retribution.

Red lunges, knife in hand.

162

LILY

'Come on, Lil, you've got this.' Lily talks to herself in a whisper. The sound of her voice combats facing the fear on her own.

She promised Chris she'd behave. It didn't take much, considering how petrified she is. Lily didn't promise Chris she wouldn't go into the house if she got there first. The back door is open.

'Be brave, Lil. You're a lion who finally has his heart. Remember how we used to say that, Sarah?' Lily isn't losing her mind. She knows Sarah can't help but the thought of her friend gives Lily courage.

The kitchen is a bloodbath. Red liquid covers the floor.

'Bloody hell, did the carnage begin here?' Lily asks.

Shattered glass confirms it's wine. Lily's shoulders loosen.

'Someone's been clumsy. The hob's covered in sauce. Did an altercation take place? Were Hayden and Sarah involved?' Lily lists her questions, wishing someone would answer.

As she treads into the dining room, Lily spins in front of the doorway, and whispers, 'Clear!'

In the adjoining lounge there are similarities with Ruth's

385

sparse home. It's more about hiding than an interior decorating decision.

'The Hawkins family certainly have enough secrets to hide,' Lily says, reflecting on her meeting with Ruth.

Muffled voices travel into the room. Lily follows them to the hallway. 'Where the hell are they coming from?'

She stands still. In the silence, the sounds become louder. There's a door.

'Well done, Naomi, for buying a house with a basement.' Lily keeps her voice soft as she approaches. 'It's a cliché but perfect for a criminal.'

Soon, Lily will be seen. Stealth is no longer an option. She has to move fast, using the element of surprise. No mean feat for someone with long clumsy legs.

As Lily runs down the stairs, she glimpses Hayden, tied up and lifeless. Despite her distress, Lily must focus on the redhead, running at Sarah with a knife.

Lily rushes at the redhead, tackling her to the ground. She sprawls on her front. The knife slides away. Lily leaps and collapses on a killer. The woman grabs Lily's ankle, preparing to fling her aside. Lily rises into the air.

'I've got you.' Chris holds Lily aloft. She falls against him.

A PC handcuffs the woman Lily assumes is Esther, thanks to Ruth's revelations. Paramedics arrive. Until now Lily was running on adrenaline and purpose. All she could think about was saving Hayden and Sarah.

'Sarah! You're alive!' Lily cries as she sees her friend tethered to a beam.

Naomi's bloodied body is no consolation. Lily figured the sisters were in this together. She didn't think Hayden's friend would kill him though. Did Esther kill Naomi?

Esther fights against the handcuffs. 'Let me go! I need to be with my sister.'

Lily notes the family likeness of the Hawkins women. Older Esther hasn't changed much from the young woman in Ruth's photograph.

As soon as the PC releases Sarah from the restraints, she runs to Hayden. 'Please, let me see him,' she cries to the wall of medics working on him.

Lily pulls Chris back as he prepares to take Esther away. 'Can I say something to this *thing* first?' Lily asks.

'Please do,' Chris replies.

'Esther,' Lily begins. 'I've met your mother. She's a hard woman with a lot to say about you. None of it is good.'

'It's Red, not Esther.'

'If I hear that one more bloody time,' Sarah says while trying to see Hayden.

Lily is almost toe to toe with Red. 'Okay, Red. Bit of an obvious name, by the way. If you've killed Hayden, there will be a special place in hell for you and it begins right here.' Lily swallows. 'Ruth told me some of the things you've done to your family, throughout your miserable life. You're nothing but a screwed-up girl with mummy issues.'

'You know nothing about me!' Red shouts. The PC holds her back.

'I know you took my daughter, *Scarlett*,' Lily says. 'I took a shot of a photo Ruth had of you and sent it to Freya, on the way here. She confirmed you abducted her. Promise I wasn't on my phone while driving.' Lily grins at the PC before turning back to Esther. 'You're lucky I was off my game, Esther, and didn't find out about you sooner. I should've checked all birth certificates linked to Ruth. I got there in the end though. Take her away and book her, boys.'

'Lily,' Chris says. 'It doesn't work like that.' He smirks at Lily before he takes Esther away.

Lily approaches Sarah. They watch the paramedics

surrounding Hayden's body. While Lily can't look, Sarah refuses to turn away.

A man in a fluorescent jacket approaches the grieving women. 'He's breathing, just. We need to get him to hospital, straight away.'

163

SARAH

ONE YEAR LATER

Hayden recovered from Red's drugs cocktail. Red isn't as accomplished with dosages as she thought. I'd like to challenge her on it but I've talked too much of my past. I told Mags about how James made me inject him and trying heroin myself. She was devastated for me, not by the revelations. I should have known Mags wouldn't judge me. Shame destroys trust.

When Hayden heard Naomi died, he wept for his childhood friend and half-sister. He forgave Naomi for the part she played in Red's plans, acknowledging Naomi didn't have a choice.

Whenever Hayden apologises for not telling me about Red, I reassure him it's not his fault. Naomi was terrified of her sister and pleaded with Hayden to keep Red a secret. Besides, Naomi didn't tell him her sister was back. If only we'd known.

I don't blame Naomi for what she did. Red had a powerful hold on her sister and Naomi had no choice. She was a victim of her sister's spite and her parents' lies as much as the rest of us.

Freya and Lily still have monumental arguments but love is at the heart of them. I'm glad Lily's filed for divorce from Gareth and things are getting serious with Chris. It's useful and tricky for Lily

LISA SELL

to be getting cosy with a copper as she's setting up her own private investigation business. She decided to learn more and train with other PIs. This is the first time Lily has stuck with something and we're all proud of her. Lily and Chris have agreed not to discuss their work. Bless him, Chris doesn't know Lily as well as he thinks.

Lily's first case will be trying to find Kayleigh. I've realised the connection between a birth mother and her child is precious. My mum, Denise, understands. No one could replace her. I need to know how Kayleigh is though. She sacrificed a relationship with me for my safety. I'm hoping she's not with James. Facing him again would be difficult.

It will come as no surprise that Imogen and Myles are living "deliciously in sin", as she likes to put it. I think Myles is a good influence on her. Someone has to be the mature one in a relationship.

Steve and Reuben are planning their wedding. Lily and I will be bridesmaids. I cried at how choked up Hayden was when Steve asked him to be best man. It'll be one hell of a party. The Lawsons could do with something to celebrate.

Mags came to terms with Paul's lies and the devastation of his secret daughter's death. I hadn't considered how Mags once knew Naomi and even trusted her to babysit Tamsin. Mags doesn't bear Naomi any malice. The events have brought Mags closer to Damien and they've recently renewed their wedding vows.

Mags insisted Tamsin's funeral was a joyful occasion. Black was banned. Hayden, Lily and I wore scarves, knitted ridiculously long, like the original. We added *Doctor Who* badges. I had a moment of panic, wondering if it was in poor taste, reminding Mags what Tamsin was wearing when she was killed. When Mags saw us, she cried happy tears, declaring Tamsin would have loved it.

Hayden and I often visit Tamsin and Naomi's graves. We leave flowers for Naomi. Tamsin gets a badge to add to her new scarf, secured to her gravestone. Unfortunately, Ruth vetoed Mags' idea to bury the half-sisters next to each other. Old wounds don't always heal.

∼

'I can't believe it's ours.' Hayden and I stand in front of the house, our new home.

'Let's get going then.' Mum's voice is muffled from behind a large box she's carrying. 'This move won't do itself.'

Hayden takes the box from Mum. 'I'll carry this before you buckle underneath it.'

'I'm so excited you're living around the corner.' Mum sits on the doorstep.

When Hayden and I saw the property in Thame, we knew it would be ours. Before, we were squashed in my house. Hayden left his flat after an altercation with his noisy neighbours. He left them a parting gift of an old stereo turned up to full volume in the lounge.

We had expanded and needed space. I wanted to be closer to my mum. After witnessing Red's warped version of family, I appreciate the woman who chose me even more.

'I think this little one wants her grandma.'

Mum reaches for Charlotte, Hayden's and my precious daughter. Charlotte Tamsin Naomi Lawson, to be precise.

Finding out I was pregnant was a surprise, particularly as the dates confirmed I was carrying our child when Red drugged and held me captive. Whenever Hayden and I regard our daughter, we know it's a miracle she has both parents.

Mum blows raspberries on Charlotte's tummy. My daughter's giggles are a balm to my soul. Only one thing is ruining this tranquil moment.

'Why the frown?' Hayden whispers in my ear.

I look at Mum, holding Charlotte, sitting on the doorstep. 'The door needs repainting. No more red for us.'

164

'It shouldn't have ended like this. Why did you get in the way? I had it all figured out.'

Naomi can't reply in the photograph or in person.

'Why didn't you understand I'd do anything for you?'

She grips the photo. The edge slices her thumb. Blood speeds to the surface. Red. What use is Red now? Her blood mingles with Naomi, smudging the image.

Naomi was always the one; the reason for revenge. She was love. Love for Naomi gave her purpose. Love for a boy and a man who never wanted her, led to bitterness.

Hayden was no better than Paul; making a girl believe she stood a chance. Hayden should feel lucky to be alive.

The saying goes: if you want a job doing well, do it yourself. She should have followed the advice. Esther is locked away. Her impulses caused trouble. Esther hadn't planned Tamsin's death but it set everything in motion.

If Tamsin's body hadn't been found, the past would have been left to rest too. The discovery of her corpse stoked latent anger. It dredged up memories of rejection and hatred.

Sometimes Esther acted rationally. She buried the body in the right place. She hadn't dug deep enough.

When you come home and find someone standing over a body, you have leverage. You can make them do anything, particularly if they're your daughter.

Ruth didn't ask for much; a few favours to guarantee her silence. She directed Esther to kill Hayden and Sarah. It was a gift for Naomi, from her mother and sister. Without Hayden, Naomi could get over her obsession with being his sister.

Esther sends letters, begging for forgiveness. Ruth hasn't replied because Esther must learn who's in charge. It's comforting Esther won't confess about her mother's role. Ruth knows too much. Esther would rather die than people hear she was a mother too.

Once, Esther carried Paul's child. She made the mistake of taunting Ruth with the information. The woman with a new opportunity with Paul's offspring was abhorrent. Paul was Ruth's. Naomi was Paul's only daughter.

Unfortunate Esther fell down the stairs.

Ruth can take children's lives too, even her grandchild's.

Paul had to die. He didn't reconcile with Naomi after Tamsin died. There are only so many times a father can reject his ex-lover and his daughter, and get away with it. Ruth would have done anything for Naomi. Killing the man who'd let them down wasn't a chore.

Ruth met with Paul the night he died. The Lawsons were out. As a cover for his meeting with Ruth, Paul feigned a headache. She expected his acceptance, perhaps even the beginning of an affair. Instead Paul listed the reasons Naomi and Ruth had to remain a secret. Although his words cut deep, Ruth was prepared.

She got him a beer, sprinkling in prepared crushed paraceta-mol. Ruth watched Paul die. His pain and horror were Ruth's release. She left the empty pill packet next to Paul's body. No need for gloves to avoid fingerprints. Who would suspect Ruth?

Everyone thought Paul's death was suicide. He missed Tamsin. It was a shame he wanted the wrong daughter. Such a tragedy he didn't want the other woman who gave him a child. They could have been such a happy family.

Ruth manipulated the meeting with Lily by dropping clues. Esther was in place to kill Hayden and Sarah. So what if Lily saw Esther in the photo and worked it out? Who cared if the police got there and caught Esther? Ruth didn't. As long as the job was done, Ruth was satisfied.

Naomi's sweet face was guaranteed to ignite Esther's obses-sion. At least Naomi died knowing her sister hadn't revealed how Naomi and Ruth joined Esther, staring at Tamsin's body on the floor. Ruth wasn't sure who was most shocked at the scene: Ruth coming home early, Esther at killing a child, or Naomi who'd been hiding when she heard Esther and Tamsin come into the house.

Using her ingenuity, Ruth proposed burial in the allotments. She didn't even flinch as she and Esther pushed the child's form into the suitcase. Ruth couldn't swear but she's almost certain Naomi smiled at the sound of Tamsin's arm breaking. Ruth's daughters are the jealous type.

Ruth once thought Naomi was pure. Now Ruth's not so sure. Ever loyal, Naomi didn't tell Ruth that Esther was back in her life. When Ruth heard why Naomi was in the basement she was horrified. Esther made Ruth doubt her love for Naomi.

Choosing love, as ever, Ruth kisses Naomi's face on the photograph. Blood covers Ruth's lips. She places her mouth on the letter to Esther, leaving a stain. Ruth is ready to communi-cate. Esther will understand the mark of red as a call to action.

Esther might not be Naomi but she's still Ruth's child. They have much in common. Both go to extremes for love. Esther may have occasionally frightened Ruth, when Esther was a child, but the power play was exciting.

Maybe Esther deserves a reward. She took her punishment in court and kept the family secrets. Esther isn't such a bad girl.

Ruth regards the ruby pendant in her hand. She fiddles with its twin around her neck. Naomi has no use for it. Ruth bought them to signify the mother-daughter bond. The necklace will be Esther's. She's always liked red.

Ruth must be there for her daughter.

Mother will take care of Esther now.

ACKNOWLEDGEMENTS

Thank you, lovely reader, for picking up this book. Trite as it may sound, authors write for you. I hope you enjoyed *Trust*. Don't forget to leave a review! They're a great way to let us know your thoughts and they often give as a boost.

For those who've read *Hidden*, my debut novel, thank you. I'm overwhelmed by the positive reviews, the amount of people who bought it, and your support. It gave me the confidence to write and believe in *Trust*.

Thanks, as ever, to the team at Bloodhound Books. So much goes on behind the scenes I don't know about. Thanks for making things happen and lightening the load.

This book couldn't have happened without my beta readers. Thanks Belinda, Helen, Kate, Sarah, and Sian, for your time and help. You're absolute gems!

To the writers and bloggers who supported me from the beginning and along the way, I'm so grateful. This is a tough business. You've advised, consoled, and encouraged. I am honoured to do that for you too.

Thank you to the friends and family who are always there for me. Your consistent love and care is never taken for granted.

Belinda, you're flipping amazing. Every writer should have a cheerleading, promo whirlwind, best friend, like you. They can't have you though!

Dave, you got the dedication and you deserve an acknowledgement too. Thank you for every moment past, present, and what's to come.

If you'd like to know more about this and future books you'll find me in the following places:

My monthly newsletter: http://bit.ly/LisaSellNewsletter

My website: www.lisasell.co.uk

Facebook: lisasellwriter

Twitter: LisaLisax31

Instagram: lisasellwriter

Lightning Source UK Ltd.
Milton Keynes UK
UKHW011852270921
391272UK00004B/1214

9 781913 419387